Skytrain to Murder

Also by Dean Barrett

Fiction

Hangman's Point – A Novel of Hong Kong
Mistress of the East – A Novel of China
Kingdom of Make-Believe – A Novel of Thailand
Memoirs of a Bangkok Warrior – A Novel of Thailand
Murder in China Red – A Novel of New York

Non-fiction

Don Quixote in China: The Search for Peach Blossom Spring

Children

The Boat Girl and the Magic Fish

DEAN BARRETT'S THAILAND

KINGDOM OF MAKE-BELIEVE

"*Kingdom of Make-Believe* is an exciting thriller that paints a picture of Thailand much different from that of *The King and I*. The story line is filled with non-stop action, graphic details of the country, and an intriguing allure that will hook readers of exotic thrillers. Very highly recommended."
— *BookBrowser.com*

MEMOIRS OF A BANGKOK WARRIOR

"Funny from the first page to the last. A fine and funny book, ribald and occasionally touching. One of the better Asian reads of the past few years." — *The Bangkok Post*

"This is a funny and human book which can describe sex without descending into sheer nastiness."
— *South China Morning Post*

Published in the United States by
Village East Books, Countryside, #520, 8775 20th Street,
Vero Beach, Fl. 32966

E-mail: VillageEast@hotmail.com
Web site: http://www.deanbarrettmystery.com

ISBN: 0-9661899-6-5

Printed in Thailand by Allied Printing
Cover and interior design: Robert Stedman, Pte., Ltd.

The Man who Shot Liberty Valance
Lyrics: Hal David ©1962

Wild Turkey
Lyrics: Dean Barrett ©2001

*All of the characters in this novel are fictitious. Any similarity to real persons,
living or dead, is purely coincidental.*

Publisher's Cataloging-in-Publication Data
(Prepared by The Donohue Group, Inc.)

Barrett, Dean.
   Skytrain to murder / Dean Barrett.

   p. ; cm.

   ISBN: 0-9661899-6-5

1. Thailand–Fiction. 2. Americans–Thailand–Fiction. 3. Murder–Thailand
Fiction. 4. Bangkok (Thailand)–Fiction. 5. Mystery fiction. 6. Suspense fiction.
I. Title.

PS3552.A7337 S59 2003
813/.6   2003102110

Acknowledgements

Many people gave generously of their time and expertise in assisting me in the writing of this book. David Zaharychuk of Larry's Dive shared his in-depth knowledge of scuba diving and his love of the sea. Vincent Giordano and Hardy Stockmann shared their expertise on muay-Thai and I am very grateful to Vincent for getting me into a muay-Thai training camp of the old school. Warren Olson, a detective living in Bangkok, gave me useful pointers on the wily ways of ferreting out information in the Land of Smiles. Paul Hughes I thank for his knowledge of boilerooms. James Pate I thank for sharing his insights into various aspects of Thai society. I owe debts of gratitude to habitues of Washington Square such as Doc Dennis House, Kurt Francis, Cowboy Jon Dodd, Richard Guitard, Don Ross, MacAlan Thompson, Les Strouse and Richard Diran for their friendship.

Those who shed light on the murky world of espionage include Sauron of Bangkok's famed Chateau Jade House of Domination and George Kenning, CIA Operations Officer for thirty years. I'd also like to thank those at the American Embassy who prefer anonymity.

The downstairs of the Boots and Saddle is loosely based on Bangkok's legendary Texas Lone Staar Saloon. The aviary is based on that on the roof of Bangkok's New Square One Pub. Many thanks to the owners and employees of both those wondrous establishments.

"I feel that the East is incapable of proper footnotes and scholarly documentation. There is really no such thing as a fact in Southeast Asia."
— Carol Hollinger, *Mai Pen Rai Means Never Mind*

"I needed a drink, I needed a lot of life insurance, I needed a vacation, I needed a home in the country. What I had was a coat, a hat and a gun."
— Raymond Chandler, *Farewell, My Lovely*

DEAN BARRETT

Skytrain
to
Murder

VILLAGE EAST BOOKS
FLORIDA

DAY ONE

1

I knew from the minute the foxy blond in the blue shorts sat down she was a tease. Young – maybe 22, 23. Blond maybe bleached. Face and figure – no maybe's there. Absolutely stunning. And she knew it.

I hadn't seen her approach because the open-air beer bar was sheltered from Bangkok's traffic by a semi-circle of dust-covered, shoulder-high potted plants. Customers were protected from the sun and rain by a thatch-and-wood roof from which a few Halloween balloons and tiny plastic witches added color and annoyance to anyone trying to chug his beer. She sat where a few balloons nestled beside a tiny Buddhist shrine, and several others encircled a beribboned bell customers could ring should they feel happy enough to buy everyone a drink.

The Thai women working behind the bar hadn't noticed the blond yet; too busy admiring Goong's latest shoes – expensive leather footwear from Italy paid for by her lovesick sweetheart in France so that (unknown to him) she could wear them to discos with her Thai boyfriend. I knew this because I knew Goong, and I also knew her cop boyfriend who owned the open-air bar I was drinking at.

But most of the customers around the oval-shaped counter had already stopped talking and were quietly appraising the blond. Which in itself said a lot about her looks. Because in Bangkok beautiful women are the norm, and most foreign men who end up in the Big Mango prefer Thai women. Especially the jaded local expats and weather-beaten foreign offshore oil riggers who drink at the open-air bars off Sukhumvith Road. I had seldom seen them cast a *farang*, or foreign, woman a second glance. Certainly not in approval. But they did now. Now they threw back their Singha beer and Mekhong whiskey as before, but behind their attempts at nonchalance each was as attentive and alert as a grammar school student on his first day of school. It was as if a solar flare had sent a spectacular light show crashing through Bangkok's murky, malevolent October night sky, disrupting communications.

I motioned to Goong's younger sister, Lek, and she suddenly noticed the blond. She quickly approached her, gave her a big Thai smile and a "Hello, what you like?" The evening traffic noises were as clamorous as ever and beside me an inebriated Greg Winston –"Winny" to his friends – was talking, still unaware that he was the only one doing so, but I heard the blond order a rum-and-coke.

At first, she never glanced my way, but I could tell she was aware of the tension her presence had caused. I had seen sexually charged particles wreak havoc with a bar's magnetic field before. But none as alluring as this one. The fine sun-kissed blond tresses, the big blue eyes, the cute upturned nose, the sensual, heart-shaped lips, the irresistible charm of youth – this one had it all.

Something about the innocent yet provocative way she perched on the bar stool, the way she tossed back her short, stylish, slightly tomboyish haircut, the way she ran her hand over the smooth expanse of flesh visible between where her short-sleeved powder blue top ended well above the belt-line of her hip-hugging, powder blue shorts. The way she tilted her head down to take a drink then looked up at me from under her full bangs and mouthed a "thank you" for getting Lek's attention for her. No doubt about it. The lady was a tease.

I raised my bottle of Singha Gold and nodded in acknowledgment.

"I am telling you, Scott, whatever country I've been in it has been my experience that one out of every 11.5 women prefers older men. That is a statistical fact. A factual statistic! You just have to get through the first 10.5 to get to the right one. The one who recognizes the charms of – " In mid-sentence Winny finally stopped droning on about his latest woman theory and caught onto the new situation at the bar. He placed his huge fists on the counter and leaned his thick neck forward to look past me. He was entering his late fifties and was spending far too much time sitting at bar counters but most of his muscle had yet to turn to fat. "Well, well, what have we here?"

I lowered my voice. "What we have here, old friend, is known as a tease with a capital T."

"You see 'tease'; I see 't's as in opportunity."

"So go for her."

"Not *me*, lad, I'm too long in the tooth for that. I think you should go for her."

"Haven't you always warned me about – "

"This one is off the charts. Besides, I could be her grandfather. She's yours."

I looked over at the blond. She was cute all right. Despite high cheekbones, her lovely face was almost perfectly oval ending in a slightly narrow chin which she had cleverly de-emphasized with her wide, pageboy-style hairdo. I watched her glance up at me then quickly down again, as if she was interested but just a bit too shy to reveal her interest overtly. The act looked guileless enough. But it was an act; and a well practiced one. I'd made more than my share of mistakes along the way but I hadn't reached my mid-thirties a complete naif. "I think I'll give this miss a miss."

Winny raised his thick salt-and-pepper eyebrows. "And have it spread throughout the Big Mango that Scott Sterling was afraid to approach a round-eyed female?"

Political correctness was not one of Winny's strong points. "Look, Winny – "

Dean Barrett

I felt one of his meaty hands clamp down on my arm. "Look at her. She is sitting there pining away because no one will pay the slightest bit of attention to her. A shy, lonely young thing on her first trip outside the States. A demure, skittish, virginal waif totally confused by all the contradictory images bombarding her in the Land of Smiles: Devout Buddhist monks, naked go-go dancers, food too spicy to eat, water too filthy to drink, heat and humidity beyond belief. She's all alone and completely lost in the city of broken hearts and broken pavement. For God's sakes, man, give her something to remember when she's back in her nondescript little village wedged into the snow-covered hills of North Dakota working over a hot stove, cooking food for an unfaithful, ungrateful, unemployed, physically violent man she no longer loves. Give her something to cling to." Here his voice dropped to an earnest but histrionic whisper: "Give her the memory of *you!*"

Winny was the proprietor of the bar I had been living over for over a year, the Boots and Saddle Saloon, one of the most popular of the watering holes favored by expats. But before he had chucked in his previous existence and moved to the Big Mango, he had been an actor and sometimes director in the Big Apple. A battle-scarred veteran of the Vietnam War as well as a bottle-scarred veteran of various skirmishes with egotistical producers, arrogant directors and demanding actors in New York's Off-Broadway, he was now without doubt, a perfectly contented expat, but his thespian background surfaced abruptly whenever he started on his fourth glass of Mekhong whiskey or whenever he was under pressure.

I held my ground. "I'm telling you, Winny, I've seen the type before – she's a tease."

He released my arm and rolled his beer bottle between his palms as a potter might roll clay. "Only one way to be absolutely certain though, isn't there?"

I glanced around the bar and saw others waiting to see if I

14

would move in on the blond. Scenes from National Geographic TV specials from my boyhood flooded back to me – 'Look, boys and girls: watch the way the males of the herd observe its leader as he tries to impress the new female of the herd. If he fails, the herd will tear him limb from limb, devour him, leave his bones to bleach in the sun, and shortly after another leader will emerge.'

I looked again at the woman. As a diver, I often reflected upon similar character traits in the life forms walking above ground and those swimming in the sea. And this one reminded me of one of the most beautiful creatures I had encountered on Thailand's reefs: the lionfish; the fish with the resplendent, plume-like dorsal and pectoral fins. As gorgeous as the fish is, the one thing you don't want to do is to agitate it in any way. Because along those beautiful fins is enough poison to make curious swimmers who venture too close wish they hadn't been mesmerized by its beauty in the first place.

Maybe I'd had too much Singha or maybe I'd been a bit depressed lately or maybe it was just a juvenile reaction to a schoolboy's dare, but I felt myself getting up. I picked up my bottle of beer and walked toward her. I could feel all eyes boring into me. The blond kept emitting her shy smile like a homing beacon. A delightfully winsome smile – all for me. But something about that smile made me feel as if a red lasar dot from a 9 millimeter semiautomatic was being trained on my forehead.

I stopped beside her and leaned against the bar. I was immediately enveloped in the pungent odor of her musky perfume. "Excuse me, but the man you were supposed to meet this evening called to say he couldn't make it. And he asked me to escort you in his place."

The smile changed. It segued from diffidence and timidity into an arrogant smirk of victory. A sneer of contempt. I knew I'd been had. The lionfish was about to strike. Her voice was all feminine softness. And hard as nails. "Nice try, Romeo, but the person I'm waiting for is a woman." She turned in her seat to look past me. "And here she comes now."

A sexily dressed Thai woman in her 20's strode quickly past the outside tables and purposefully up to the bar. The outline of her nipples appeared plain as day as they pushed into her canary yellow blouse, and her curvaceous legs made impossible demands on her short cream-colored skirt. I couldn't be sure, but she seemed to be a kind of high class call girl. And her face lacked a certain softness – the kind of face a Thai woman might have after spending years abroad; or years with men who have come from abroad.

As she approached, the blond stood up and held out her arms. The Thai woman walked into them and they held each other as lovers, kissing full on the lips. A lingering kiss, neither being in a hurry to break it off. I heard a few subdued exclamations around the bar. I gripped my beer bottle and tried not to feel like a horse's ass. I pretended to take a sudden interest in the red, white and blue bars of the drooping Thai flag above the faded beer advertisements. The city's notorious pollution had transformed the white of the bars into a deep gray. I looked up at the tiny blinking lights of various colors draped about the bar and then down at the bar's ailing dog tossing in its sleep. But two attractive young women passionately kissing one another was enough of a spectacle to turn a boisterous bar into a silent movie.

The blond released the woman and sat back on the stool. She reached up and took her companion's hand. "I'm glad you got here early." She glanced in my direction. "This middle-aged Romeo was hitting on me."

The Thai woman made a face as if she'd smelled something slightly off. "I think Patpong girls are more his type." She looked me over. "Kangaroo Bar would be perfect for him."

I smiled. "The night market has screwed Patpong up. And the touts are too aggressive. I don't go there much anymore."

"Maybe you should."

"And which bar will I find you working in?"

Her face became a malevolent mask. "I suggest you fuck off. Now."

Two rules I had learned in Bangkok long before I left my CIA section at the American embassy: Never argue with a woman in love and especially never argue with a woman in love with a woman. I nodded and smiled pleasantly. "My mistake." I made the long walk back to my stool and sat down. Conversations slowly resumed. I may have just imagined hearing chortles and chuckles at my expense.

Winny slapped me on the back. "Lek, get this middle-aged Romeo a beer. On me."

The blond finished her drink, paid her bill and, holding hands with her significant other, walked off in the direction of Sukhumvith Road. I drained the bottle in front of me before speaking. "Am I going to tell you I told you so or am I going to resist telling you I told you so?"

"I think you are man enough to resist. Besides, that was a lovely pick-up line you used on her. Does it really work?"

"I tried it on my ex-wife the first time I saw her."

"And it worked?"

"Only too well."

Lek placed the beer down in front of me. Lek had opaque brown eyes, the same shade as fish sauce left a bit too long out in the steamy Thai climate during the hot season. But in the rays of the setting sun, her eyes appeared a murky, reddish brown, the exact hue of vinegared ground chili. Her skin was a coconut-husk brown and her nail color was the same odd pink as shrimp paste. Her blouse was a gingko-nut-soup yellow. Just looking at her made me hungry. Above her head, strings of tiny bar lights flickered on and off like aroused fireflies. "What mean, 'Lomeo'?"

Winny reached out to gently stroke Lek's delicate chin. "'Lomeo', my incomparable Siamese beauty, is a man who is irresistible to women. All women want him."

Lek brushed his hand away and laughed, revealing both her protruding upper teeth and her lovely dimples. "All girl want man with money; Scott no have money; he number ten Lomeo." And with that she went back to share the joke with the other Thai women behind the bar.

I peeled back bits of gold paper from the mouth of the bottle and took a long hit on my beer. Now I had been ridiculed by women of East and West: a fine ending to a fine day.

We were nearing the end of the rainy season, but when the Thai flag began flapping about like a just-landed marlin and the sky directly overhead darkened I knew that in less than fifteen minutes the day's downpour would begin. I could make it back to my apartment over the Boots and Saddle if I left now; or I could finish my beer and ride out the storm. Call me Storm-rider.

I swiveled my stool to watch bargirls on their way to work emerge from a samlor, and others sitting sidesaddle cling tightly to the back of motorcycle taxis, when something made me take a last look at the blond.

She and her friend were getting into another samlor. She turned back to me and favored me with a coquettish smile. No question about it: whether she was straight or a lesbian or a bisexual or an alien, she was gorgeous. I didn't know then that I would soon see her again. And I had no way of knowing the danger that would involve me in.

2

Living above a Bangkok bar has its advantages. At least above a bar like the Boots and Saddle. For one thing it's located off Sukhumvith Road at *soi* (lane) 22 and it isn't the kind of Bangkok establishment frequented by tourists. Tourists seldom make it out that far. Unlike the bars of Bangkok's infamous nightlife areas such as Patpong Road, *Soi* Cowboy and Nana Plaza, there are no go go dancers, no lesbian shows, no shower shows, no dildo shows, no bottle shows, no dart shows, and the music in the B&S is all Country Western. And if you don't fancy Country Western you might be wise to keep that fact to yourself. Or you might just mosey over to one of the other bars around Washington Square: the Silver Dollar, The Texas Lone Staar, Wild Country, Cat's Meow, Prince of Wales, Bourbon Street, Happy Pub, Crystal Bar and the New Square One.

There *are* young (and not so young) Thai women present in each of these establishments, and the Boots and Saddle has over a dozen of them on each of two shifts, working the bar, lounging about in booths, beating one another at darts or winning drinks from customers on one of the two pool tables at the back. And occasionally they score ladies' drinks. Just don't ask them to put on any shows for you unless you like to see women angry.

They wear normal outfits, usually blouse and skirt, but with the addition of a cowgirl hat and boots, supplied by the bar, and sit beside whoever buys them the drink, and more-or-less listen to oil riggers or ex-military types or ex-spooks with receding white hairlines and burgeoning beer bellies talk about the old days. And sometimes I buy them drinks and they listen to me. Of course they might just be staring at the various pictures of Country singers, cowboys in ten-gallon hats and scenes from the old West lining the walls, and wondering if they made a mistake by leaving the ricefields of northeastern Thailand to work in a Bangkok bar frequented by foreign men old enough to be their fathers.

The bar is one of the more spacious in the square, and besides the music, I like the incongruous combination of western *décor* and traditional Thai symbols. A Buddhist wall shrine perched above a plaque describing the venerable Judge Roy Bean, colorful garlands hung from cattle horns, and a statue of *nang kwat*, a Thai maiden beckoning all to enter and spend money, had been fixed up in such a way that it now rode a small plastic horse.

By the time we made it to the bar, Winny and I were soaked. I decided to check the mail then get on upstairs and change. As always, the lighting was low almost to the point of depressing, and a good-old-boy on the CD was singing of how he lost his true love to a fast-talking, cattle-roping, Brahma-bull-riding, rodeo cowboy. Rodeo cowboys not making much money these days, I would have thought true loves went to portly stock brokers with portly portfolios, but I was too wet to give it much thought.

While Winny went to deal with some problem in the kitchen, I stepped behind the bar and opened the leather sack marked "Pinkerton – Sante Fe Payroll" and checked the mail. My name was on the usual bills and typed incorrectly on various pleas to give generously to everything from orphanage children in Bangkok slums to down-and-out mahouts whose elephants were running out of bananas.

The one letter with no return address and a New York postmark I figured would be from my brother, Larry. A Manhattan cop, he seldom wrote and when he did it was usually just a few sentences on e-mail. I sat down, and quickly glanced over the letter. His note was just a brief summation relating to the affairs of our late father; affairs he had to continue taking care of because he was there and I was here. Dad had been a decorated detective and a legend at One Police Plaza known as Jimmy "The Tiger" Sterling. Larry, on the other hand, was stuck in License Division, and, from all appearances, might not be moving up and out any time soon.

But he included a newspaper clipping of my ex-wife marrying a high school classmate of mine who had become a partner in a stock brokerage house. I figured she got it right the second time around. And I figured I had it right about whom true loves go to.

Noy, the mamasan of the bar, stormed over to complain that I had screwed up the order of the mail again and had dripped water all over the bar receipts. Noy was somewhere in her late forties, and had managed to keep the face and figure of a much younger woman, possibly because she drank only when others were buying.

She had been married only once, to a 21-year-old American GI, an M-60 machine-gunner with the 17th Assault Helicopter Company. On her eighteenth birthday she received word that her husband had been aboard a Bell UH-1D "slick" which had been sent into a hot extraction of a LRRP team and slammed into a mountain somewhere in the A Shau Valley. Search teams hadn't recovered enough to make use of a body bag but his dog tags had been recovered. Noy wore them around her neck along with her locket containing a faded color picture of the two of them together. Noy's moods varied from playful to morose and over the years some of the girls had left because of clashes with her. A Vietnam vet himself, Winny kept her on long after another bar owner might have let her go.

When she finished complaining she asked if I wanted a beer. I put two fifty-baht bills on the counter, about US$2.50, and told her to buy herself a ladies drink and I'd be back later. In gratitude she placed her palms together and *waiied* me. Then she handed me my rent bill for the month. Noy was smart enough to know that if she'd given me the bill first, I might not have been in the mood to buy her a drink.

"Howzitgoan?"

I turned to see one of the bar regulars perched on his usual barstool in an area of shadow. Five-minute Jack was an American from Delaware in his early 50's with thinning brown hair, watery grey eyes, a pencil-thin mustache and nut-brown skin. He was thin almost to the point of emaciation. He sat facing sideways from the bar with one elbow propped on the counter. He wore a flowery Aloha shirt a few sizes too large for him, baggy blue shorts and below-the-knee length blue socks in open-toed sandals. As usual, a cigarette dangled from his small slash of a mouth (the Boots and Saddle blithely ignoring anti-smoking laws involving places serving food). One of his bony hands constantly stroked his glass of Mekhong whiskey as if someone might try to take it from him; the other roosted on his lap like a nervous Chihuahua. His cheekbones were high, his cheeks were gaunt and his attitude was that of a man for whom paranoia was a natural state. His thin, spindly legs were crossed and as he leaned forward his grey eyes roamed suspiciously about the bar from under dark, bushy eyebrows. Then they focused on me.

"Just collecting my bills, Jack, how you doin?"

He picked up his glass and used it to gesture toward the world said to exist outside the Boots and Saddle. "You know that guy sells the coconut pudding other end of the square? The fat guy with the cart?"

"Uh, yeah, I think I've – "

"Son-of-a-bitch switched from charcoal stove to gas stove."

Jack's almost permanent presence inside Washington Square bars gave rise to the saying that whatever bar you were in, if you would just wait five minutes, Jack would show up. Others said he was given the nickname because he had more than once chugged down one shot of Jack Daniels every five minutes for over an hour. Although generally lethargic, when riled, he had the stereotypical Irishman's temper. Jack and I had never had a problem but dealing with a potentially abusive drunkard is actually hard work and I wasn't in the mood. "That a fact?"

He ran his free hand over his chin stubble as if checking to ensure it was still there. "Yeah. That's a fuckin' fact! I love that coconut shit but it don't taste the same without the charcoal."

"Did you mention it to him?"

"Of course I fuckin' mentioned it to him! All he did was smile!" He angrily tapped out another cigarette from his pack on the bar counter, flicked open a three-inch lighter flame and lit up. "Fuck Thais ever do when a *farang* says something to them except *smile*?"

I nodded. "Well, I gotta be somewhere else. Take care, Jack."

"I wrote to Trink but all he cares about is bars and hookers."

Bernard Trink's "Night Owl" column appeared in the *Bangkok Post* every Friday and Five-minute Jack seemed to have it in for the columnist. Most likely because Trink never published anything Jack sent him. "Well, it is a nightlife column, Jack."

"You sayin' hookers don't eat coconut pudding? They're just whores so they're not part of the equation, right?"

Jack was a master of the lonely drunkard's technique of suckering someone into a discussion, by blandishment or accusation. I wasn't biting. "Catch you later, Jack."

He drained his glass and motioned to Noy for another. "This country is gettin' fucked up is what it is."

The stairs to the apartments were reached by an outside door so I exited the bar and opened the door to upstairs. As I did, one of the bargirls who lived in a room near mine was coming down. Her flopping sandals created a faint and slightly sinister echo. The wrinkles in her tired face seemed even deeper in the semi-darkness. Her crimson lipstick matched her tight skirt. She smiled lasciviously and said, "So-cott! I come see you soon. You like?"

As she spoke, a strong scent of some incredibly spicy, malodorous salad – the type favored by girls from northeast Thailand – enveloped me. I smiled and assured her that I would greatly look forward to her visit as soon as I returned from an indefinite stay in Cambodia. She laughed, slapped my shoulder, and continued on. Her offer to pay me a visit had become a kind of in-joke between us. Several of the bar girls lived in the rooms above the bars and thus far I had been bright enough not to begin anything I couldn't easily end.

As usual, the stairs were lined with and partly blocked by beer cases full of empties, scrub buckets and brooms, large plastic water jugs, shoes and sandals belonging to women who worked in the bar, and an overlooked bra or two a maid or bargirl had dropped from her laundry. A narrow, dark hallway off the second floor landing led to a small, ill-ventilated kitchen and beyond that to Winny's windowless bedroom. I climbed the stairs to the top floor, jiggled the key in the lock and entered the apartment, the only apartment at roof-level, and the only one which had Winny's raucous macaws and mynah birds as neighbors.

I listened to the message machine while relieving myself of much of the beer I had unwisely consumed. "Hi, Scott, George here. Expecting you at the Halloween party. Don't forget! Most people are bringing bottles but if you bring Winny you don't have to bring a bottle. About eight. Ciao!"

Halloween was actually still several days off, and I'd forgotten about the party, so it was good that I didn't have to bring a bottle. George was one of the Washington Square regulars who hung out in the Boots and Saddle. He also owned Len's Diving shops in Bangkok and Pattaya Beach where I freelanced my services, teaching students to dive.

He was somewhere in his early 50's although he looked older. He had turned prematurely bald long ago, his large and somewhat bulbous nose was reddening, his belly was thickening. He had a small mouth, large, projecting ears and no one he wasn't buying drinks for would ever describe him as handsome.

George had failed at a lot of things in life except the important one of having had very successful, very loving parents. He'd apparently been left a lot of money b y his real estate father and he'd married into a prominent Chinese-Thai family down on its luck.

According to George, the family had a long and prestigious pedigree but had lost a fortune in Bangkok's economic crash and was using its beautiful daughters to recoup as best it could. One of the daughters had become a *mia noi* (minor wife) of a politician and it was an open secret that at least two of the other daughters were available for an evening's entertainment at a gentlemen's club to anyone well-heeled enough to afford them. Or, as George liked to say, they "sold the family ass to save the family face." They apparently lost still more face by allowing a foreign-devil to marry one of their daughters but at least managed to stay afloat with the money George had paid for the privilege of doing so.

The only thing that puzzled me was why George was inviting me at all, let alone calling to make sure I'd be there. Although a friend of Winny's, and the owner of a dive shop which threw some business my way, for various reasons, George was not one of my favorite people, and we were not exactly drinking companions.

His apartment was in a relatively quiet and clean section of Bangkok off Wireless Road. But at least three times a week, he'd be ensconced inside the Boots and Saddle debating or commiserating with Winny, on everything from Vietnam War tactics to the sad demise of the *pasin*, the Thai-style sarong, which was rapidly going the way of the Chinese *cheongsam*. Whenever someone teased George about what his Chinese-Thai wife thought about his nights away from her, he'd laugh and say he'd bought his freedom just like a slave. According to him he'd showered her with enough gold chains so she didn't need to keep him on a chain as well. George also bought the girls lots of ladies drinks.

As Winny liked to say, "I don't need a bar full of customers; just give me one free spender." George filled the bill perfectly.

I showered, shaved, put on a clean pair of slacks and short sleeve shirt and went back downstairs. This time I passed nobody except Maew, one of the cats that made their home on the series of rubbish-strewn landings outside. Maew used to rub against my leg, look up at me expectantly and give me a cute meow. When she got nothing substantial in return, she stopped. Maew knew how the game was played as well as the girls in the bars.

The rain had lessened to nothing more than a fine drizzle which was good because the only umbrella I had was in a Thai lady's apartment across town. Winny had wandered off to the Silver Dollar for a quick Singha, then to the Prince of Wales for another quick Singha, and by the time I had found which bar he was in he was in the middle of a pool game. So I ordered a quick one while watching him lose to one of the bargirls and he ordered another quick one while waiting for me to finish my quick one and a ladies drink for the girl because she had beaten him and in gratitude she bought us both beers. To make a long story short, we arrived at the party late. And none too sober.

3

The Skytrain, an elevated electric public transport system, ran above Sukhumvith Road and would have gotten us close to where George lived but we decided that traffic on a weekday would not be so bad so we hailed a taxi. We were wrong. But we both knew we had taken the cab because we were too lazy to walk up to the nearest Skytrain station.

George's apartment was on the ground floor of a modern and well guarded building. For the money he paid – which I knew for a luxurious Bangkok apartment even after the crash was still considerable – he got the garden as well. Someone in a demon mask opened the door and was almost immediately pulled back into a conversation.

We slid our shoes off and slipped our feet into the leather sandals provided for guests. It took a while but I found a pair that almost fit. A woman wearing a witch mask pushed her way through the crowded room, handed us each a demon mask, and told us in Thai to put them on. Then she kind of kissed us on the cheek, mask to mask, and pointed toward the bar.

I grabbed two Singhas off a waiter's silver tray, handed one to Winny, and looked about the room. About two dozen people were conversing and laughing in that familiar way that suggested they'd started their drinking early. Beautifully arranged azaleas covered teakwood tables, hardbound books covered teakwood shelves, and an expensive looking carpet with colorful swirls and spirals covered the floor.

Winny got buttonholed by a couple of Vietnam vet acquaintances, so I headed toward the garden. Whereas the living room's Tiffany-style lamps provided an elegant stained glass effect, Japanese lanterns had transformed the garden into areas of light and shadow; a partly sheltered retreat from Bangkok's noise and pollution populated by pairs and groups with still more Halloween masks. Many had removed their masks while drinking or smoking but I nodded politely to ghosts, phantoms, devils, imps, vampires, ghouls, deformed monsters and Count Dracula. Split-leaf Philodendron were silhouetted against a white wall by strategically placed spotlights, creating ominous shapes and sinister shadows, a perfect Halloween effect.

The mask was interfering with my drinking so I simply moved it about to the back of my head. As others had already done the same, in the darkness it appeared as if ghosts and goblins and witches were floating backward. I passed through a short path lined with Chinese Fan Palms sprouting from large porcelain cats and started to turn. And then I saw her. She was dressed in a dark blue-and-white blouse and dark blue slacks. The contrast of the blue with the yellow of her hair was every bit as striking as she no doubt thought it was. Even when she wasn't kissing another woman on the mouth, she was a cynosure of attention.

She was standing with two others, and all three had removed their masks and held them in the hand which wasn't holding the drink. I spotted her girlfriend from the beer bar, and a large man with a red face and beady eyes named Frank Webber. Frank and I had worked at the embassy together. Frank and I had sometimes gone drinking together. Frank and I had had a falling out. The kind of falling out so fallen out that my painful death would have pleased Frank greatly.

In many ways, Bangkok's expatriates move within a small world of their own and seeing someone twice on the same day in a different part of town had happened to me before. But sometimes there is that inner voice that tells me there may be more than meets the eye.

I stood with my beer in my hand and stared at the blond. She turned toward me and stared. Webber said something to her. I knew it wouldn't be anything flattering to me, but, whatever it was, it didn't prevent her from striding right up to me. She stood in front of me and glanced back at her girlfriend and Webber as if to emphasize her defiance, then turned back to face me.

"I'd say he doesn't like you much."

"An unfortunate misunderstanding."

"Involving a woman?"

"His wife."

"You hit on his wife?"

Her question conveyed no sense of shock; only curiosity. "She hit on me. I resisted."

With her lovely indigo morning glory eyes fixed on mine, she took a sip of what looked like rum and coke. "Until you didn't."

Again no suggestion that she was judging; just a fact-gatherer. "Something like that." I waited until several people laughing boisterously at someone's joke passed by. "Anyway, I got the impression you didn't like me much either."

"You just looked a little too sure of yourself."

"So did you."

"So why'd you make the approach?"

"Ask the moth that question as he approaches the candle flame."

She shaded her eyes with her mask as if protecting herself from some imaginary glare of sunlight and looked me over. "What do you do? No, let me guess. Over six feet. In shape despite the fact that you seem to have been born with a beer bottle in your hand. You look like a cop."

"My brother's a cop. My father was a cop. I was working at the embassy."

"Not the visa section, I'll bet."

"No."

"So you quit?"

I could hear the sound of a glass smashing onto the walkway. People at the party were obviously having a great time. And making it obvious. In the doorway of the house, I could make out George engrossed in a conversation with Winny. "Kind of a mutual feeling that my leaving would be best for all concerned."

"Da says Frank's getting a divorce. Some kind of scandal. You wouldn't be the heavy in that story, would you?"

So her girlfriend's nickname was Da. "As we Americans love to say, *I'm* the victim here. But what about you? What do you do? Besides lead men on siren-like and then dash their hopes on the rocks, I mean."

She waited for a well-dressed couple with ghoul masks to pass. "I was working in a New York publishing house as an editorial assistant then I discovered that a woman out here with a bit of style and attitude can earn a lot more than she can as an editorial assistant in a New York publishing house." She reached out and flecked something invisible off my shirt. She brushed her hand against mine then took a step back. "And have more fun."

We turned as Da called her name: "Lisa!" Da and Webber were still standing in the doorway. Da's stern expression almost matched that of her mask. "Come on, we're leaving."

"Your girlfriend?"

"Why is it men assume every time a woman kisses another woman with a bit of passion they must be lesbians?"

"Yeah, why *is* that?" I glanced at Da but it was impossible to guess from her expression if they were really lovers; she might simply have been impatient to get out of a noisy party full of inebriated people. Actually, so was I. I turned back to Lisa. The lights of nearby lanterns intensified the lustrous blue of her eyes and transformed her blond hair into the golden shade of an expensive champagne. She made no move to leave. "You want me to ask you out?"

"Getting bored with Thai women and need a change of pace? Or just want to see if you can get me into bed?"

"I was actually offering you a change of pace: a chance to go to bed with a man who doesn't pay you for it."

"I'd slap your face for that but you're probably the type of man who would enjoy it."

While she reached into her purse I tried to think of a clever retort. I had only had my face slapped once by a beautiful woman and although I can't say I enjoyed it, it wasn't so bad actually. When a woman feels so strongly toward a man that she wants to cause him pain, it seems to me they've already ventured close to some kind of sexual passion. And sure enough in my case that is precisely what happened shortly after I'd been slapped. Unfortunately, the slap that had led to the sexual passion had eventually led to marriage which had in turn led to divorce.

She took out a pen and scrap of paper. She spoke as she wrote: "Name…address… phone number. You can tell your overweight friend you scored big time." She handed me the paper. "I'll expect you tomorrow night around ten. Call only if you've got a better deal and can't make it. Or if you can't find your Viagra."

And with that she strode off to rejoin her friends; neither one of whom seemed pleased that she had spent time with me.

Winny ambled over and stood beside me, watching the three of them disappear into the apartment. "That wouldn't have been a phone number she was giving you?"

"It was. She said to tell my overweight friend that I scored big time."

"A pity."

"What is?"

"The lady is obviously too young to appreciate the difference between a man who is 'overweight' and a craftsman who is painstakingly cultivating a beer belly."

"She also said at one point that she would have slapped my

face but that I was probably the kind of man who would enjoy it."

"Yes, well, I believe it was Schopenhauer who remarked that 'life is the pursuit of pleasure and the avoidance of pain.' But for some the pain *is* the pleasure."

"So it would seem."

"Yes. The problem is once you've lived in Bangkok long enough you tend to lose track of which is which."

and then put his life savings into a Bangkok condominium and an SUV, both in her name. He had married her and they had moved into the condo. Then one night when he returned to Thailand from a trip abroad, she picked him up at the airport in a taxi rather than in their SUV. Paul Sr. had thought it also strange when she took him to a hotel, rather than to their condo. She had in fact sold the condo and the SUV and was letting him know she was moving in with a Thai boyfriend. Paul Sr. was left penniless.

When Dang unwisely approached Paul Jr. to cadge a drink, without looking up, he swung out his right arm and knocked her back into a booth, startling the girls sitting there and spilling Five-Minute Jack's Jack Daniels-on-the-rocks onto his mauve Hawaiian shirt and tawny trousers.

In a flash, an incensed Five-minute Jack began shoving screaming bargirls out of the booth so he could get at Son-of-Loser Paul who was already off his stool and spoiling for a fight with the much smaller man. Along with Winny and a few other regulars, I jumped up to prevent yet another bar brawl. Unlike Winny and a few other regulars, I somehow got in between the two would-be combatants. And while Five-Minute Jack was being pulled in one direction I found myself alone trying to talk some sense into a drink-enraged, red-faced, wide-eyed Son-of-Loser Paul. Not caring who was actually in front of him, he clenched his large fist and prepared to throw a wild punch in my direction.

Anyone with experience in fighting knows that attempting to throw a roundhouse right is almost suicidal. In John Wayne westerns, the combatants may be dumb enough to simply trade punches without ducking or countering, but not in real life. Nevertheless, I could see Son-of-Loser Paul was actually drawing back his arm to throw such a punch.

There are any number of ways to counter such a stupid move: Akido, jujitsu, karate, muay-Thai, Western boxing – they all had their techniques; and I knew several. Unfortunately, it is very hard to counter such a blow while one is lying on his back on the floor. Which is where I was at the moment. Because I had chosen simply to move my head out of the way and try once again to talk Son-of-Loser Paul out of fighting. But while attempting to run past me, a frightened Dang had bumped into me and my head had ricocheted off the crown of her cowgirl hat, keeping it (my head) in place, positioned perfectly for Son-of-Loser Paul's "stupid" move. And a roundhouse right that actually connects – which this one did – is a good move indeed.

Unless someone had suddenly started ringing the bell to buy everybody drinks, my hearing was affected; and for a few moments, it was a bit like being underwater – I couldn't tell which direction sounds were coming from. But my sight was fine. I could see Son-of-Loser Paul take a step closer to me. Possibly because he couldn't believe his good fortune, or possibly because he was off balance or possibly to see who it was he had knocked down or possibly to finish me off.

Whatever the reason, it gave me the opportunity to place the instep of one foot behind his heel and the sole of my other foot firmly against his knee. With his foot locked into position, I thrust my leg out hard against his knee and over he went. Backward. Down. Hard. I sat up. He groaned.

Fight over. I had a black eye. He would have a big bump on his head. I was awake. He was semi-conscious. I could stand up. It would be a few minutes before he could. I guess all that meant I had won. But as some of the bargirls ran to get some ice for my eye, I didn't feel like a winner. I felt stupid. Stupid for being in a bar fight and stupid for getting nailed with a roundhouse right by Son-of-Loser Paul.

6

To be honest, I wasn't quite certain why I was taking up Lisa Avery's invitation. And I felt a tinge of guilt at doing so. Nothing in Thailand is ever black and white, so, although I didn't exactly have a girlfriend, in a way I did. Thitagan, nicknamed Dao ("star"), was everything a man could desire: if a man desired a beautiful 26-year-old muay-Thai boxer from Korat who could probably deck him with one thrust of her curvaceous leg. But our unspoken agreement was that she could do as she liked with other men and I could do as I liked with other women. Although I hadn't failed to notice that whenever she thought I had in fact been with another woman her mood changed and our bedroom scenes resembled more of a boxing match than a love match. Which led me to sometimes wonder if unknown to me we had a second unspoken agreement that neither of us would actually act on our first unspoken agreement.

Maybe the blond was right: maybe I just wanted a change of pace. But although I might be imagining it, I thought I had seen something beyond the cool, cavalier, flippant nature of her invitation; something intangible just beneath the surface that suggested she might need help. It was either a kind of sixth sense I had developed for people in trouble or else just a hopelessly out-of-fashion notion that most women still needed to rely on big strong men. Whichever, I was about to find out.

She lived in a five-story building off Sukhumvith Road on *soi* 31. It was actually no more than a 20-minute walk from my apartment but I was running late, my eye ached, and even a short walk in Bangkok usually resulted in a shirt soaked with perspiration, so I hopped on the back of a motorcycle taxi at the Sukhumvith entrance to Washington Square. The strong smell of whiskey on the driver's breath wafted back at me and as he made his near-suicidal, against-the-light run across busy Sukhumvith Road I remembered I had forgotten to wear my Buddha amulet.

Lisa's building was on the corner of *soi* 31 and what was called the "Green Route," a series of back roads running between Petchaburi Road and Sukhumvith Road, which, in theory, offered drivers an alternative to the constant traffic jams on both. Like most theories, it was fine so long as it wasn't tested.

I had visited the apartment building once before at a friend's urgent request. His Thai wife had found a receipt for an expensive lady's watch, a gift she had never received, and had refused to let him in. I had met her a few times and we seemed to have hit it off, so he had asked me to use my Thai and whatever persuasive powers I might have in an attempt to calm her down. I had stood in the hallway of the fourth floor, pleading his case to his wife from behind a firmly closed and locked door. Although I remember thinking that if I were her, I probably wouldn't let him in either. She did eventually relent and grudgingly opened the door, but the marriage ended less than a year later.

It was one of those not untypical Thai buildings which served various purposes. On the ground floor was the office of an equipment supplier for swimming pools, fountains and spas, a Thai restaurant and a Western restaurant, and the floors above had apartments with the occasional small workshop or storage room wedged in here and there. Whether it was more residential than commercial was something no Thai zoning official would ever worry about. Everyone in Bangkok knew that a zoned city was a Western concept bearing little relevance for Asian town planners.

The restaurants faced the stylized yin-yang symbol of a brightly lit Korean restaurant and karaoke across the street, but the door to the apartments was at the side entrance facing the more sedate Euro Inn, a small hotel favored by Japanese businessmen. A sign near the road, as well as the address Lisa had jotted down, said the apartments were the "Leman Apartelle," but words painted beside the doorway informed me that the apartment building I was entering was the "Gaiete Inn." Six of one, half a dozen of the other.

I walked through a dark, gloomy hallway, turned left to avoid entering the Thai restaurant, and walked up the stairs to the third floor. The pungent odors of spicy Thai soup followed me all the way up. From somewhere in the outside darkness off a third floor balcony, a Gecko lizard made its presence heard. I found apartment 302 just beside the lift. There was no sound within. I knocked.

Within seconds she opened the door. I wasn't certain what the short, sheer, diaphanous bluish-white dress she had on was made of, but from its translucent nature, it was clear that foundation garments were not something she felt essential. Her hairstyle gave her the same tomboyish appeal as before and when she smiled there was in her blue eyes that same indefinable expression, balanced somewhere between mischief and malice. She seemed to have applied a minimum of makeup but a scent of flowery perfume assailed my nostrils. "Right on time."

It was a one-bedroom apartment with low ceilings and only a sliding, corrugated, metal divider served as a door between rooms. I got a quick glimpse of a bedside table on which were framed personal photographs taken where snow falls, and a copy of a book with the word "detective" in the title. The screensaver on the living room computer displayed a forest of pine trees partly covered with snow, and a swirling ceiling fan gave off a loud click with each revolution. Through the partly drawn curtains I could see the lights of the Korean restaurant across the street.

The apartment was clean, neat and certainly spacious enough for one person, but I had expected something a bit more flashy, or at least less practical; something that matched the unconventional if not outright outre personality of the girl. Or at least the personality I had perceived at the Halloween party. I half wondered if this was really her apartment. In my experience, people usually fit their apartments; this one didn't. There was also a surprising temporary quality to it. Folding tables and wickerware. Almost everything that could be sold quickly or else simply left behind.

She led me through the living room and out to a balcony. We sat in chairs on the balcony behind a rail covered with pink bougainvillea still glistening from rain. "I love it out here late at night."

Her statement conjured up a Manhattan taxi driver's almost exact words when he was driving me down a nearly deserted Fifth Avenue about 2 a.m. I had just seen my father take his last breath but the taxi driver's enthusiasm for the Big Apple at two in the morning had helped me remember that life is worth living. But the Bangkok street below Lisa's balcony was far from deserted.

I took the cold Singha beer she handed me and thanked her. I gestured toward the book on the table beside the chair. The title was *Crazy Cock*. I could see from where the bookmark jutted out that she was near the end. "I see you read Henry Miller."

"I love him. Have you read him?"

"The *Tropic's*; not that one."

"Did you know when he lived in New York his wife seduced a wealthy old man and used to show the old guy what she said was *her* writing? So the old guy gave her money as long as she kept writing."

I took a long hit on my beer. "I didn't know that."

"But it was *Henry's* writing." Her voice took on a conspiratorial tone. "She was sleeping with the old guy for *him* and pretending it was her work to make money for both of them."

"Sounds like Henry. Underneath it all, a romantic at heart."

"It *was* romantic. Until she ran off to Paris with a lesbian."

"That must have been a blow to Henry."

"It was." Her lips curled into a sardonic smile. "Some men don't have the capacity to understand how a woman can love someone from either sex."

I noticed that here on the balcony her royal blue eyes had enough shade of red to be described as violet. If Lisa Avery had a flaw in her appearance, I certainly couldn't spot it. She could accurately be described as adorably cute and undeniably sexy. "Wouldn't surprise me if some of those men are right here in Bangkok."

Her smile briefly evaporated and her eyes narrowed. She seemed about to respond but instead favored me with a coquettish smile. "So, was it about me?"

"Was *what* about you?"

She nodded toward my eye. "The fight."

"It wasn't actually about much of anything," I said. Like most bar fights, I thought.

"Would you like me to put some ice on that?"

"Someone already did, thanks."

"I don't think it did much good."

"I didn't think it would. But it made a few bargirls happy to play nurse for awhile."

"You didn't strike me as the Patpong type."

"Washington Square."

"I thought those bars were reserved for men over one hundred."

"They are. Sometimes they let a few of us younger lads in. But you have to know somebody."

On the street below, a motorcycle roared through one of several large puddles, sending a spray of water onto a seller of late-night Thai snacks. The vendor never glanced at the motorcycle and continued to wheel his dimly-lit cart unhurriedly along the wet street.

"So Frank Webber says you're a genuine New Yorker."

"That I am."

"How long have you been in Asia?"

"Five years in Beijing. With the embassy. Five here with the embassy. Over one year on my own."

"You speak Chinese?"

I nodded. "Mandarin."

She leaned back and stared at me, then her lovely lips curled into a playful smile. "Divorced?"

I nodded again.

She grew thoughtful. Knitted brows. Slight pout. I had no doubt she knew how cute she looked with knitted brows and a slight pout. "So your job with the embassy ended over a year ago. But you're still here. What do you do really?"

"A bit of this and a bit of that."

She gave me a knowing smile. "Quicksand."

"Say what?"

"The kind of guy who gets sucked into Bangkok and can't get out. The Thai Tar Baby's got you and she won't let go."

In the windows above the Korean restaurant, Karaoke girls stood before mirrors intently reapplying their makeup. Red and blue neon advertising the restaurant reflected in the street's scattered puddles lending the scene the fractured texture of a disturbing dream.

I had the feeling that finding what made Lisa tick might not be that easy. And I sensed she was in a very different mood than the night before. I was about to learn ho w right I was. I decided on a direct approach: "Enough about me. Tell me about yourself."

"There isn't much to tell. And, to be perfectly honest, I don't believe I need you now; yesterday I did."

"Need me in what way?"

"I've been looking for a way to…deal with someone. For a long time. But something happened."

"And?"

Her voice hardened. "And now I think I am about to find out all I need to know to make that someone pay for what he did."

"And whatever happened happened after you saw me at the party."

"Right! And in just a couple of hours, I should know all I need to know." She tilted her head and looked at me with concern. "Oh, but don't worry." She glanced at her slim gold watch on her slim white wrist. "That doesn't mean we can't go to bed for a bit."

I took a swig of beer. "That's a relief."

For just a moment she grew serious. "You don't like me much, do you?"

"You don't reveal enough of yourself for me to decide." She stared at another vendor appearing and disappearing as he peddled his food cart through the street's lights and shadows and remained silent. A small dark boy in a large shiny rain hat sat crouched in the front of the cart looking up at us without expression. "What made you think I could help you find someone?"

She smiled enigmatically. "A friend of yours."

"In Bangkok?"

"No. In New York. A fellow named Chinaman."

I couldn't help but react to that one. Chinaman, or rather, Liu Chiang-hsin, which translated as 'a mind as sharp as a sword.' And it was. I had first met him as a kid when Dad adopted him. Even though we grew up together, he was never outgoing; given his experiences as a child, I couldn't blame him for keeping his feelings to himself. In Mao's China, he had learned at an early age that expressed opinions can be dangerous. "Did he say you could call him 'Chinaman'?"

She nodded. "He did."

"Then he must have liked you, because only his friends call him that."

"He said I was lucky you were out here."

"The Manhattan yellow pages are full of detectives. How did you get onto him?"

"Well, the first one I called had just gone out of business due to some technicality over an illegal search, the second was too expensive, the third only specialized in seducing somebody's spouse or fiance to see if they were faithful and the fourth I met in an East Village coffee shop. He was a lot cheaper than the second but he spent the whole time talking not to me but to my tits."

I made certain my eyes were fastened to hers and tried to convince myself that nothing existed below the lady's chin.

"And Chinaman was my fifth and lucky try."

"I take it he talked to you, not to your tits."

At that, she grew serious. "That man looked right through my eyes and into me like no one else ever did."

I waited.

"What do you know about him?"

"He's my brother."

Her lovely blue eyes widened. I decided they were a moonstone blue; the shade of blue a man could become lost in forever and be happy about it. The shade of blue a man could desert his wife and kids and job and friends and self-respect for.

"I mean my father adopted him when he was a boy. He's descended from a scholar family. His father had loved Chinese tradition and culture, and that hadn't set too well with the Red Guards so they killed his father and drove his mother mad during Mao's Cultural Revolution. Chinaman had been a child at the time. He was smuggled out of Beijing into Hong Kong and eventually into New York. By a friend of dad's."

"And he became a private detective in New York City."

"A creative writing teacher then a detective." I stared into her eyes. "So that chance meeting we had at the bar?"

"Ummm, not exactly a chance meeting. I wanted to look you over. Chinaman described you pretty well and gave me your address. Not many foreigners your age and build living over the Boots and Saddle. A girl burning incense just outside the bar told me you and your portly friend had gone to the open-air bar down the street."

"And you took it for granted that your womanly charms would cause me to hit on you."

"Didn't they?"

"With a bit of encouragement from my portly friend."

"I must remember to thank him."

"So why did you brush me off?"

"I told you: You seemed a little too sure of yourself."

Actually, I had the impression she was about to loosen up just when Da arrived – "early," as she had said at the time – but I decided to drop it. Despite her surface confidence, there was something fragile about Lisa Avery. And I didn't get the feeling she understood Thailand and the Thais all that well: people deservedly known for their beautiful smiles and graceful charm and yet people with the highest murder rate in the world. Sometimes it took years of living in the kingdom before one learned a very simple truth: Thais are the nicest people in the world – until they're not. But I had learned early in life that you can't force protection on people who don't want it, so I decided if she didn't need anything I would get back to my own life.

"Speaking of friends, how's yours?" When she didn't seem to understand, I added: "The lady at the bar."

"Oh, Da. She's fine. She's been showing me the ropes here." She reached over to pour more white wine into her glass. I did my humanly best to ignore the outline of her breasts beneath her dress. I was already ignoring the curves of her legs. More or less. At least by Bangkok standards, I was doing an amazing amount of ignoring. "What does she do?"

She smiled. "Let's just say Da is a party animal."

"How long have you been out here?"

"A bit over three months."

"You waited a long time before you contacted me."

"I thought I'd see what I could do on my own."

My eye was beginning to pound more than it had before and my head ached and – I suppose a good sign – I had feeling in my finger just enough to know that it also ached. And neither the beer nor the humidity was helping my condition. "So you were willing to go to bed with me when you thought you might need my help. Now you don't need my help."

"But we can still go to bed." Something about the way she said the line made me feel as if she were offering alms to a beggar; I could have a handout whether I deserved it or not. She must have noticed my reaction because she added: "If you like."

I let that sit for several seconds. "Did you go to bed with Chinaman?"

"Hey! A lady never tells."

Actually, something else was bothering me about Lisa Avery's "You-can-still-have-it-anyway" attitude. In Pattaya, I had recently visited a friend, a former diving student and now the general manager of a hotel. While we talked beside the swimming pool, I had noticed a barefoot, bikini-clad Thai girl enter the stairway to a wing of the hotel. Her thin, elderly escort was saying something in broken English with a heavy German accent that made her throw her head back in loud ribald laughter. The laughter could be heard even when they disappeared briefly then reappeared on the second-floor landing and entered the room.

One of thousands of excited and contented male tourists from Europe, America and Australia spending their two- or three-week vacations with newly acquired Thai girlfriends in a luxurious Pattaya beach hotel room behind a door secured with a magnetic-mechanical variable code lock; a lock capable of being magnetically recoded in a few seconds with any of up to four billion codes. German steel workers, Italian businessmen,

American servicemen, Japanese farmers – like the keys themselves, completely interchangeable instruments with the correct financial code to feminine locks also capable of infinite recoding. Magnetic-mechanical unions of two-or three-week duration after which the recoding of the keys, locks and people could begin again. I couldn't help but get the impression that to Lisa Avery I was just one of these interchangeable instruments. I had nothing against the Pattaya scene – it was what it was; I just didn't feel like indulging in a magnetic-mechanical union with someone who acted as if she was doing me a favor.

I saw that the rain had stopped. I finished the beer and stood up. I dug a namecard out of my wallet and handed it to her. "This being the rainy season, I think I'll take a rain check."

Wrinkles of puzzlement lined her smooth brow. "You sound like you're insulted."

I allowed my eyes the brief luxury of roaming over her short, sheer dress. "I'm beginning to suspect you specialize in humiliating men. Or is it just me?"

For just a second, her eyes narrowed but then she must have decided a playful response was best. "You're saying I'm a dicktease? A man-hating lesbian?" Her smile widened as she gestured toward the book. "Or that I'm cock crazy?"

"I'm not sure what you are. But I think you're very pretty and I think you know that. What I think you don't know is that you may be far more naïve than you realize, and Bangkok can be a tricky place for pretty, naive American blondes on the hustle. Remember Kipling's warning about what happens to those who try to 'hustle the East.'"

Lisa stood up. "Remind me."

"Never mind. My eye hurts. I'm going home and go to bed." I walked just ahead of her to the door. She opened it for me. "Thanks for the beer."

"Anytime. Thanks for the advice. Maybe we'll meet again?"

"Maybe."

"Until then, I'll try not to hustle the East."

I waited in the street for a motorcycle taxi in a fine drizzle lost in thought. Something bothered me about Lisa Avery. So did the picture of a younger Lisa Avery on her table by her living room door. She stood hugging a woman who could have been her sister, her girlfriend, her anything. I knew I had to let it go: she was a big girl and could take care of herself. But why did I have the feeling she was far more vulnerable than she made out to be?

I glanced up to her balcony but it was empty. Clusters of bougainvillea still clung to the rail as if unable to decide whether or not to swing up and over or to give it up and let go. Immature chauvinist that I am, I couldn't help wondering if Chinaman did go to bed with her.

I looked up into the night sky and watched glistening beads of rain flow gracefully along electric wires like exquisite jewels and then – one by one – plunge abruptly into the darkness. And I thought of Lisa. And I thought of Kipling.

> *...And the end of the flight*
> *Is a tombstone white*
> *With the name of the late deceased,*
> *And the epitaph drear: A fool lies here*
> *Who tried to hustle the East*

DAY THREE

7

Benjasiri Park fronts Sukhumvith Road and serves as a small but welcome green oasis not quite overwhelmed by the pollution of the area. Its northern boundary runs beside the Emporium, one of Bangkok's classier shopping malls, and one especially favored by young Thai women out shopping with their elderly foreign boyfriends.

Three times a week I roust myself out of bed about 7 a.m., throw on some old jogging clothes and Adidas sneakers and make the five-minute walk to the park. A paved road curves around the park and here I join other joggers – some local, some foreign, and some hotel guests of the Imperial Queen's Park – and jog. I try to make at least a mile or two in decent time but the idea isn't to go for distance; simply to sweat off as much beer as I can.

I had just finished my un and sat on a narrow concrete ledge near the park's small lake. Billowy white clouds scudded leisurely across a light blue sky. Pigeons hopped anxiously about, ready to brawl over scraps of food. A few dozen followers of Falun Gung were in the midst of cultivating their moral qualities through various sets of exercises. Beyond the white blossoms and dark green leaves of frangipani trees I could glimpse joggers as they passed.

I was still puffing hard and wiping sweat from my face with a towel when I heard someone approach from behind. I turned to see a thin young Caucasian in his late 20's dressed in short-sleeved white shirt, blue-and-red paisley tie, tan slacks and loafers. He stopped just a few feet away from me.

He had wavy blond hair, bright blue eyes, a pointed nose and a pointed chin. His skin appeared pasty and reddened, as that sometimes seen on foreigners in Thailand whose complexions never quite adjust to the Asian sun. He was sweating more than I was and his posture suggested he was about to wilt in the heat. He had the look of a young missionary as described in the travel writing of Somerset Maugham: resigned to his situation even though it wasn't what he thought it would be. It never was.

His voice was high-pitched. His accent was middle-class British. "Mr. Sterling?"

The young man looked vaguely familiar. I nodded.

"Father Mike told me where I could find you about now. My name is Kenneth Wade. We met once in the slums."

Then I did remember him. It was at some kind of Catholic charity benefit for slum children. I had helped Father Mike, an eccentric Catholic priest, locate a man who had a penchant for chatting up very young female flower sellers at intersections and luring them into his van for sexual purposes. Only one family had been brave enough to press charges. I had tracked down the man and got a measure of satisfaction when he thought he could fight his way past me but he had the last laugh as his ties to corrupt, high-ranking police had eventually won the day. Father Mike had the girl sent far from Bangkok to avoid repercussions.

I stood up and reached my hand out. "Yes, of course. I remember you. From Manchester, right?"

"Yes." His hand was moist and smooth; his grip weak. "May I sit down?"

I sat down again and motioned for him to do so.

"Father Mike has a problem he thinks you might be able to help him with." He paused as if waiting for a reaction from me, then, getting none, continued on. "You may know about the loan shark situation in our slum area, I think."

I nodded. "I know they're more dangerous than sharks in the water."

"Yes. Well, even in slum dwellings, people have rents to pay. Sometimes they simply don't have the money so they are forced to borrow."

I wiped my neck and placed the towel over my shoulders. "At extremely high rates of interest."

"Yes. Then they owe still more money. So the loan sharks threaten them and sometimes beat them. Then they have no choice but to sell whatever they have of value. The loan sharks also demand a guarantor of the loan, usually a friend or neighbor in the slums."

He paused here almost lost in thought. It couldn't have been more than six months since I had seen him but he seemed to have aged six years. Perhaps he had been affected by the depressing nature of his job. One can only see destitute slum dwellers having their lives ruined by gangs of thugs protected by the rich and powerful for so long before being affected by it.

"So now we have a case where an elderly woman borrowed nothing herself but signed as a guarantor for a friend. The friend couldn't pay and fled Bangkok." He put his hand to his neck and made an unsuccessful attempt to pull his tie away from his prominent Adam's apple. "Now the loan sharks are after the guarantor. She sold her radio, kitchen utensils and even her Buddha amulets but each day she's deeper in debt. She says she is old and doesn't care about herself but she has a twelve-year-old granddaughter." A brief flicker of anger clouded his bright blue eyes. "The men have been making noises about taking the granddaughter and using her to recoup the debt."

"And what is it Father Mike wants from me?"

Kenneth Wade seemed apprehensive as dozens of unruly pigeons swirled about and edged closer to the ledge. "The girl doesn't want to go to another province. She won't leave her grandmother. Not for long, anyway. Father Mike said you might be able to hide the girl for a short period of time; while he and I try to work out something with the loan sharks."

"Have you dealt with them before?"

"Yes."

I knew how tough Father Mike was beneath his affable facade; he had to be; protecting the poor in a country where corruption flourishes was a tough business. But at least on the surface Kenneth Wade appeared ill-equipped to deal with the Bangkok heat let alone the intricacies and pervasiveness of bribery and intimidation. Still, people often had resources that surprised me. "And they're open to reason?"

"Sometimes. Or sometimes they are a gang protected by senior police officers. We make an appointment with the police officers and explain our problem, never suggesting for a moment, of course, that the officer himself is involved. That technique we can use only a few times." He ran his hand slowly along the back of his neck as if the sun were burning him. I decided he had a bad case of seborrheic dermatitis, reddened skin foreigners in Thailand get thanks to pollution. I knew what it was because I'd had a touch of it a few months after I arrived. I had made the mistake of washing it well with soap. I wanted to warn him not to use soap as it would make it worse but I decided another man's rashes were none of my business.

I could tell he was trying to think of the best way to ask something else. "One other thing. We think we are being watched by the gang. We know the grandmother is. They don't want the girl to disappear. That's their leverage." He hesitated, as if embarrassed to ask more, then continued. "Father Mike wonders if you will come and take the girl."

"What about the grandmother?"

"She said she won't leave her home and doesn't care what they do to her."

I didn't respond right away. I looked over at the growing horde of pigeons scrambling brazenly about for crumbs and then looked up to watch a skytrain pass. Large letters advertising a phone network were on the cars of the train: "A Beautiful Life – A Beautiful Orange." It wasn't that I didn't want to help; I just try never to promise anyone more than I can deliver. "I might be able to help. I should know in a day or two. Give me a number where I can reach you or Father Mike."

Kenneth Wade handed me his namecard with his new mobile phone number printed on the back. He stood up, shook my hand, thanked me for my time and said he had to get back to work.

I watched him carefully avoid the pigeons scampering for food as well as the Falun Gong practitioners meditating on the grass, and walk off in the direction of Sukhumvith Road. A young man with a pasty complexion, a bad case of dermatitis, a high-pitched, reedy voice, a birdlike nose, and a lot of guts.

8

Two hours later, I hailed a taxi outside Washington Square and headed for Thitagan's training camp on the Thonburi side of the Chao Phraya River. As the tiny, elderly, bespectacled, taxi driver gripped the top of the wheel, thumbs touching, his wrinkled brown hands fluttered and flapped in spasms like the wings of a dying butterfly. He looked out at the confusing swirl of traffic before him by sitting up very straight and peering between two large Buddha statues affixed to his dashboard, and squinting beneath Buddhist amulets and a fresh garland hanging from his rearview mirror. His straight white hair was long in back but when, at the first red light, he turned to ask in broken English if this was my first trip to Thailand, I could see he was losing the battle of male pattern baldness.

I had learned long ago that in Thailand even simple things could be complicated, so I considered my response carefully. If I said yes, and pretended to be a visitor who spoke almost no Thai, he might pester me to hire him to see some tourist destinations or to try an overpriced massage parlor, or to shop at a gems store; most likely the type of store notorious for poor quality gems at high prices. If, on the other hand, he learned that I was an expatriate who spoke fluent Thai, rather than relaxing, I would spend my time responding to the usual questions about my origins, work, marital status and, of course, whether I had (or would be interested in having) a Thai girlfriend. He had already seen me hail his taxi, Thai-style, by holding my hand out, palm down, and slowly lowering it, a dead giveaway to a Thai that I wasn't a new boy in town.

The ploy I used was to inform him in a hoarse voice while gripping my throat that I had visited Thailand a few times before and loved the country but had some throat problems and it hurt to talk. This was always accepted with good grace, as it was now, and I customarily made up for my lack of conversational skills due to sudden and mysterious illness by tipping well.

The weekday traffic wasn't as horrendous as I had thought it would be and I managed to reach my destination in just under half an hour. I paid the driver, wished him good luck, and began walking.

The way to the camp was through a maze of alleyways and narrow lanes which at times resembled the Thai countryside more than an area within a crowded city. On dirt paths, chickens clucked excitedly at having to flutter out of my way, badly scarred *soi* dogs eyed me warily, and vegetable gardens stretched out to the horizon. Then the dirt path ended abruptly and I walked on a paved path lined with modern lampposts past recently constructed lower-middle class town houses.

In a yard partly hidden by bottle palms, a thicket of tall, slender yellow bamboo swayed in the breeze, repeatedly concealing and exposing a black, concave, satellite dish pointed toward heaven. The sun illuminated pink and purple sashes tied to the post of a spirit house and coruscated along beer-bottle colored shards of glass cemented into the top of a wall. A small boy pushed a still smaller boy on a swing while a teenage maid in a Thai-style sarong swept a wooden porch with a short Thai-style whiskbroom. The hiss of the pliant twigs and bamboo bristles along the teakwood floor merged with the creaking of the swing, the laughter of the children and the chatter of small birds.

As I rounded a bend and the roof of the two-story wooden house of the training camp came into view, I heard the unmistakable sounds of muay-Thai: gloves whapping with force and determination against practice pads, the hissing of boxers as they practiced their kicking, the slapping sounds of sparring partners and the whaps of jump ropes hitting the wooden floor of an outside training area.

The boxing camp might not even have been recognized as such in the West. The tin-and-wood roof over the outdoor ring looked as if it might be blown away during a serious storm, and the equipment – from gloves to heavy bags to ring ropes – had seen better days. Except for a small sign with the name of the camp, and the usual spirit shrines, the wooden house itself might have been a slum dwelling awaiting razing by the government. But the reputation of those who taught there, and the dedication of those who learned muay-Thai there, was as respected as in any training camp in Thailand. Those who trained here regarded this camp (*Daochalatfa* – "Never-extinguished Star") as being very different from camps that accepted Western students. Here there was no music, and no one was left to practice alone. No one would ever be matched too early against a more experienced opponent simply for a promoter's financial gain. Here it was understood the path of a champion was not only through boxing skills but through pain. The ability to absorb pain and continue on to victory was regarded as no less important than *khaeng raeng* (strength) and *jai su* (fighting spirit).

The fronds of banana trees reached over a low green hedge flecked with orange clusters of Ixora flowers. Behind the hedge a shoulder-high bamboo fence ran the length of the lane fronting the house. I pushed open the wooden gate and *waiied* the boxers. Dao's elder brother, Narong ("battle"), was training one of the professional boxers, and I stopped to congratulate the boxer for handily winning his last fight at Lumpini Stadium and apologized for missing it. The boxer grinned and *waiied* me with gloved hands. Sweat from his forehead and chin dripped onto his gloves.

I nodded to her father, Amnart ("power"), who was correcting a beginning boxer on his kicking method. Each time the boy kicked, Amnart would slightly move his leg, torso and hands to their proper position. The boy paid strict attention. In Thailand, teachers were still highly respected, and the relationship between a muay-Thai trainer and his students was that of a father and children. The boy's faulty hip movement showed he apparently wasn't getting the hang of it and I heard Amnart tell the boy to pay attention to what he was saying because he wasn't going to waste his time playing his flute for a water buffalo. The boy's head hung forward, his thin shoulders drooped and he gave his teacher an up-from-under look replete with remorse and contrition.

I spotted Dao beyond the training area near the house, dressed in white T-shirt, blue shorts and cheap sneakers, her long black hair tied back in a ponytail with a red barrette. A tire had been placed flat on the ground and she was exercising by standing on top of it, legs apart, and rapidly jumping up and switching both feet in the air, first in one direction and then jumping up and placing them in another. It was an exercise she enjoyed after her regular workout and just before taking her shower. Her breathing was heavy, her forehead glistened with sweat and her attention was internally focused on her training As I approached, I allowed my gaze to linger: The bouncing pony tail, the determination clearly evident in the beautiful face and the smooth muscled curvature of her powerful brown legs.

I knew she couldn't talk until she had finished her exercise so I went into the house and joined two teenaged boxers on a cheap sofa watching a live bout of muay-Thai on a television which had seen better days. Her father ran a very strict camp and I knew that these two would not be watching television unless their training session was finished. There was an ancient phone with a lock on it which in any case was to be used only by trainers. Cellphones were reluctantly allowed in the camp for those few who could afford them but they were never to be used during training. On the wall above a shelf full of trophies a sign in Thai read "What do you have?"

Dao had explained that it was asking the boxers what they had in reserve during a fight. When they felt the pain unbearable, when they couldn't catch their breath, when they were blinded by their own sweat and could taste and smell their own blood, when they knew their powerful opponent was trying to finish them off – what did each boxer of this camp have left inside? Her father had spoken to me once at length as to how essential it was to find out what a boxer has in reserve and how it was his job to find the best way of working with what he found there.

I had visited the house several times and I knew the sleeping rooms were even more spartan than the living room. There were no beds, only bedrolls, no photographs, only pictures cut from magazines or a calendar with the king's picture. A few of the rooms did have pictures of modern Thai muay-Thai champions as well as grainy black-and-white photographs of Thai boxers from an earlier era; before gloves were used. The boxers hands were wrapped with rope, hemp or cotton soaked in glue. It was said some fought with bits of glass glued into the bandages. On the wall above Dao's bed was a picture of a very young man, her father, hardening his instep and shin by a method long gone – kicking against the trunk of a banana tree.

There was no air-conditioning, only fans, there was little privacy as even Dao had nothing to herself but a portion of a room curtained off. Each boxer washed his own clothes and, under a trainer's supervision, took turns preparing dinner for the rest.

In an outside area behind the house, traditional water-filled *klong* jars with scoops served as baths. And of course the toilet was not of the sit-down, flush variety. Amnart only recently installed a refrigerator but I noticed it had a lock on it. Dao had described the camp as "like an orphanage or a monastery."

It was also just a bit like a prison. Lights were out early and everyone was supposed to be in their room. There was officially no opportunity for sex while one lived at the camp. Early morning runs at Sanam Luang, daily exercising, contact sparring, intense training and preparations for bouts, pushed such thoughts from their minds. Most Thai boxers went "home" after a fight, back to their village or town where, as might be expected, they would quickly find some outlet for their sexual drives.

Nevertheless, well after sunset, twice a week, usually Tuesday and Thursday, Dao made her escape by pushing through her window, circling around to the front of the house and climbing the bamboo fence or locked wooden gate. She would then walk to the main road and take a taxi to my apartment over the Boots and Saddle. But the barking *soi* dogs were a dead giveaway that someone was outside the house in the yard and Dao had no illusions that her father and the other boxers knew nothing about her nocturnal activities. This was the only exception he allowed to his rules; and it was never acknowledged. If it had been, she would have been barred from training. The truth was professional trainers who worked daily with the same students could instinctively tell from the energy level if a boxer had been neglecting his or her rest; and Dao was experienced enough to know this.

She was almost always back by 5 a.m. in time for the Sanam Luang run. Twice she had been late but had had the presence of mind to buy some fruit and vegetables to create the fiction that she was returning from early morning shopping.

She appeared in the doorway of the living room with her hair down and wearing a white blouse, khaki slacks and casual shoes. She spoke in Thai. "All set. Shall we eat something?"

"Sure. But I need to speak with your brother and father. It might be best if we all go, all right?"

She seemed a bit surprised at this but nodded. She spoke to them and they agreed to join us in a few minutes. The two of us headed out into the lane and walked in silence, the sounds of muay-Thai gradually fading behind us. The sky above was still a canopy of light blue punctuated by fluffy wisps of white clouds. Partly in deference to Thai customs and partly due to simple common sense, Dao reserved demonstrations of affection for my apartment.

We reached the lane's popular open-air restaurant and sat down on plastic stools as purplish red as the crimson bracts of nearby ginger bushes. The rickety table was just large enough to serve four, if the four didn't mind one another's elbows. We were partly shielded from the mid-day sun by a traveler's palm whose dried-up, fan-shaped leaves had seen better days. Crates of soft drinks were piled behind the restaurant separating it from a long stretch of green lawn leading to rickety one- and two-story wooden houses nestled cheek-by-jowl.

The restaurant's Buddhist shrine was crowded with offerings of oranges, joss-sticks and tattered peacock feathers rising out of rusty Ovaltine cans. The tables were almost all occupied and the owner and her children bustled about serving customers.

A dark-complexioned girl about twelve expertly employed a cleaver to cut bite-size pieces of duck on a Tamarind wood chopping board. When she noticed Dao, she smiled and quickly took our orders for four. She gave the order to a slightly older girl who began grinding peppercorn, garlic and coriander roots with mortar and pestle. A few feet from our table a small boy with a frowning face employed a celery stick as a spatula to place pork inside square-shaped soup patties. As he wrapped each piece his hands turned white from flour. Flies used my own hands as jumping off points to buzz about kaleidoscopic bits of red and green Thai chilies in a small pink dish.

Food constantly simmered in a wok placed on the flanges of an earthenware pot filled with charcoal. Family members carried trays filled with round balls of chicken and beef-on-sticks, crisp noodles and fresh vegetables. Two overfed tabby cats stealthily prowled after them like sharks following garbage scows.

For several moments, I stared at Dao in silence. She was every inch the daughter of a respected trainer of muay-Thai in Korat. She had been brought up with her brothers and the other boxers as if she was one of the boys. And although she had been expected to feed chickens and clean and cook and sew, she made it her business to learn Thai boxing well. Despite her obvious beauty, she was as tough as the men.

Her face could not be described as delicately sculptured or light-complexioned, hence, in the eyes of many Thais, she would not be thought beautiful. But to a discerning observer, there was a keen intelligence in her dark brown eyes, and a special loveliness in her long, naturally curving eyelashes, her full, generous lips, and small but almost Caucasian nose. Even the tiny boxing scar above the eyebrow accentuated rather than spoiled the symmetrical beauty of her face. But, when annoyed, her face also clearly revealed strength of character, and I had more than once been on the receiving end of a smoldering defiance which was delivered with a direct stare and firmed-up line of her strong jaw. But when in a playful mood, her Thai smile could light up a room while the sound of her laughter could make anyone who heard it laugh with her. A lady of many moods who could take heavy punishment in a ring, endure it, and come back to win. I often thought that I admired her as much as I loved her.

She seemed more than a bit on edge and I knew why. Although men from abroad learning muay-Thai did only fairly well against native boxers, women from abroad did very well against Thai women boxers. Many of these women were taller and more muscular than their Thai opponents and often snared victory. Dao had lost only once in her several fights, to a thick-bodied American woman from Pennsylvania who had learned Thai boxing. In three days she would have a rematch with the same woman, a woman who had knocked her out in the second round with a kick she hadn't even seen coming. A kick that had given her a tiny scar over her right eyebrow.

The sanctioning body for the fight was the International Women's Muay-Thai Association. At 108 pounds, Dao was in the Junior Flyweight division. After her defeat, she had dropped from second to fourth place. She had been knocked out and scarred as well. In her mind, she had been humiliated and had let her father and her camp down. I knew by now that she was always moody before her matches, but she was especially moody before this one.

Her English wasn't fluent but she could usually hold her end of a conversation. But I decided to speak to her in Thai and I addressed her by her fighting name, *Sangdao* (light of the star). "You look very beautiful today."

"You must want something, yes?"

"You mustn't be so suspicious."

"Why do you need to speak to my father and brother?"

"I need a place for a child in trouble to stay. For a while. A safe place."

The woman placed a small bowl in front of Dao. Slices of light green mango were partly immersed in a murky dark brown fish sauce with bits of chili and onion. There were so many tiny pink specks of sun-dried shrimp on the mango it looked as if each slice had broken out in a rash.

She looked up at me, placed her hand on my chin and slightly turned my head. "Does the eye hurt?"

I wondered when she would get around to mentioning that. "Not much."

"It has to do with the girl in danger?"

"No. This was just from a bit of horsing around in a bar." When she said nothing, I continued: "A girl didn't hit me and the fight wasn't about a girl. A drunk got lucky when I tried to calm him down. All right?"

She picked up her spoon and fork. "All right. Please don't act like I am such a jealous type. I just care about your health."

"I know you are not the jealous type," I lied. "I just wanted it to be clear." She stared back at me as she began eating. I gave her a smile. "Anyway, you really do look beautiful today."

"In my dream last night, I was bitten by a snake." She pointed to her waist. "Here."

I waited. Over the years I had learned that every dream a Thai woman had could somehow be interpreted to mean that her husband or boyfriend was being unfaithful.

"That means I will marry someone of my own class. Too bad the snake hadn't bit my head. Then I would marry rich."

"What if he had bit your foot?"

"Oh, no. Then my husband would be very poor."

"What if you dream of a boyfriend getting a black eye?"

"Then he probably deserved it."

Dao's father and brother appeared and returned greetings from several customers. Her father was tall, slim and ramrod straight. He had hair short enough to pass as a Marine guard and he carried himself with something close to military bearing. Beneath thick eyebrows his dark eyes seemed to be constantly assessing anyone speaking to him. He was quiet and observant and everything about him said that this was not a man who tolerated bullshit. His own career as a boxer had been spectacular. He had been known for his lightning speed and for ending a fight with a barely visible blow from one of his elbows.

Narong's face and body were wider than his father's and in the ring he was slower moving. But what he lacked in speed he made up for in power. And stamina. I had seen his handsome face, strong jaw and thick neck absorb enormous punishment and yet he never flinched or revealed in any way that he felt pain. His career had been very respectable but it had never approached that of his father's success and fame. He was now in his late twenties and his retirement from the ring would not be far off.

After a brief discussion of fights coming up at Lumpini and Ratchadamnern stadiums, and the strengths and weaknesses of the fighters involved, I raised the subject of the slums. I told them about Father Mike's request and the girl's situation. I said I could think of no other place that might be as safe as a respected muay-Thai training camp. I also mentioned that it was possible news of her whereabouts would leak out and there could be danger.

While I was speaking, the girl placed a tray of brown duck eggs in a sauce of spices in front of them. The dish resembled barren islands isolated from one another in the midst of volcanic liquid fire. I glanced at the food on the other tables. What was being eaten varied in texture, shape, color and degree of exotica, but with most dishes, green and red chilies were ever-present: embedded in curries, floating in soups, mixed with salt, sprinkled on fried fish and poured onto any dish deemed lacking in spice.

Amnart picked up his spoon. "Which slum is the girl in?"

I told him while accepting his offer of a duck egg.

He spoke quickly to Narong in Korat accent. Narong replied in the same accent. The discussion continued for a few exchanges before Narong turned to me. "We will take the girl. She is welcome to live at our camp until there is no danger."

"Thank you."

He ate one of the duck eggs with the enthusiastic enjoyment of one who loves good food. "On one condition."

I waited.

"We will go with you to pick her up."

"I thank you for your offer but that's my responsibility."

Narong finished chewing another duck egg. Amnart cleared his throat. "You know my son, Buen."

"I do."

"He was a monk for two years. But before he found the proper path, he had fallen in with bad people. He did things we are not proud of. But he has spent time in slums. He knows Bangkok's slums well. He will help. Go see him and tell him I said to help you."

What worried me was that Amnart's insistence that "they" would help would include Dao. To include her placed her in danger; to leave her out insulted her ability and courage.

I chose my words carefully. "I will see Buen and I know he will help. But there is no need for you to accompany me to rescue the girl. This is a situation with some danger."

Amnart glanced at Dao and back to me as if reading my mind. "No, this is an opportunity to make merit. For all of us."

Amnart and Narong finished eating and returned to the camp, allowing Dao and me a few minutes alone. I reached into my wallet to pull out a five hundred baht bill and a slip of paper fell to the ground and fluttered toward Dao. She reached down, picked it up and stared at it. "What's this?"

"That is…the name of a woman who asked for my help. As a detective."

She continued to stare at the paper. "And did you go to see this 'Lisa'?"

"Yes, I did." I held out my hand. "Now would you mind giving it back to me?"

"She is a client?"

"Look, I told you about my adopted brother in New York, remember?"

"Chinaman?"

"Yes! He had her get in touch with me. She seems to need help."

She took one last look at the scrap of paper and handed it back to me. I knew her English was good enough and her mind sharp enough that she had it memorized.

"Is she pretty and young?"

"Dao, remember – "

"Perhaps I could help her. Maybe I should pay her a visit."

"Thitagan!"

I knew the extent of her jealousy and was determined to deal with it but an outdoor café near her father's training camp wasn't the place and a few day's before her fight wasn't the time. I paid the bill. We didn't speak on the way back to the camp. I said goodbye at the gate. She smiled and wished me a pleasant day. The rainy season had just gotten several degrees colder.

9

The early afternoon sun beat down on Bangkok's Chinatown boldly enough, but as its rays swept through the narrow lanes leading away from Yaowarat Road, its intrusion became more tentative, less confident, and – until completely surrendering to shadows – it yielded far more glare than warmth. The area was Bangkok's oldest, and traffic was as it always was – congested and chaotic.

I got out of the taxi a few blocks away from my destination, and made my way through noisy jumbles of streetside stalls selling everything from noisome animal innards to silk tapestries of the Great Wall so gaudy that the emperor who had ordered it built would turn in his grave.

As I approached the shop, I thought of how I had first met Buen. It was on a weekday in late January, just after he had been hired to protect the elderly American owner of a Nana Plaza bar. I knew the bar owner well from my CIA days, so when he called close to midnight and said he had had some threats and expected trouble, I quickly grabbed a taxi.

Just as I arrived, I saw three rough looking Thais walking up to the owner who was standing beside a well-built, very dark complexioned Thai with shoulder-length hair somewhere in his early 30's. The three men had slicked back hair, muscle-revealing, short-sleeve shirts, and the aggressive attitudes of schoolyard bullies.

The second they raised their voices demanding something from the owner Buen politely placed his hands on the owner's shoulders and moved him aside, and stepped in front of the men. He stood placidly, with a serene smile on his face and his hands at his sides. His facial expression and body posture revealed no trace of hostility or nervousness. The closest and most aggressive of the Thais shouted something and when he got no reaction he kicked out at him. That was when all hell broke loose.

I saw that it was three to one so I pounced on the third man, spun him around, and, avoiding his punch, brought up my left wrist to trap his arm and to force him down, facing forward and away. He had almost enough strength to break the grip but I managed to grasp my left forearm with my right hand, locking his arm firmly in place. I applied pressure and he went down on one knee. But I wasn't sure how long a simple *jiu jitsu* technique could tame the lion heart of a muay-Thai boxer.

Suddenly Buen was beside me, politely thanking me for my help. I wondered why someone in the midst of fighting two men had broken off to thank me then saw that both of his opponents were lying on the pavement, out cold. I realized then how skilled he was and how my involvement had been totally unnecessary.

He bent over and said a few sentences to the man still trapped in my armlock. When the man nodded, Buen motioned for me to let him go. The man rose and quickly roused his friends. The three of them left without a word.

Buen and I had spent some time drinking that night and several times after that, discussing the various systems of self-defense. Over the years, several schools of martial arts experts had come to Thailand to try their skills against Thai boxers. The experts had quickly learned that they faced incredibly tough opponents inured to pain. Almost all – from Chinese kung fu to Dutch Chakuriki to Japanese kickboxers – had gone down in ignominious defeat. Thai boxers so easily demolished those with foreign fighting styles that disappointed Thai audiences began avoiding such fights and promoters lost money.

Buen liked the fact that I was interested in muay-Thai, and

one day, about six months before, he invited me to visit the training camp where he had once trained as a professional muay-Thai boxer. And that is when I met Amnart, his father and owner of the camp, Narong, his brother and the camp's head trainer, and his sister, Dao.

Buen had been a professional boxer with a real chance at winning a title. But he had been more fascinated with firearms and the world outside the ring than with constant training. Finally, his father had kicked him out. Enough time had now passed that if there was a coolness between his father and Buen, at least Buen was still considered a member of the family.

The Celestial Delight Gold Shop sold gold and silver jewelry and had been bought with the corruption money of a senior Bangkok police officer who had made his fortune protecting Bangkok's illegal gambling dens, but other than that it had little in common with other goldshops in Chinatown. Its name was spelled out along the first floor of an ancient three-story building in English, Thai and Chinese. A slice of sunlight had managed to penetrate its wide show window transforming an assortment of expensive figurines, Buddhas, necklaces, bracelets and rings into a glittering golden wonderland.

A uniformed but unarmed Thai guard stood beneath the pedimented doorway of the shop. I nodded to him and entered. At the nearest counter, a young couple was being shown an assortment of gold necklaces. The girl was shyly trying on a necklace before a counter mirror while her beau looked on with a mixture of pride and bashfulness. At two other counters, female shop clerks sat on stools reading Chinese language fashion magazines. While the displays of jewelry were bright and dazzling, the rear of the room was almost dim.

The shop space was only a few times wider than its show window, its ceiling was high and its chandelier lighting was the product of another era. Over many decades, fancy wall molding and elaborate ceiling molding had begun the slow process of deteriorating, and the green-and-red ceiling rosette set in the midst of oval-shaped applied molding had darkened. The room was air-conditioned but the ancient flush-mounted ceiling fans slowly turned, casting strange shadows. Century-old wood and glass wall panels displayed scenes from famous Chinese operas. At either end of the room facing the street, interior green shutters remained open inside recessed windows.

A wall shelf held the usual Thai Buddha, garlands and other offerings, while beneath it was a narrow wooden table of various Chinese legendary heroes and deities, their dust-covered swords and hands decorated with fresh garlands. A faint scent of incense permeated the room.

An elderly brown man wearing a brown Sun Yat-sen jacket sat behind a wooden desk near a rear inner door, working with an abacus. The clicking beads echoed off the walls of the room just loudly enough to be heard over the sounds of traffic. He gave me the slightest of smiles and reached under the counter to press a button. He nodded toward the rear of the room. I had called ahead and I knew Buen had told him to buzz me in.

I crossed the aged parquet flooring and pushed open a paneled wooden door. I stepped into a poorly lit alcove devoid of furniture and decorated with a half dozen examples of expert calligraphy framed along the walls. I knocked on a much thicker door with a peephole. The peephole darkened briefly. When light reappeared, I could hear bolts being thrown and a key turning. Buen welcomed me in with a *wai* and immediately threw the bolts and turned the key.

In contrast to the front room, this smaller room was as bright and white and shiny as a 1950's kitchen commercial on American TV. Beneath fluorescent lighting, rows of gleaming steel boxes lined the entire rear wall. Another wall was lined with a spotlessly clean glass counter, on which were magnifying glasses, a microscope, velvet-lined trays and Chinese-style scales and weights. Against the wall to my left was a late-model computer on a modern beige desk beside a fax and telephone. The screensaver displayed the head and shoulders of Kuan Ti, the Chinese god of war. I had been here twice before and I knew the alcove at the rear had a sink and a small refrigerator. The room had no windows and no other exit.

I also knew there was a large hidden space inside the rear wall; a space filled with various weapons and boxes of ammunition Buen had bought from a Thai middleman who in turn had bought them from Cambodian soldiers. More and more impoverished young men were joining the Cambodian army and then as soon as possible deserting and selling their weapons, ammunition and uniforms to the highest bidder. It was the latest wrinkle in the Southeast Asian arms trade.

Buen's jet-black hair was long and thick and it continued down in natural waves past his shoulders. His face was slightly triangular, a large forehead tapering down to a strong square chin. His goatee was thick and lustrous. His eyes were a deep coal black and his nostrils were slightly flared. His lips weren't as thick as those on Cambodian Buddhas, but almost. If someone didn't know his background, they might mistake him for an artist. Unless they insulted him or threatened him. Then, assuming they were perceptive enough, they would notice a certain look in his eyes; and a certain stillness descend on him. But it was the same stillness that might pervade the atmosphere just before the cyclone appears.

He was dressed in a black short-sleeved polo shirt, square at the bottom, and worn outside and over his tan trousers. I knew he was very devout in his own way and three of the five Buddha amulets he wore on a gold chain around his neck were visible. He wore black slip-on loafers.

When I refused any refreshment, he pulled up two grey office chairs and we sat facing each other while I filled in the details on the plight of the girl. I told him how his father had agreed to take the child for as long as necessary. I also told him his father insisted he and Narong and Dao would accompany me to the slum and assist me in getting the boy. I told him I didn't feel they should go but his father had said that was the deal; and his father was a hard man to argue with.

At that, Buen smiled. He spoke in Thai. "You think there will be no problem in getting the girl?"

"I'm not sure. She's with her grandmother. We just have to pick her up. But…."

"But there are some men who would like to stop you."

I nodded. "I don't like the idea of putting your family in any danger but your father insisted they would go. All three of them." I had little doubt that Buen understood that if events escalated, I especially wanted his protection for Dao. But it was not something I could simply tell him; it would be almost an insult to suggest his sister could not protect herself. And, if she knew, she would never forgive me for doubting her ability. It would also be casting aspersions on her father's training.

He stood up and walked almost soundlessly over the grey tile floor to the steel jewelry boxes. "I think this: If you can get the girl safely away from these men, and this is known in the slums, then they lose face. And then people aren't so scared of them anymore." He motioned for me to join him. "And the men who want the girl can't allow that to happen."

He placed a key in a lock inside the door of a steel cabinet at least three foot square, and turned it, first one way, then another. He grabbed the handle and yanked the door open. He pulled out the top drawer filled with boxes of jewelry with the store's logo on each box. He jiggled the drawer and lifted it out. He motioned for me to pull down a nearby drop shelf and he carefully placed the drawer on it. Then he returned to the cabinet, reached his hand into the back, until he had made the sound of three clicks. He reached in and brought out a drawer cleverly made to hide inside the recesses of the safe. He pulled the top off, reached in, and brought out a 9mm, polymer-frame, semi-automatic, Glock 19.

He wiped it with a rag and handed it to me. "Unregistered." I handled it with genuine admiration. "One in the chamber plus fifteen in the clip, right?" He nodded. "When my father was a New York detective, he owned a .38. Never wanted a semi-automatic. Too many stories of them jamming. But now New York police have been issued with these."

Buen shrugged. "I never heard of a Glock jamming."

I nodded, played with the weapon a bit more then handed it back. "I'll stay with what you gave me before."

He smiled. "Like father, like son?"

"Something like that."

He put the weapon back and sat down. "All right. Let me know when. And let me know the address of the grandmother."

"I will. But it might be difficult to find in the slums. That area is – "

"I know the area well. I used to hang out there. The things I did I am not proud of. But rest assured I know the area. And I know the people. Just get me the address and let me know when." We chatted for a bit. About guns, about fights, about lots of things. But underneath it all, I didn't feel good about myself. I was about to involve friends in a dangerous undertaking. And if the sharks were in fact protected by high ranking police, they would certainly feel no qualms in doing whatever they had to do to retain their hold on people in the slum.

I got up to leave. Buen walked me to the door and opened it. He smiled. "My sister?"

"She is fine."

He smiled and nodded toward my eye. "I mean, did she give

you that?"

"No. Not *this* one. But I think she will give me another one soon."

"She has an important fight coming up."

"Yes, I know."

"If I were you, until it's over, don't get on her wrong side."

I laughed. "Good advice." Of course I also realized that if she lost, even being on her 'right side' would be no guarantee of safety.

"And don't worry about her during our mission. I will be there. And I have given her some personal protection as well."

I stared at him. And then at the Glock. In Thailand, "personal protection" could mean anything from a knife to an Uzi. "What kind of personal protection?"

He grinned. "Don't worry. She will be fine."

DAY FOUR

10

The following morning was sunny and bright. I called Kenneth Wade and let him know we would pick up the girl and when. He gave me the name and address of the grandmother and thanked me profusely. Then I called Buen and gave him the name and address. I was in the process of calling my local server about lack of proper internet service when the phone in my apartment went dead as it often did during the rainy season. Rain or no rain.

I stepped around cases of empty Singha bottles and a dozen pairs of sandals and continued on up the stairs to the roof. I pushed open the door and made my way carefully through a small area crammed with ladders, old bird cages, buckets, mops, a laundry basket and broken barstools.

The roof was large but most of the space had been given over to serve as an aviary, a wire cage for Winny's macaws and mynahs. The cage was about nine feet high and six feet wide and ran in a horseshoe shape around three-fourths of the roof giving the birds plenty of room to spread their wings. Winny had fixed up a double gate to prevent birds from flying out when the maid or a well-intentioned bargirl went in to feed them. Nevertheless, the average macaw being just a bit smarter than the average bargirl, two had almost escaped. Winny was now considering triple-gating the cage.

Winny was as protective of his birds as he was his bar employees and he had recently built a small light blue hip roof of corrugated metal over the cage area to protect them, although in the event of a storm they would quickly fly through holes in the concrete wall into their inside "playroom."

The day's bright sunlight made its way around the edges of the roof like a clever thief and warmed the tiled floor. The interior tiles of the cage were littered with ping pong balls and other toys, corn cobs, papaya, mango, grapes, bananas, birdseed, sesame seed, pans of rice, leftover chicken, bird droppings and feathers.

Winny was standing inside the cage turning on a water faucet in the middle of what vaguely resembled a run-down miniature Chinese rock garden. The rock formation had a circular water pond and Winny was overflowing the pond to upset a nearby colony of red ants who would then indignantly pick up their eggs and stream out – making a perfect meal for the macaws.

Paying particular attention to all this were half a dozen alley cats on an opposite roof all dreaming of the day they might somehow make it through the wire. Although once bit by the macaws' beaks they might wish they hadn't.

Regardless of whether they were male or female, Winny had given his birds the names of real or legendary cowboys including Liberty Valance, John Ringo, Jesse James, Wyatt Earp and Hopalong Cassidy. His pride and joy was Liberty Valance, a feisty, loud, gorgeous and incredibly expensive macaw. Liberty was well aware that my kitchen window – should I foolishly draw open the curtains – looked out into his playroom and although he was used to heavy rain, lightning and thunder still drove him into a frenzy. In case I wasn't able to hear all of the hysterical squawks and earsplitting screeches that made their way through my tiny kitchen window and into my bedroom, Liberty made sure I heard the noise by banging his body against the window. I wasn't sure why but I was quite certain Liberty didn't like me much.

At the moment, Ringo was punishing a ping pong ball as he propelled it along the floor, Jesse was messily splashing about in his bath, Hoppy was asleep on his perch, Wyatt was squawking angrily while failing to get his beak around a rubber ball, and Liberty was eyeing me as if I had stolen the greatest love of his life.

Everyone delighted in teaching the macaws and mynahs to talk and in their high-pitched nasal voices, their vocabulary ran from "Pay your fucking bill!" in English to "I love you" in Thai. Three of the blue-and-gold macaws streaked toward their rope perches near Winny and made ungodly noises while waiting for the ants to fall for the ruse.

Rays of the sun backlighted their emerald green crowns, blue heads and saffron yellow bodies. Their cold blue eyes looked toward me, dismissed me as of no particular significance, and then stared at the emerging ants.

Like the bargirls themselves, the birds were very much individuals – moody, bold, temperamental and with distinct personalities. But they would happily perch on Winny's head or shoulder whenever he gestured for them to come. As he did now.

I had got a late night phone call from Winny's girlfriend, Malee, in which she had tearfully told me about Winny having to go into the hospital to have a tumor on his neck cut out; after which doctors would know for certain if it was malignant or benign. Apparently, the cells in the tiny sample of the tumor drawn with the FNA (Fine Needle Aspiration) hadn't made it clear one way or the other. I had calmed her down the best I could and told her I would always be there for Winny. And for her.

Winny stood with Liberty Valance perched proudly on his shoulder watching the emerging ants. After a bit of small-talk about the birds, I spoke as nonchalantly as I could. "I hear you might have to go into the hospital shortly."

He turned toward me so that Liberty's green crown wasn't blocking his view. "And who told you that?"

I nodded toward Liberty. "A little bird told me."

He waved the news away. "No big deal." He briefly let his fingers run over a small bump on the left side of his neck. "Some half-assed tumor has to be taken off."

"Where you going?"

"Bumrungrat."

"They're the best," I said. "When you going in?"

"Couple 'a days."

"Anything I can do you let me know."

"Thanks. I will. But it'll be a piece of cake."

I had seen my aunt's head-and-neck cancer begin with a neck tumor diagnosed as malignant. And I had seen what followed: the surgery, followed by heavy doses of radiation, the weight loss, the temporary destruction of taste and smell, the depression, the permanent loss of her saliva; the way it had aged her. I had no doubt Winny knew exactly what he was in for if the tumor was malignant. "OK. See you later."

"Oh, by the way, I'll double-pane your window as soon as I'm out. I was gonna do it tomorrow."

"That's about the last thing you should worry about."

"Well, it'll be done next week."

As I turned to leave, Texas John Slaughter, a glossy black Thai hill mynah, stretched its wings a bit then gracefully opened and closed them while balancing on its perch. His head and body movements while stretching always reminded me of a teenager trying out exaggerated movements to get attention on a dance floor. Texas John had puffy yellow wattles, short yellow legs, and a bright orange beak, and he glared at me from under his tiny crest. He spoke in the stock phrases and exact tone and timbre of voice of his previous owner. "You're not so tough."

"I never said I was, John."

"Pay your fucking bill!"

"I will," I said, "as soon as I've got the money."

He laughed raucously, then emitted a kind of guffaw suggesting he had heard that lots of times before and continued to glare at me. Even after dozens of such confrontations, it was still hard to believe I was having conversations with mynah birds but there was probably about as much real communication between us as between the bargirls and me; only difference was I didn't have to buy the birds drinks.

11

I usually read the Bangkok papers in the morning and the *New York Times* main stories on line later in the day. If I have time. But it wasn't a jogging day, and I'd got up late. Then, after I'd left Winny, I spent time teaching scuba diving to two beginning Japanese couples in the swimming pool. They were eager but not so able, so I had stretched the lesson a bit to help them out. And so it wasn't until late afternoon when I entered the Boots and Saddle for a quick beer. Winny sat back in his usual booth and looked at me with a strange expression.

I sat on a stool at the counter facing him. "What's up?"

"You haven't seen the paper?"

"Nope. Let me guess: some general pulled off a coup and all *farangs* have twelve hours to leave the country."

He reached onto a wall shelf and handed me a folded, beer-stained copy of the *Bangkok Post*. "Bottom of the first page."

My eyes focused on a story about more amphetamine factories being set up just inside Burma along the Thai border and then I saw it.

AMERICAN WOMAN FOUND DEAD IN APARTMENT

An American woman was found shot dead in a Bangkok apartment late Wednesday morning. Police said yesterday that the body of Lisa Avery was found in the bedroom of her serviced apartment in Sukhumvith soi 31.

Avery, who was from New York, was believed to be in the entertainment business. Staff in the apartment building said Avery had been a resident for about three months. She was found by a maid at mid-morning when she went in to clean the apartment.

Lt-Col Sombat Phahurat, an inspector at Thung Lo Police Station, said his team was treating the case as homicide and that Avery's body was being kept at the Police Hospital's forensic division pending notification of relatives.

Noy plunked a bottle of Singha Gold on the counter in front of me. I took a long hit.

12

The phone in my apartment was still out of order, the one in the Boots and Saddle offered no privacy, and the week before I had gone to Pattaya to teach a group of students how to dive and I had somehow managed to lose my cellphone. On the boat. In the water. Along the beach. In the taxi coming back to Bangkok. Wherever. It simply meant I had spent a long, tiring day teaching diving with nothing to show for it but memories of two hostile sea turtles and a black cloud of cuttlefish camouflage in the face.

I walked out of the Boots and Saddle and along Sukhumvith in the direction of the Emporium. The sky was a patchwork of ominous darkness interspersed with areas of pale blue. The dark patches expanded and contracted by the minute as if teasing those of us below to guess what the weather would be like in an hour. But the low pressure front over Bangkok, courtesy of a typhoon in the South China Sea, was pelting the city with daily downpours and it didn't take an expert to know that flooding was a real possibility.

I rang the American Embassy from a Sukhumvith Road phonebooth so stifling hot that it could have served as a sauna room. As I hadn't had any kind of serious paycheck for over a year, it seemed wise to cut expenses wherever I could; and cellular phone service was one of those items I had decided I might try to do without for a while. So what to the average Thai bargirl was a necessity had become for me an unaffordable luxury.

I asked for the DI (Directorate of Intelligence). A female voice all bright-eyed and bushy-tailed spoke with a slight southern accent. "Extension Three-one-seven."

Great. Betty had at last remembered to answer the phone by repeating back the extension number to anyone calling in on an insecure line. That way the caller gained no more information than they already had. Who says the Agency wasn't on top of things? "Yes, good morning, Betty. I need to speak with Frank."

"May I know who is speaking?"

"Scott Sterling."

"Oh…One moment, please." Betty and I had never been close but we'd joked around some and, on occasion, covered one another's back. But from the cool tone of her voice I understood her loyalty went to whichever male of the office herd emerged victorious. And that hadn't been me.

I was already drenched in sweat so I opened the door to cool off but the traffic noise forced me to close it again. Exhaust fumes from passing busses pressed up against the booth like shabby, malevolent ghosts. Which was appropriate considering that Halloween was just a few days away. A non-air-conditioned bus lumbered by, and passengers sitting by the windows held handkerchiefs or hands to cover their mouths from Bangkok's pollution.

I caught a distorted reflection of my face on the dirt-streaked glass of the booth. The damaged blood vessels were at last constricting and the swelling around the eye had begun to recede. The bruise was changing from black and blue to what in a sunset would have been oohed and awed over as a splendorous magenta. The eyelid still had a noticeable area of sucker-punch purple.

While I waited, scenes of unpleasantness between Webber and myself churned about in my memory bank. I tried to think about how to get information out of someone I had thrown over an embassy desk. Someone who had once threatened to kill me.

His voice crackled over the phone line. "Webber."

"Hi, Frank, this is Scott. How you doing?"

"Scott...How am I doing? That's why you're calling?"

"Well, actually, I was calling to get a line on the Thai woman you were with at George's party."

"You called for my help in getting you a date?"

"No. I called for your help in locating a Thai woman who was seen in the company of the American blond found shot to death on *Soi* thirty-one."

He seemed to think that over before responding. "Aren't you forgetting something?"

"I didn't say 'please'?"

"You're forgetting that I don't like you. In fact, you're forgetting that I hate your guts. So why in hell should I help you?"

What I wanted to say was that if I hadn't let my temper get the best of me, I'd still be there, and a barely competent Foreign Area Specialist like Frank, a plain old case officer grunt, would never have been moved over to the DI section, let alone promoted to Deputy Branch Chief. But I had a better card to play. "Well, look at it this way, Frank. I'm on the trail of the person or persons who murdered an American woman in Bangkok. It's quite possible they're well connected. I figure there is a very good chance that if I'm the least bit careless or unlucky they'll murder me as well."

In the several seconds of silence I could almost hear him thinking. "Yeah. Yeah, there is that. OK, her nickname is Da. I think her first name is Wattana. Something like that. I took a visiting fireman from Langley out to the Emerald Club on Petchburi. Maybe three, four weeks back. The guy took her out for the night. Next day, he raved about her. When he left, I tried her out myself."

"And how was she?"

"Sexiest woman I ever met. She does it all and she does it well."

"You never saw the blond before?"

"Nope. Hey, gotta go. Here's wishing you lots of luck, Sterling."

The phone clicked in my ear. I hung up and stared out at the traffic. A middle-aged taxi driv er stuck in traffic stared back at me.

Some people playing detective get leads through a contact in the police department or through an old girlfriend or simply because people want to assist in solving a crime. I got my leads because people who supplied the leads hated me enough to hope maybe one of those leads would get me killed. It was enough to make a body think.

DAY FIVE

13

Late the next morning I was sitting at a booth in the back of the Boots and Saddle working on a Mehkong and Coke and what passed in the bar's kitchen as a ham-and-cheese sandwich. I had finished my jogging and made a few phonecalls in an attempt to find a bargirl who had absconded with a tidy sum of money from a local go-go bar. But mainly I had done a lot of thinking about Lisa Avery and what if anything I should do about finding her killer. Thus far, in my quest for justice, I had managed to kill off several bottles of Singha Gold.

I had considered making my way down to the Police Hospital morgue but I couldn't see how viewing Lisa's body would be of any use whatever. And I knew an autopsy of a foreigner murdered would be automatic. I had been to the morgue there before. Down a back lane which ended beside the office of the Forensic Police. Large open door to a small non-air-conditioned room with autopsied bodies partly covered with white rectangles of cloth so thin and shopworn they looked as if they'd been stolen from short-time hotels. Outside, a few white coffins with gold trim. Monks and others sitting about patiently waiting to do whatever it was they came for. Very Third World. And very depressing for anyone viewing the corpse of a loved one or friend in that atmosphere. And there wasn't a damn thing I could do for Lisa Avery by seeing her one last time.

But there was another reason I didn't want to head down there. And that was because except for the murderer I was probably the last person to see Lisa Avery alive. And the police might not unreasonably conclude that I was the chief suspect in her murder. And with a quick wrap-up in sight, they might stop looking too hard at any other possibilities. And there wouldn't be a lot I could do to catch her killer if I were in jail or under investigation.

The only piece of good news was that the phone in my apartment suddenly began working just as suddenly as it had stopped working. Actually, there was one more piece of good news. George had called and said I'd left my mobile phone in Len's Dive in Pattaya and they were sending it up to Bangkok. Then I remembered taking it off when I was trying on a new BCD. I wondered if not remembering things like that meant I was getting old.

I had made one more phone call which I hoped might just pay off. Inside Officers, i.e., those working at the Station inside the Bangkok Embassy, are Declared or Non-Declared to the Thai government. I had been Declared, hence, although my main job had been Intel, the collecting and reporting of intelligence, an important part of that job had been to conduct joint liaison operations with Thai Intelligence. With a friendly country such as Thailand, many liaison functions are overt, but there is a lot of collection activity that exists beneath the surface. In other words, with the Agency's money and knowledge, I paid Thais in high places for information. I had befriended one very high-ranking police general with many friends in immigration.

On the phone I had made it clear that I now had nothing to offer him for his information, but we had long ago hit it off as friends. He agreed to find out what he could about Lisa Avery's death and get back to me. I made a mental note to send him a bottle of Johnnie Walker Black.

I had a copy of a local paper open to a photograph of a killer of a banker and his wife reenacting the scene for the press. In the apartment of the victims, a policewoman was playing the role of the wife while the murderer held a knobby stick and pretended to press a knife to her throat. I wondered if having murderers reenact their crimes was exclusively an Asian thing. I was never quite certain what value such scripted scenes served, but the killers invariably wore embarrassed smiles or suitable looks of remorse. This killer seemed to have the embarrassed smile but only the policewoman looked remorseful.

Although the Land of Smiles always had plenty of murder and mayhem, it was only fully (and lovingly) covered in the Thai language press. There, gore, carnage and bloodshed in text and photographs reigned supreme. For those of us who neglected to learn written Thai's forty-odd consonants, nine vowels and diphthong forms, five tones, and whatever else, and were limited to perusing only the English language papers, Thailand had few crimes indeed. We would have to be satisfied with the occasional but familiar account of a drugged up or inebriated foreign male tourist falling (or being pushed) to his death from his hotel balcony in such beach resorts as Pattaya and Phuket. Or, very rarely, the murder of a female tourist. Lisa Avery had been no tourist. I was convinced of that.

Winny was at a booth near the front door working on bar receipts. The two female cooks were playing pool and, lacking customers to hustle, the bargirls were sprawled out in booths or slouching over the bar, heads down, more asleep than awake. Winny let them have any fallen macaw feathers and a few had a macaw feather sticking out of the bands of their cowgirl hats. They had finally got around to decorating the bar for Halloween and the girls lay about sleeping beneath witches and cobwebs and bats and goblins and ghouls. Anyone not familiar with the scene might have mistaken the girls for fanatical adherents of a bizarre Jim Jones-type religious cult who had just committed mass suicide by drinking poison.

The lead-gray sky had been threatening all afternoon with just a few drops of rain every ten or fifteen minutes, then whisking the dark clouds away and teasing the Big Mango with lighter skies, then dashing all hopes and darkening again. Something about the scant lighting thrown from small shaded wall lamps at each booth and the constant gloom of the bar itself seemed to intensify the soul-destroying gloom outside.

The door opened and a tall, distinguished looking man with a full head of gray hair stepped in. He was dressed in an open brown sport jacket over a beige shirt, well pressed trousers and what appeared to be dress shoes. He looked about the bar with little attempt at masking his disgust. The bargirls hardly stirred but I had no doubt they were watching him as mongeese would watch a snake. The eternal questions: Could he be induced to buy ladies' drinks or not? Is he the ATM machine with legs who will change someone's life from Bangkok bargirl to expatriate housewife?

Noy put her love story comic down behind the bar and stood up. "Hello, sit down, please."

The man ignored her and looked at Winny. He spoke with the tone of a man who brooked no nonsense. "I'm looking for Scott Sterling."

Dress Shoes had an English accent with an Australian overlay. Or the other way around. Winny took his time replying, not certain if the man was a friend or foe. "I can get a message to him."

I spoke above the sound of Honky Tonk music, a twangy and gliding guitar backing up yet another rodeo cowboy spilling out his tale of lost love. "I'm Sterling."

As he walked toward my booth, I noticed he was in fact wearing tasseled dress shoes. I tried to remember the last time someone with tassels on his shoes had walked into the Boots and Saddle. Customers had been thrown out for less. He stopped close to the booth and nodded toward the seat opposite me. "May I?" I nodded and closed the paper. "Make yourself comfortable." He reached out his hand. I wiped my hands on a napkin and gripped his hand. It was as cold as his personality.

Noy approached the booth. I asked her question for her.

"What's your drink?"

"Maker's Mark on the rocks."

He dug an expensive looking leather wallet from an inside pocket of his jacket and pulled a namecard from it. As he handed it to me he said, "So at last I meet the 'diving detective'."

I smiled outwardly and winced inwardly. One of my diving students had turned out to be a journalist and he had done an article in a popular Bangkok magazine on "Colorful Personalities in the Big Mango." And he had done his homework well. He had described me as the ex-CIA "detective diver" who split up his time between diving and detective work. It made me sound colorful, remorseless and invincible. I hadn't much cared for the me who appeared in the magazine but the article had found its way onto an internet site and I had gotten a few minor cases from the publicity.

His card announced in elegant (almost tasseled) script that "John Morrell" was managing director of an engineering firm in Sydney. I placed the card on the table, far from my plate, to avoid upsetting Mr. Morrell by getting mustard on it, then took the last bite of my sandwich. "What can I do for you, Mr. Morrell?"

"I'd like you to find someone for me. I have reason to believe he is still in Bangkok."

I wiped my hands again. Oy moved in with his drink and took my plate away. "Caucasian?"

"Yes."

I looked the man over. Some men seek out a detective to find if their wife is cheating or maybe simply to find a missing girl-friend. John Morrell didn't look the type. He struck me as the facial peels/bleached teeth/manicure type. He was clean-shaven, imperious, all business, egotistical. His main concerns in life would be financial. "He owes you money?"

"Yes."

"How much?"

He hesitated. "He got three hundred thousand dollars out of me."

I assumed he meant Australian dollars. Still. "He was your partner in business?"

He took a hit of his Maker's Mark. "No. The man is a professional telephone liar. And a very good one."

It was then that the penny dropped. "Are you saying you were scammed by a boileroom boy?"

"I didn't know they were called that but, yes, that is precisely what I am saying."

I had read about boileroom boys in the local papers. The brassy salesmen at fly-by-night operations who set up in Bangkok and fleece investors in Australia and New Zealand over the phone. Investors who let greed and the well practiced techniques of skilled salesmen cloud their judgment. I had also known one. An American. In his early retirement he would hang around Washington Square bars, get drunk, ring the bells, buy drinks for one and all, and sing the boileroom chant: "ABC: Always be calling; Always be closing!" Some of the bargirls could still sing that line, even if they didn't know what the hell it meant.

He would get soused and brag of his success in cheating "laydowns" by which he meant "suckers" out of their money. Until the day a gorgeous Thai woman half his age suckered him out of his. Then he crawled in a hole somewhere and disappeared. What others had lost to greed he had lost to lust. I got the impression nobody paid attention to the Seven Deadly Sins anymore; at least not before it was too late. And by the time anyone washed up in Bangkok it was always too late.

He cupped his hands around his glass the way a man might practice strangling someone. "These people, and I use that term for such scum loosely, highly praised a stock in a pharmaceutical company. They made me think I was getting in on the inside – "

"Mr. Morrell, I'm going to save you some time. I don't think I would want the case."

Morrell's brow furrowed and his eyes narrowed; a captain of industry bewildered and discomforted by the rare sight of someone not only interrupting but also not complying with his wishes. "May I ask why?"

"Stop me when I'm wrong, but if I have this right, some type of sleazebag called you and claimed to work for a capital management-type company and offered you the bargain of a lifetime. An initial public offering, maybe. You bought some. The stock went up. You made money. They offered more of the same or a chance to get in on an even better IPO. You bought a lot. That's when the stock tanked."

He drained his glass without taking his eyes off me. "Go on."

"That's when you called what you thought was their company phone number and it turned out to be an answering service. And when you complained to some regulatory body about it, you found out you weren't the only sucker. There were lots of them. And the stock was nothing but a pump and dump. The boileroom boys had pumped it up themselves and then, when the turkeys were ripe for plucking, they dumped it. And then you eventually learned that the so-called capital management company consisted mainly of some slick brochures, glossy pamphlets, a few fax machines, a bank of phones and a fancy website."

Morrell cleared his throat. He seemed annoyed and impatient. "Have it your way, Mr. Sterling. I was certainly a victim of my own cupidity. Why would that preclude you from helping me in getting my money back?"

"You're not going to get your money back. You know it and I know it. Even if you find the man who pitched you he would have been a lowly account opener who made, maybe, ten percent, and has already blown it on drink, drugs and women. And even if you find the one who owned the company, assuming he's still here, this is Thailand. Boilerooms are a gray area here. You would spend a fortune on legal fees and get nowhere."

The door swung open to the sound of heavy rain and Death Wish Don stomped in followed by West Texas Andy and Son-of-Loser Paul. The afternoon storm had started in earnest. The three of them were soaked. With barely a glance toward us, they headed unsteadily for a booth on the other side of the bar. All three were already drunk. Noy knew their drinks and was already getting their beer. West Texas Andy slumped into a booth. "Goddamn rainy season supposed to be over!"

Death Wish Don tried to dry his wet hair with his bandanna – without removing the bandanna. "Supposed to be. But you never know about October. Cool season gets delayed sometimes."

Son-of-Loser Paul pounded his fist on the table. "That's right! October is the ladyboy month. It could go one way or the other, AC or DC. And if you check back outside you'll see that Mr. Rainy Season has jist thrown a surprised-as-hell Mr. Cool Season over the bar and is fuckin' him up the ass!"

Death Wish Don emitted an old man's wheezing, high-pitched, chuckle which could have passed on Old Time Radio as a perfect horse's whinny. "You missed your calling. You could'a been a weatherman on TV!"

"My calling, as the Thais say, is to 'shoot a rabbit'! Now!" Son-of-Loser Paul headed for the men's room.

After a brief glance at the men, Morrell had turned back and stared into his drink. While they had shouted to one another he remained completely motionless with an expression of distaste on his face; not unlike that of a Thai bargirl being pawed by a disagreeable drunk but one who was buying her drinks. As soon as the bar was quiet, he lowered his voice and continued.

"What you say may be correct. Still, I would like you to try to find this individual."

"And when I find him?"

He hesitated. "I would get some of my money back."

"Or you might just spend a bit more of your money to hire

Mok the Motorcycle Man. Isn't that the plan?"

"Your role would end once you had found him. And I would pay you well to do so."

I wondered if Morrell would give as much care and attention to the choosing of a hit man as he did to the cutting and tailoring of his hand-tailored, camel's hair sport jacket. I shook my head. "Sorry, Mr. Morrell, you'll have to find somebody else."

He stared at me as at someone incapable of recognizing opportunity. "Well, I should congratulate you on your successful lifestyle. It seems you have the luxury of not taking every case that comes your way."

"I've found sometimes it's better not to."

"Isn't it nice that you can pick and choose?"

"Picking and choosing a bit more carefully is precisely what you should have done, is it not, Mr. Morrell?"

He glanced at his 18 Karat yellow-gold Cartier watch, stood up, threw a five-hundred baht bill onto the table, turned and walked out.

Noy waited a decent interval after the door closed, maybe all of five seconds, before swooping down and grabbing the bill off the table.

Dang walked slowly over to my table, her bleary, brown eyes half closed in sleep, her black eye makeup in need of repair. Even her macaw feather had seen better days. She set a Singha Gold on the table in front of me. I looked up to tell her I still had one nearly full when I saw her point toward the other side of the bar. I looked between two shelves of bottles over the bar and saw Son-of-Loser Paul holding up a bottle of beer. It was the custom in the bar that when you had a falling out with someone – someone you preferred to know – you bought him a beer. If he accepted, all was normal again; if he didn't, the feud continued.

I picked up the bottle of Singha Gold, returned his salute, and took a long drink.

14

The Emerald Club had been built at the end of a lengthy gravel driveway lined with perfectly kept flower gardens and carefully tended thickets of bamboo. The closer I got to the building itself, the quieter it became, so quiet that the sound of my shoes on the gravel seemed almost an embarrassing intrusion. I wondered if members were given special tire wrappings so their car tires would make no noise.

Strategically placed lawn lamps illuminated white fluted columns with ionic capitals framed by travelers palms. The lights were all at ground level or even recessed and whoever had been hired knew well how to create a magical atmosphere through landscape lighting. The mood was that of Somerset Maugham; the architectural statement – not to mention the BMWs and Rolls Royces in the parking lot – suggested power, money, privilege and class. When the Thai economy crashed, several members clubs – along with much else that catered to the newly and briefly rich – closed their doors; but the Emerald Club remained the favorite of those who could still afford such luxury.

The light pouring forth from the windows of the immense two-story wooden structure had a rich golden warmth, and I could almost see pampered playboys, their jackets off and ties loosened, drinking their cognac while surrounded by adorable and adoring young women.

I had seen no one and no one had challenged me but now I caught a glimpse of someone standing at the far end of the parking lot. I had no doubt that a club as opulent as the Emerald would have guards stationed discreetly about. I stepped onto a plush red carpet, walked up several stone steps flanked by mythological Thai figures, and rang a diamond-shaped brass bell.

After just under 20 seconds a young *luk krung* (Eurasian) woman opened the door. She too could have passed for a mythological figure. Her skin was the purest shade of white I'd ever seen. Her flawless makeup and abundant, perfectly-in-place, swept-back hair were obviously the work of a talented professional, and her emerald green earrings and necklace contrasted in a lovely way with her chartreuse gown. I knew that ladyboys did the hair and makeup of the girls working in many of the upper class bars in Bangkok and I wondered if one of them had done hers. Men at various stages of transforming themselves into women doing the hair and makeup of women so the women can attract men. Welcome to Thailand.

She threw me a huge, bubbling-all-over, public relations smile, a smile which conveyed how pleased she was to see me, how wonderful it was that I had taken her away from whatever mundane task she had been performing, and how anxious she was to hear what I had to say. There was not even a hint that she noticed what was left of my black eye. I wondered if she had previously worked in hotel P.R. I gave her my best grin and asked in English if I could see the manager.

She responded in perfect English with a slight British accent. "Do you wish to become a member?" As she asked the question her lovely hazel eyes widened and her very feminine voice rose in breathless anticipation, as if my joining would be nothing less than the happiest event she could ever imagine. My first thought was that maybe Miss Happy was working on commission. My second was that maybe I'd interrupted her while she was snorting white powder up or popping happy pills down. The thought also occurred to me she might have been a fine actress; most likely when it came to faking orgasms for club members she was.

"Not at the moment. I just need a few minutes of the manager's time." I dug a card out of my wallet and handed it to her. A Len's Dive Shop card with my name on it as 'Chief Instructor' and a logo of a man wearing scuba gear observing a fish. George loved to give even freelancers like me an impressive title to make customers feel that they were being well looked after by his top people; hence, I was the Chief Instructor but there was also a Head Instructor and a Master Instructor and a Principal Instructor.

As Miss Happy held the card between her elegant slim fingers and lovely, perfectly manicured, cherry-pink nails, her eyes widened even further as if my role in teaching tourists to dive made me a very important person indeed. "If that would be all right," I said.

Despite her dashed hopes that I might be membership material, she held her smile in place and ushered me in. She motioned toward a chair and lifted her forefinger and lowered her voice to a breathless whisper as if she were sharing something confidential, "Just one moment, please," and swept her hourglass figure balanced on shiny black high-heeled shoes across the thick ruby red wall-to-wall carpet down a long hallway toward one of the inner rooms. The scent of a subtle, high-priced perfume lingered after her like a naughty promise.

While I waited, I sat in a straight-backed emerald green chair near the front door facing an upholstered emerald green couch with intricately carved woodwork, a profusion of plants and yet more statuary on gold-trimmed, marble-topped tables. Chandeliers glittered above and large paintings on the wall with antique gold frames displayed palaces of various monarchs of the Chakri dynasty. I could just make out the sounds of happy voices and soft laughter and even softer piano music from somewhere within the building.

Miss Happy was back in less than five minutes. As she approached, her smile increased with each step to where I thought

I might soon be face to face with Alice's Cheshire (now Siamese) Cat. She gave me a slight bow and asked if I could please follow her. Her beautiful, bright hazel eyes seemed almost to light up with pleasure at the thought that I might accompany her. And then and there I decided to rename Miss Happy. To me she would forever be known as Bright Eyes. And, for those who could afford it, following her bewitching walk across that ruby red carpet might well have been wor th the cost of membership in the Emerald Club.

As we walked down the hallway, the sounds I had heard before increased in volume, then we changed direction, and passed through several well appointed rooms with plush couches and chairs and walls lined with thick wine red drapes. Each room also boasted huge glittering chandeliers, well stocked bars and friezes of naked women cavorting along mountain streams. A few open doors revealed smaller, more private, rooms off of the one I was passing through. With the exception of a few fleeting glimpses of other women in chartreuse gowns and bouffant hairdos gliding silently across carpets, I saw no one. Apparently, non-members were not allowed even a hint of the Promised Land.

Bright Eyes walked ahead of me up a circular staircase to the second floor, holding a banister for support and stepping carefully in her high heels. The plush elegance of downstairs quickly gave way to a down-to-earth business area. No carpet, no paintings, no drapes, no statuary. Open doors revealed bespectacled Thai men in casual clothes working at computers and typewriters. From one of the rooms I heard the sound of beads rapidly being clicked along the wires of an abacus: some Chinese-Thai no doubt checking computer printouts by his ancestors' own tried-and-true method.

Bright Eyes's heels clicked loudly on the hardwood floor in counterpoint to the abacus. At the end of one of several corridors, she knocked softly on a door with a frosted glass window. A male voice from within said something intelligible to her if not to me, and she opened the door and motioned for me to enter. She beamed a bright "Goodbye" and closed the door behind me.

There were no overhead lights: The small room was lit by floor lamps and table lamps only, giving the four men in the room a sinister, conspiratorial air. Sections of the walls were lined with battleship gray filing cabinets, open shelves and an oval table upon which a blueprint of some sort was being held open by cut glass paperweights in the shape of squabbling cats. The shelves held stacks of manila folders and framed photographs of what must have been the grand opening of the club. There was a wooden liquor cabinet about the size of my living room and a sideboard covered with bottles, a bucket of ice and half-empty glasses. The drapes of the room's sole window were half open and the window looked out upon the lights of a luxury apartment building some distance away. Beyond the building, the pulsating blood red light on top of a TV station's mast pierced the darkness.

The man behind the desk staring at my namecard as if it were a strange if not repugnant insect was about thirty, of medium build, casually dressed and in need of a haircut. His eyes were an unusual shade of brown, not unlike fried baby clams with chili. The lazy way he drummed his fingers on the desk reminded me of whip coral caught in a mild current. And as his fingers moved, light glinted off rings any one of which could probably have bought the Boots and Saddle with enough left over for a down payment on a Chinatown brothel.

Two of his even more casually dressed friends sat in chairs not far from the desk, their tight shirts revealing their muscular physiques and penchant for lifting weights. They both looked about thirty which meant they were probably closer to forty. One had a flattened nose, a puckered scar on his chin, and a few nicks here and there. The other had so many scars, nicks, welts and poorly healed cuts, he almost looked as if he had undergone tribal tattooing. I had no doubt they knew their way around a Thai-style boxing ring. They stared at me the way their boss was staring at my namecard.

The man in the chair behind me was slim, wiry, swarthy, mid-30's and dressed all in black. His face was gaunt and pockmarked and his slicked-down, gleaming black hair was long enough to get him kicked out of Singapore. His shiny black pupils had a slight greyish tinge, not unlike the seeds of a papaya. He leaned back in a leather chair, a cigarette in his hand, staring through me as if not really seeing me until he had specific orders to do so. Had there been more light in the room I most likely would have seen the outline of his gun under his shirt.

I congratulated myself on my smart move: I had stumbled into a snake's pit with a Thai underworld boss and his muscles and his artillery. Need a nosy-Parker foreigner carrying a bag of sliced mangoes for his girlfriend roughed up on a deserted lane? Here they were. Need a nosy-Parker foreigner walking home from buying cigarettes at the 7-11 shot dead by a guy in black on an unidentifiable Yamaha or Kawasaki? Look no further. For a split second I harbored the chimerical hope that maybe somebody was making a low budget Thai gangster movie and that somebody would soon yell "cut."

The man behind the desk took his time putting my card down and looking up at me. His English wasn't perfect but it wasn't bad either; just delivered with a thick, almost unintelligible, accent. "You a diver?"

"I'm a diver."

"So what you want here?"

"I want to ask you about a woman who works here."

"So why come to me? Ask the manager. Downstairs."

As he said the word, "downstairs," he turned his fist over and stabbed the air with his thumb and his manner of speaking left no doubt that "downstairs" is where people like me belonged; not upstairs bothering the boss.

"This woman is a Thai, and was friends with an American woman who was murdered recently. It's possible the American woman also worked here. I'm not sure."

Long seconds ticked away as he stared at me. Other than the droning hum of the air conditioner there were no sounds in the room. I continued on. "I just want to talk to her. Find out what she knows about the dead woman." Several more seconds passed. "Her name is Wattana. Nickname Da. I don't know her last name."

He took a long drag on his cigarette, let it out and looked up at the ceiling. The fingers of his other hand did the whip-coral-in-current movements again. His body language suggested he was getting bored with me. Maybe even irritated. And I had no doubt his muscle-bound boys were paid to make sure irritating people didn't stick around long. "We don't talk about anybody who works here with anybody." He looked straight at me with narrowed, unfriendly eyes. "Understand?"

"Sure. A good policy. But I need to talk to this woman."

"Why? You the boyfriend of the dead American?"

"No. I only met her a few times."

"So why you so interested?"

It was a good question. I knew I was interested partly because I think someone who takes a human life should be punished and Thai police weren't always up to speed in solving murders of foreigners, partly because I thought there was more to Lisa Avery than a good-time girl who had come to Bangkok to party and make money. I hoped it was *not* because prying into the life of a woman who humiliated me twice gave me a certain satisfaction, a puerile sense of voyeuristic vengeance for insulting my male dignity.

"She was in her early twenties. Her whole life was ahead of her. All the joy and all the mistakes. Somebody took all that away from her. He had no right to. And he's still out there."

He shook his head, picked up my card and held it out for me. "You go now."

I didn't move. "Not until I've talked to Wattana."

With a bored expression and half-closed eyes, he nodded toward his muscle-bound companions. A nod that spoke volumes about just how worn out my welcome had become. They stood up and took a step in my direction. I could almost feel the eyes of the man behind me boring into my back; he was probably already deciding where best to dump my body – the canal or the river? A mango orchard or a lamyai farm? I wondered if Thai cops referred to bodies in the river as "floaters" the way New York cops did. I crossed my arms at my chest. "Why are you so interested in protecting a murderer? Do you have something to hide?"

His "bullshit" was barely audible but what counted was that he'd said it in Thai: *I kee kawk kow!* In fact, it was Korat Thai. Which I knew a smattering of thanks to having a girlfriend from that town.

I said "not bullshit" in the same dialect: *Ya I ha gin kow!*

At that he stiffened and spoke again in Korat dialect. *Khun phut phasa korat, dai nee?* (You speak Korat dialect?)

I knew my knowledge of Korat Thai would quickly be exhausted so I smiled, shrugged and spoke in central Thai dialect: "My girlfriend is from Korat."

As he pointed to my black eye, his lips parted crookedly into just a suggestion of a smile. "She give you that?"

In fact, it wasn't exactly a black eye, anymore. It had now assumed the coloration of the street stall version of crispy fried chicken: dark reddish brown tinged with yellow in which appeared isolated bits of black. "No. But she probably could. She's a muay-Thai boxer."

He looked interested. "What camp?"

I told him.

One of the musclemen actually managed a smile. "I know Master Amnart. He's a good man."

"A very good man. Once a champion and now a man who

produces champions." I was going to add that my girlfriend was his daughter but it seemed too much like hiding behind a woman's skirts. Not that I haven't done worse. But I was definitely more afraid of being thought afraid in their eyes than I was afraid. Assuming that makes any sense.

But the man with the scarred face couldn't resist asking. "Master Amnart teaches females now?"

I could understand his confusion. It had been only a few years since female boxers were allowed in muay-Thai rings, and they still weren't allowed in the most professional boxing rings in Bangkok. But now I had to say it. "Only his daughter."

Several tense seconds passed. Babies were born. Old people died. Only the air conditioner hummed along. Another lifetime of seconds passed before the man behind the desk seemed to make a decision. He waved the musclemen back into their chairs, waved me into the empty chair facing him and came out from behind the desk. The power of his wave reminded me of Mandrake the Magician.

He walked to the filing cabinets, pulled out a drawer and quickly pulled out two folders. He handed them to me and sat down. He continued speaking in Bangkok Thai: "We read about the woman's death. Lisa was working here. Da used to work here. Not now."

I opened the first folder. A full black-and-white head shot of Lisa Avery taken against a plain curtain backdrop. She looked out at me with her hair nearly covering one eye and her lips formed into a sexy, playful, whimsical smile. The message I got was "Are you ready to play?" I made a mental note to tell Winny that the Emerald Club shots of employees resembled headshots for New York actresses. On the back of the print was her name, birth date, address, phone number and a New York City address. Assuming this information was accurate, Lisa was twenty-three. The only other item in the folder was a piece of paper written in Thai with the usual garuda symbol on top, stamped and signed by more than one bureaucrat. I don't read Thai but I figured it to be some kind of work permit.

The man behind the desk gestured toward the cabinet. "You want a drink?"

"Thanks, no, not right now."

The second folder had a full face shot of Da AKA Wattana Boonsong. It was a bit grainier and not in sharp focus. She wasn't smiling but she did have her lips formed into an undeniable sexy pout. Her eyes stared out at me with a kind of suggestive defiance. The unmistakable message was "Are you man enough?" She was twenty-six and lived in the Banglampoo area of Bangkok. There were two phone numbers and a home address in the northern city of Lampang. There was nothing else in the folder. "Can I copy this information down?"

He removed Lisa's work permit and handed me back the folders. "You can have them. They don't work here now."

"I appreciate that. Where is Da, do you know?"

He glanced beyond my shoulder to the man behind me as if they shared some secret then looked at me and smiled. "Try Jezebels."

"Jezebels?"

"You don't know Jezebels?"

When I confessed that I didn't he made the motion of cracking a whip. "Bangkok now has *two* whip houses." His face was that of a proud city tourist official telling an important travel agent that his city now has two five-star restaurants.

"Houses of domination?"

He nodded. "Off the Pattaya highway." He picked up his phone and asked someone for the number of Jezebels. While we waited he motioned for one of his underlings to mix him a drink. He stared at me. "You American?"

"Yes."

"How long you live Thailand?"

"About six years."

"Your Thai very good."

"Thanks. So's your English."

He picked up a pen and wrote down the number and spoke slowly: "A-n-g-s-d? OK." He handed the slip of paper to me. "You ask for Mistress Ang-stah." I thanked him and headed for the door. I nodded to the musclemen who smiled and nodded back. When I glanced at the artillery I found that he still possessed the ability to look at me without quite seeing me. And yet I was certain I detected the slightest of smiles. The effect was as if someone had slapped a happy face sticker on the barrel of an Uzi.

15

Like most Thai women, Dao took at least two showers a day, morning and night. Like most Western men, except during the hot season, I tried to make do with only one, always in the morning. So that meant that she spent more time in the bathroom and I spent more time in bed. Although as a compromise, I washed up at the sink before climbing into bed. This prevented her from sniffing my body with her sensitive nose and telling me (as she had early in our relationship) that my armpits were "dangerous."

While she was still splashing about in the tub, the phone rang. My police contact called to say that all identity in Lisa Avery's name was false. Her real name was Janet Burgess, as stated on her passport. In searching her apartment, the police had also turned up a New York address and phone number which didn't match the ones Lisa Avery was using. I wrote everything down, thanked him profusely, and hung up. Then remembered I should have asked him if he knew the caliber of weapon that Lisa AKA Janet had been shot with. I picked up the phone to call him back but decided I would find that out another way. He had done enough. Now I knew my hunch was right: Lisa Avery was not simply a high class callgirl making a good living in Bangkok. She was here for a reason. And whatever the reason, she had created a completely new identity. Which suggested someone in Bangkok might have known who Janet Burgess was by name but not by sight and she didn't want them to know Janet Burgess was in town.

I decided to tuck the information away into my subconscious

until after Dao left the next day. Insights never came when I was with someone else and they sometimes came the fastest when I wasn't pushing to solve something too hard.

I undressed and slipped under the sheet intending to begin reading my serendipitous and highly prized find from a Sukhumvith Road used bookstore: a slightly warped paperback version of *The Real Cool Killers*, one of the late Chester Himes's Harlem novels starring the inimitable police duo, Coffin Ed and Grave Digger Jones. I had paid far too much for it but for a lover of mysteries bored with sensitive modern male detectives and feisty modern female detectives, to revisit the honest if politically incorrect emotions and powerfully written violence of Coffin Ed and Grave Digger Jones was worth almost any price. Especially if for a few hours it took my mind off real murder in real life. Which, given my profession, sooner or later might place me in real danger.

At least that had been my intention. But before I had finished the first chapter, the bathroom door was ajar and Dao was standing at the sink wearing nothing but white panties and red-and-white slippers, her proud brown breasts and the rest of her perfect brown body profiled against the ivory-yellow bathroom light. She glanced over and saw me watching her and smiled. I put the book down. Coffin Ed and Grave Digger Jones would have to wait.

Without inhibition, I watched as she rubbed some kind of cream into her face and again when she used the hairdryer on her shoulder-length hair. The way she held the dryer and dipped her head was as feminine as everything else she did. And I especially watched her when she slipped out of her panties and out of her slippers, and jumped onto the bed.

She lay on her stomach favoring me with a teasing smile. I never failed to be mesmerized by the curves of her body. The pronounced arch of her back gave way to the beautiful curve of her perfectly formed buttocks. The bathroom light spilled out and turned her skin a lustrous golden brown. Then, just as I made a move in her direction, she reached over and handed me the small, cylindrical container of "Boxing Liniment" and said, *nuat lang hi noi* ("massage my back a bit"). Unfortunately, I had forgotten that before her fights, her training was more important to her than any pleasure I might provide her.

I poured several drops of the liniment onto my palm and almost immediately the powerful and pungent smell permeated the entire bedroom. As she lay on her stomach, her head resting on her arms, I began massaging it into her back and shoulders; slowly and with force to penetrate her muscles. Under the liniment, her skin glistened like mouth-watering caramel.

Suspicions I didn't even want to acknowledge kept crowding my thoughts like obnoxious panhandlers. Dao was a beautiful and, beneath her cool composure, a very jealous woman. She also knew where Lisa Avery lived. What bothered me the most was that she hadn't mentioned Lisa again, and it wasn't like her to let that kind of suspicion simply drop. I told myself she was preoccupied with the coming fight or else was simply determined not to be consumed by jealousy.

But I couldn't forget that she also had received "personal protection" from Buen. I needed to know what weapon he had given her. But I knew any attempt to interrogate her could end in disaster. I decided the best course of action would be deception.

"Sweetheart."

"Hmmm."

"I was thinking. You know Buen and I will be armed when we go to the slums. Maybe I should ask Buen to give you some kind of weapon, as well."

"I will be fine."

"Well, it wouldn't hurt – "

"Massage my buttocks, will you?"

My hands would inevitably be drawn to her buttocks during

massages as she already well knew. I kneaded them for several seconds and then, dropping any pretense of giving a massage, simply ran my hands slowly over them in admiration. The liniment seeped into the pores of her flawless skin. "You have a beautiful ass."

"Have you told that to other women?"

"None with an ass as beautiful as yours."

Bak kwan! ("sweet mouth").

I again began massaging her back in earnest. After nearly a minute of silence her playful mood seemed to have left her. "You're doing it wrong."

"So, show me again."

"I'm not going to play my flute if there is only a water buffalo to hear it."

I knew exactly from whom she had learned that expression. I said nothing. I knew that before a fight, her moods could change from minute to minute. And I knew there was no point in trying to deal with each one; by the time I had worked out a defense, she would have entered into a totally new one.

Her voice was barely audible. "Sorry."

"Never mind."

After a few minutes, I pronounced her "finished!" and put the liniment away. I reached out and turned her over onto her back. "Hello, beautiful woman."

She smiled coquettishly. "You want something from Thai girl, *farang* man?"

When she felt (or more often caused) my erection, she would use one of several Thai expressions to describe either the condition of my male organ or of my state of arousal.

Now, when her hand found my erection she kissed me playfully on the neck and whispered softly into my ear that my "dove was cooing," *nok khao khan.*

But when I started to lie on top of her, she pushed me away.

"No, you will get liniment in my hair. Anyway, I have a fight soon. You will tire me too much."

I tried my best smile. "I'll be very gentle."

She shook her head.

I gave her my most pained expression. "So you mean until the fight is over we can't – "

She placed her fingers against my lips to shush me and rolled off the bed. She got up and turned off all the lights. She then slithered down along my nearly naked body, snake-like, to press first her chin and then her cheek and finally her lips and tongue against my growing erection. Then at the familiar tug on my underpants, I raised my midsection and she whipped them off.

The only windows in the apartment facing the out-of-doors were in the living room. But on the wall opposite the foot of the bed a curtained window was clearly outlined by the dim light from a back hallway. By day a dirty window covered by a worn dull brown curtain flecked with tiny stains; by night the window curtain transformed into a mysterious horizontal rectangle penetrating the darkness, serving as a softly lit backdrop against which Dao expertly and uninhibitedly performed her oral magic.

Lying on my back with my head propped against a fluffy, over-sized pillow, I looked down to see her bare brown shoulders and jet black hair outlined against the rectangle. As she pleasured me with her tongue and lips and hand, her head moved ever-so-slowly in different directions and her hair sometimes fell outside the rectangle, leaving me with – until I inevitably closed my eyes and let go – a view of her masses of jet-black hair.

Earlier in the evening, she had eaten an *Essarn* (northeast Thailand) version of somtam, and its spicy, piquant odor still scented the apartment, coalescing with the boxing liniment into some kind of potent, repulsive, yet undeniably erotic elixir. The only sound in the room was the barely audible ticking of a cheap Thai clock which inexplicably seemed to enhance the sensual nature of the experience. Almost as if in counterpoint to the soft ticking, Dao exerted pressure in her fingers at the base of my cooing dove and flicked her tongue teasingly against its tip.

And then I felt the dove exploding and I placed my left hand on the top of her head, and grasped her wrist in my right hand to slow her strokes. The clock ticked away seconds of pure pleasure. And then she was gone. Seconds later I felt her gently cleaning me with a warm, damp towel.

Within minutes I had forgotten about Lisa Avery and my dark thoughts about Dao. I dreamed of Coffin Ed and Grave Digger Jones running beside a Thai *klong*, and I saw Coffin Ed draw his .38 revolver with its long, nickel-plated barrel from his shoulder sling and I watched him blaze away at a shadowy figure in the darkness. As he fired, I felt a sudden pain in my side. I rolled over and saw Dao back under the sheet staring at me, ready to pinch me again. *Siaw*, she said. "I'm horny."

16

The clock rang just before five. I let it ring. I was on my back dreaming and in my dream I was floating over the Thai countryside – ricefields, temples, villages, market-places. Children riding the backs of water buffalo waved. I waved back. It was a good feeling. Then suddenly I was inside the village, beside an open-air boxing ring, acting as a second for Dao. Everyone in the packed auditorium was waiting for the judges' decision. Above the ring there hung a beautiful blue-and-yellow striped punkah being gracefully pulled back and forth to provide a modicum of moving air. But as she turned toward me, the scene suddenly transformed and everything was underwater. The punkah had become a huge striped surgeonfish and Dao had transformed into a boxer crab.

The boxer crab has a tiny anemone attached to each of its front pincers giving the appearance that the crab is wearing a pair of fancy, tufted white boxing gloves. When diving, I had seen these boxer crabs raise their "gloves" in defense and feint left and right jabs just like a boxer. In my dream, Dao had become just such a crab.

My laughter woke me up. Dao reached across me and shut the alarm off. Her hair fell across my face. I stopped laughing. I brushed her hair from my eyes.

She kissed my lips and leaned on one elbow. "What is so funny?"

I knew that with her match just days away, any dream of mine involving boxing might in her superstitious mind presage disaster and so I made up a story about dreaming of a humorous child-hood incident. It was a lie but it was safe. I had learned as all men living with women eventually do that keeping the peace is far more important than adherence to literal truth.

I looked at the clock. "You *Essarn* girls get up early."

"What are you talking about? I'm not from *Essarn*."

True, Korat could be called the gateway to *Essarn*. And as *Essarn* was the poor northeast – the provider to Bangkok of most of its laborers, samlor and taxi drivers and bargirls – not everyone from the area might want to admit they were from there. But I had been abruptly pulled from my dream and was in the mood for a battle. "Oh, well, pardon me all over the place, but you are from Korat, right?"

"Of course I'm from Korat. But do I speak Lao? Do I eat things like *phak loom phua* (forget-your-husband vegetable)?"

I looked over at her feminine form in the semi-darkness. She was now sitting up; and ready for battle. She had slipped into one of my "Been there - Dived it" T-shirts during the night and beneath it I could see her nipples jutting out from her breasts. I could feel myself backing down. "OK, have it your way, you aren't from *Essarn*."

"Turn on the light."

"Say what?"

"Turn on the light!"

"Jesus, what, have you got a map of Thailand on you?"

She reached up, turned on the light above the bed, then grabbed her T-shirt and yanked it up. She pushed her breasts close to my face. "You see?"

"See what?"

"Pink! Korat girls have pink nipples! *Essarn* girls have black or brown nipples!"

Certainly her nipples were close to a dark shade of pink; depending on time of day and source of light their shade was somewhere between damask and sepia. The thought occurred to me that I had accidentally entered the most creative geography class I would ever have. And if Miss Van Orden had taught geography the same show-and-tell way in the 5th grade, I would have paid a lot more attention.

She gave me a sniff kiss on the cheek and went into the bathroom. I lay on the bed thinking of bacon, eggs, coffee and toast. Like many *farang*s who have acquired a taste for Thai food, I drew the line when it came to breakfast; in the morning hours, only western food would do. Dao was not fond of "bland" western cuisine and seldom wanted to join me even when her training allowed it. When she came out of the bathroom, she was dressed in T-shirt and panties. Just for form sake, I asked if she had time to join me.

She stopped brushing her hair long enough to shake her head. "No, thank you."

I headed for the bathroom to brush my teeth. Before I reached the bathroom door she added: "I had a dream."

I felt a sudden nervousness in the pit of my stomach. Because when you live with a Thai woman long enough you learn that almost every dream she has can be – will be – interpreted to mean the man she is with has cheated on her. I entered the bathroom and, with the door open, began brushing my teeth. She brushed her hair. I waited for whatever was going to fall to fall.

"My brother needs cigarettes."

Now I knew the situation was much worse than I had thought it would be. She'd had dreams about her brother needing things before. And I knew which brother it was. It was the brother who had been shot dead in a land deed dispute many years before.

She seldom mentioned him but from what little she had said, I understood that Buen had avenged his brother's death – and then some. Illiterate farmers who had been swindled out of their land title deeds near Korat soon knew whom to contact for help.

Buen had acted as a one-man Robin Hood against gangs who preyed on the poor. On one such mission, he had been shot once and knifed twice but managed to kill three thugs sent to kill him. And it was shortly after that sanguinary act of revenge that he had joined the monkhood for two years.

In any case, if her late brother needed cigarettes, this meant she would be visiting a temple to make offerings, including cigarettes, to a monk and to pray for her brother. I knew it also meant she would like me to go with her. I brushed harder and tried to think of a response. She was not without a sense of humor but I knew if I said something about smoking being bad for her late brother's health it would most likely be bad for my health.

She came into the bathroom, whipped off her T-shirt and threw it into the laundry basket. She turned and pressed her breasts against my chest. "It won't take long; I have to get back to the camp. Would you like to go with me to the temple? It's not far. We can take the Skytrain."

And so it was that instead of relaxing in an air-conditioned coffee shop reading a local paper, and sipping coffee, I was standing beside a malodorous *klong* (canal) behind a nondescript temple holding a small wooden cage with nine sparrows and in the other hand a transparent plastic container of several small eels. The idea, of course, was to release the birds from their prison, return the eels to their habitat and gain good karma from an act of merit.

But the birds acted as if I were the one who had captured them and they pecked angrily at my fingers. The hideously ugly eels Dao called "sea snakes" and assured me they don't bite. Whatever she assumed they were, I had no doubt if they could get at me, they would do what damage they could. My lack of caffeine had made me irritable and just as I had made up my mind to "accidentally" drop everything into the canal, Dao took them from me.

She opened the door of the bird cage and the sparrows flew off into the light blue sky. While I held the bag of eels, she opened it, then dumped them out. They fell, still in a cluster, and disappeared with hardly a sound beneath the filthy water.

She smiled. "There. Now, don't you feel better?"

17

Dao took a taxi to camp and I headed back to Washington Square. I had no sooner returned to my apartment when one of the girls from the Boots and Saddle brought up a message. George had called and desperately needed somebody to teach an afternoon class for beginners – a husband and wife, and all of George's regular instructors were out of town leading diving groups in Pattaya. I told her to tell George I would be there in an hour; and to tell him that my phone was working again.

Sooner or later I would find out the caliber of weapon Buen had given his sister. Which meant that the one thing I needed to know now was the type of weapon used in Lisa's death. I still had a few friends at the embassy so I called one I had dated a few times. Nancy Evans and I had never been an item but had had a few drinks. It wasn't long before we realized we were destined to remain friendly acquaintances and nothing mor e. The strange thing is once we knew where we stood we got along very well and continued having a dinner and seeing a movie together now and then.

I didn't envy her one aspect of her job: After confirming the death of an American citizen, it was her responsibility to locate the NOKs (Next of Kin) and inform them of their loved one's death and express condolences on behalf of the United States government. I imagined murder cases were especially difficult. And then she might also have to tactfully discuss costs to cover the disposition of remains, be it by shipping back to the States, by burial or by cremation, as well as the packing and shipping of personal effects. I also knew beneath her professional veneer, her job deeply affected her.

I had seen her really angry only once; a colleague had referred to her as "the bird lady." When Nancy asked why he called her that he said it was because she deals with NOK's and the word nok in Thai meant bird. To say the least, Nancy hadn't found it amusing. No one called her the bird lady again.

Nancy's Thai was fluent and far better than mine. In fact, every woman who worked at the American Embassy seemed to speak Thai better than I did. I had once accused Nancy of being a Mormon missionary in a past life; she had laughed but she hadn't denied it.

A secretary put me right through and Nancy's voice, still with more than a bit of mid-Western drawl, came on the line. "Nancy Evans."

"Hi, Nancy. Scott Sterling."

"Scott Sterling! Now there is a name I haven't heard for awhile. I heard the Mafia got you."

"Mafia?"

"Somebody said you were swimming with the fishes. Get it?"

"Very good, Nancy. I do indeed swim with the fishes. I teach scuba."

"Well, good for you. I haven't seen you since your late misunderstanding with Frank Webber."

"Least said, soonest mended."

She laughed. "Right. Anyway, what can I do for you?"

"You know of the death of Lisa Avery."

In the brief silence that followed I could almost feel Nancy becoming more cautious. "Of course."

"You're in charge of Lisa Avery's affairs?"

"Her affairs?"

"I mean you send out the Direct Relay Casualty Message Hand Deliver telegrams to the NOKs, right?"

"Scotty, telegrams were phased out about the time the

Burmese sacked Ayudhya. It's e-mails and faxes, now."

"Oh. OK, I'm in the two per cent that didn't get the word. But have you located any relatives yet?"

"Not yet. There seems to be some confusion over her identity. I've already contacted State. What's your interest in this?"

"Informal investigation. I knew her slightly. I can give you her real name and former New York address if you'd like."

"Of course I'd like. Wait a sec'. OK, let's have it."

I had no doubt that Nancy already had the information and quite possibly had Lisa's passport on her desk. But she was too professional to allow anyone to know what information she might already have. And she was perfectly willing to let me think I was doing her a favor. I gave her what information I had then chose my words carefully. "Have you read the police report on Lisa?"

She hesitated. "I have a copy, yes."

"Does it say what caliber the weapon was?"

"Even if it does, there is no way I could give out that information except on a need-to – "

"Nancy, the dead have no rights under the privacy act."

"Scott, we are talking about an American citizen here. And ACS officers don't routinely discuss the affairs of deceased Amcits with anyone who happens to be curious."

"I was thinking after I finish up this case, you and I might try the Normandy Grill at the Oriental Hotel some night."

She laughed. "I don't believe it. Scott Sterling trying to bribe an American Citizen Services Officer with a meal at a fancy restaurant."

"Best shrimp in town."

"Listen, mister, and listen good: you try that on some twenty-two year old in a mini-skirt, not on a middle-aged lady."

"OK. You win. I tried. But let's have that dinner, anyway."

"Sure. Call again soon, Scotty. You brighten my work day."

I rang off. I couldn't help but smile. Nancy was still as sharp as ever. And I had listened good: A "twenty-two year old in a mini-skirt." In other words, a .22 caliber mini-revolver. She would definitely get her meal at the Oriental. Now I just had to find some way of learning what weapon Buen had given Dao and hope it wasn't a .22 caliber mini-revolver.

I walked downstairs and over to the nearby Bourbon Street Café where I managed to talk the waitresses into making me some bacon and eggs even though everyone around me was ordering from lunch menus. But the girls serving were used to my strange ordering habits by now. I surprised them by not ordering my usual Bloody Mary but I still have enough common sense never to drink when I dive. Since I had left the embassy, I had been drinking more and enjoying it less.

Bangkok is the kind of town that presents you with every vice known to man – and if you've got a modicum of character and something to keep yourself busy, you'll only dabble. It's when you've got time on your hands that you begin to understand the true nature of the city's seductive powers. I had little character and lots of time on my hands.

I finished brunch, reentered the hazy glare and started the ten-minute walk over to Len's Dive Shop. My least favorite students were husbands and wives. The problem with teaching couples about diving is that one or the other in the relationship is usually dominant, sometimes domineering. More often than not it's the man. And that can quickly lead to a problem, although the types of husband or boyfriend who cause trouble are as different as night and day. The first is usually an overprotective sweet-heart who tries to do everything for his mate, making it difficult for her to learn and making it almost impossible for me to teach her. That type I can deal with without losing my cool.

The second type is something else again. It's a man whose overbearing attitude makes the woman more nervous than she already is. An exasperated impatience that only adds to the problem. That's why, if possible, I like to split couples up and pair each with a separate "buddy." On one or two occasions, in fact, the male students were such idiots that I came close to hauling off and smacking them – lawsuit be damned.

The bull-necked husband with the gruff manner waiting for me in the shop was one of the most disagreeable I'd ever encountered. And I just wasn't in the mood for an obnoxious student. He must have been a year or two shy of thirty, and if he had smiled during the time I was with him and his wife in the shop, I must have been looking in the other direction. In response to my introducing myself, he mumbled over his first name and brusquely introduced his wife as Sally.

I had no doubt women would have described him as ruggedly handsome. He stood about six feet two inches tall, and his presence was commanding. His wavy, jet black hair was the type women loved to run their fingers through. His deep-set eyes glanced upon all they surveyed from under full brows, and his jutting jaw was that of various American military officers or the actors playing those officers. His eyes were a hypnotic bluish green, the kind of shade centuries old, recently dug up, Buddha statues turn on first exposure to air. A Greek god with a flawlessly chiseled nose, the well-trimmed mustache of Clark Gable and the perfectly placed chin dimple of Michael Douglas.

I retrieved my mobile phone and pushed the "balance check" button to see how much time and money I had left after every bargirl in Pattaya had most likely used it. I was both surprised and pleased to find that I still had nearly three hundred baht of phone time.

I hailed a taxi to take us to the swimming pool and the three of us sat in the back seat, the wife in the middle. George had said on the phone that they were beginners who wanted to get started right away, but whatever I had to say was met with polite if quavery responses from the woman, and either silence or a barely audible grunt from him.

At six-foot-two inches, he was exactly my height, but he had an extra thirty pounds on me, some of it in the right places, some of it not. From the tight, chest-hugging T-shirt he wore, I figured it was safe to assume he thought his physique was worthy of display. His whole attitude was that of a bull dog looking for someone to bite. I only learned two things about him. First, he was a computer specialist from somewhere on the East Coast who had been transferred to his company's Bangkok office, and, second, it had obviously been his idea to learn to dive; not hers.

His wife was closer to middle age, maybe eight or nine years older than he was. She was still attractive and youthful looking or maybe her shoulder-length red hair, bright green eyes and girlish freckles made her look younger than she was. Yet years of living in fear of her husband's disapproval had cast a shadow over her features which seemed to have aged her. Her manner was diffident and her smile was nervous, and as I watched her fidget with strands of hair, I couldn't help thinking of the proverbial long-tailed cat trapped in a room full of rocking chairs. And it was clear that the bright Bangkok sunshine pouring out of a brilliant blue sky wasn't doing anything to calm her nerves.

The pool was only about a twenty-minute taxi ride from Len's Dive Shop and we were about halfway there when he asked me how long I'd been diving and how many dives I'd had. It wasn't the question I minded so much but the way he had asked it; in a tone that suggested I might not really be qualified. Besides, I knew George always explained my credentials to new customers. But I could tell how nervous his wife was, and I thought it might calm her down a bit if she saw my qualifications.

I reached into my pocket and dug out my leather card case and opened it to the PADI page. I explained how I was a member of the largest of the dive organizations, the Professional Association of Diving Instructors, and how each of the black photo ID cards qualified me for a different task. I read them off as I quickly flipped through them: "Open water scuba instructor, master scuba diver trainer, underwater videographer, underwater photographer, night diver, wreck diver, deep diver, search and recovery diver, dry suit diver, underwater navigator, multilevel diver, boat diver, drift diver, equipment specialist, underwater naturalist – "

I had just got to "enriched air specialist" when he waved his hand impatiently and said, "Yeah, yeah, enough." I knew then for sure this fellow and I would never throw back some Singha beers together.

The swimming pool and the four floors of luxury apartments with balconies surrounding it belonged to a wealthy Thai friend of George's. The building had been almost finished during Bangkok's real estate boom but final construction had ended abruptly when the economy collapsed. The apartment complex had been done in a kind of faux-Spanish style and was well kept but some of the apartments had not been finished and none had been furnished.

The story George had told about the manipulations between the owner and the banks and some other lenders and their family connections had been a bit too complicated for me to follow but what it came down to was that a beautiful swimming pool surrounded by eerily empty apartments was kept in perfect working order as an attractive bonus for occupants at other apartments owned by George's friend; apartments which did not have swimming pools. After we'd changed into swimsuits, we sat by the side of the pool. His suit was black edged with a gold border and brief enough to emphasize the muscles of his thighs. Her suit was green with red stripes and although it covered too much of her smooth white flesh to be described as a bikini, it did nothing to hide her feminine curves. I wondered if there had been a point early in the marriage when they had been happy and how long before she had realized the enormity of her mistake.

Despite ominous gray clouds rushing in from the horizon, sunlight penetrated the water, reflected off the bright white tiles surrounding the swimming pool and glittered along the red and white tiles of the "Spanish" balconies above.

His wife and I sat in the shade of tasteless white statuary surrounded by tall green plants. He had sat down well outside the shade and he obviously felt no discomfort as his leathery skin absorbed the sun.

I explained what each piece of equipment was and how it was used: The wet suit, the air tank, the weight belt, the BCD (Buoyancy Control Device), the regulator with octopus and pressure gage, the fins, mask and snorkel. I emphasized the importance of not holding one's breath and explained more than they wanted to know about how the air in the tank is the same as the air we breathe: twenty-one per cent oxygen and seventy-nine per cent nitrogen. The deeper a diver goes the more nitrogen his body absorbs. And although it was a bit early to talk about the effects of decompression sickness (the bends), I had seen enough divers experience its unpleasant consequences to make certain everyone I taught understood the dangers involved in diving right from the get-go.

The husband had positioned himself barely within my line of vision, impatiently waiting for me to finish my lecture. He made no attempt to hide the fact that he was daydreaming while I spoke. The cold bluish-green eyes beneath their heavy brows never focused on me nor did he have any questions when I'd finished. I decided he must be the type of man used to being in control – control of his wife, his employees, his life; the type who resented encountering a situation in which he is the student rather than the one in charge. Just about the last kind of fool I would ever want to go diving with.

I helped them on with their scuba gear and got them into the pool. The wife was of small frame, and, fully loaded down with the BCD and the tank and the weight belt, she seemed almost a child trapped in equipment meant for adults. She stood beside her husband in water which reached just below her breasts. Even if she hadn't been visibly shaking, any fool could tell she was extremely tense and, thanks to her husband's impatient bullying, she was working herself up to a full blown anxiety attack.

I began explaining how the mask creates an air pocket for the eyes and how to clear it underwater. Despite her discomfort, he interrupted me to berate her. "Oh, come on, it's no big deal, you've been in a pool before, haven't you? Don't be such a big baby!"

I swallowed my anger and gave him my most charming smile. "We can stop for awhile, if you like. There's no need to – "

"We're not stopping! If she can't do what she has to do here, how is she going to do it under the ocean?"

She stood just out of his line of vision and I saw her give me a slight nod to continue. I wondered if inside their home he was more than just a verbal bully. I motioned for him to go under. "All right, fine. Let's get started."

At first, all went well. The woman seemed to grow more confident as I instructed her and her husband seemed to be paying a modicum of attention. And then, while underwater, the husband got water up his nose while trying to clear his mask. As soon as he'd started to cough, he spat the regulator from his mouth and made a strenuous effort to surface.

I was wearing extra weights on my belt for exactly this reason. When beginning students encountered what he was experiencing, they would usually attempt to shoot to the surface immediately. Which would sooner or later prove disastrous: if they got into the habit of shooting to the surface to deal with a problem, how would they deal with it under thirty feet of water in Pattaya Bay?

It was my practice to hold them under while gently pushing the regulator back into their mouths and making them breathe through their regulator. It was the kindest thing I could do for them. If they picked up any potentially fatal diving habits it wasn't going to be on my watch. I prided myself on the fact that no student of mine had ever gone to the surface to solve that kind of problem.

So when the husband started coughing, I held him in place. Needless to say, he was not the type who appreciated it. And while it was true that I usually gently placed the regulator back into a student's mouth, in his case, I shoved the regulator into his mouth. Hard.

After he stopped thrashing about and began breathing normally, I released him and let him surface. He started sputtering, then glared at me. He walked toward me as best he could on his fins, twisting his body with the effort of moving through the water, an animated cartoon – the menacing expression of Mike Tyson and the comical moves of Charlie Chaplin. "You son of a bitch!"

If I had been looking for an excuse to end the session, that was it. "That's it. Lesson's over!" I turned my back on him and swam to the ladder. Once I'd reached the tiles, I removed my mask, fins, weight belt and BCD. The sky had darkened and raindrops were already pelting the pool and nearby plants.

He followed me up the ladder, stripped off most of his own equipment, then strode quickly over to confront me. He pushed out at me and I backed up. "Bullshit! You didn't have to shove it into my mouth! You practically broke my jaw!"

As he pushed, I moved backward, while warning him to cool off. Fighting with a client – even one who had already paid for his lesson – was a no-win situation, and I figured he'd calm down after a few verbal exchanges. But my retreat must have given him the impression that he was cowering me, and he pushed harder. I wondered if this is how he did it with his wife.

I moved back still farther, closer to the edge of the pool. He reached out again to push and that's when I suddenly and simultaneously did a number of things. I stepped forward, grabbed the wet suit covering his left arm with my left hand, bent my knees to lower my center of balance, threw my right arm around him, turned my body, and slammed my right hip into him. With my right arm around his waist, and firmly grasping his left arm, I used his own momentum to throw him over my hip and onto his back into the water. Yes, Virginia, sometimes if you practice a text-book move often enough, and if you're lucky as well, the technique actually works in the real world just like in the diagrams. Or, in my case, just like in the martial arts classes my father got me into as a boy. This one worked like a charm.

I had thrown him into the deep end of the pool, that is, into about twelve feet of water. As he still had his weight belt on, he sank like a stone. All he had to do was to snap open his quick-release buckle and dump it, but, as expected from a beginner, he panicked, thinking only about clawing his way back to the surface. He seemed to be doing it without much trouble but I decided to dive in to help him. That's when I heard her shout.

"No!"

The almost deranged fury his wife managed to inject into that one word caused me to turn to look at her. She was resting on the underwater ledge which ran around the pool. She sat with her back to the side of the pool, propped on her elbows, her legs in the water. As she stared back at me, something in her eyes suggested she might have been perfectly content to live with an unfortunate accident.

As he thrashed harder, he broke the water's surface. Once he'd finished gulping air, he shouted something at me. Thunder drowned out his words but it was clear that he was not a happy man. That was clear from his swearing in between coughs and threats of a lawsuit in between bouts of throat-clearing. But while he was not happy, he was no longer aggressive either. Except in his legal threats. "You'll be hearing from my lawyer about this!"

"The hell he will!"

He was so shocked at his wife's insubordination, that it took him several seconds to resume his intimidating manner toward her. His voice was as ominously grating as he could make it. "What did you say?"

She raised her voice to him. "I said there won't be any lawsuit. He was only doing what he was supposed to do." Her green eyes had widened, and her jaw was set in unflinching defiance, and she boldly held his gaze. I suspected there was also something in her relaxed posture that conveyed to him a newfound confidence in his better half. "It's important that you learn proper techniques in the pool. After all, if you can't do what you have to do here, how are you going to do it in the ocean?"

The light rain had now turned into a downpour. He stared at her for nearly half a minute, then went into the area we used as a dressing room. As I followed him in to change, I turned back to look at his wife. She lay back in the pool, still propped on her elbows, her face turned to the sky. Her eyes were closed and as the rain pelted her face, she was smiling like a contented cat.

18

By the time I made it to the Boots and Saddle, most of the regular drunkards had worked their way through their money or their anger or their lust and had fallen asleep in the booths. The joke was that the bargirls would occasionally pass through and check their pulses to see if they were still alive or not.

For many of the regulars, the bars of Washington Square represented but one angle of a Golden Triangle, the other two angles being the bars of *Soi* Cowboy and those of Nana Plaza. With the exception of visa runs to Cambodia or Laos, if life existed outside the parameters of this triangle, none of the regulars would have been particularly interested. The once famous Patpong Road had been written off as something now suitable only for tourists and in any case lay well outside the Golden Triangle. As far as Khao San Road and the backpackers went, that area might as well have been on another planet.

As I looked over the booths, I noticed an old acquaintance, but we studiously avoided each other for lack of knowing whether either of us was 'operational' at the moment. I'd last seen him at Fort Bragg's former stockade, called the Compound. He was a Major at SFOD Delta, the antiterrorist unit and the Compound was its headquarters. I knew he'd served in Afghanistan and Iraq and had a dozen questions to ask but there was no way I could chat him up without knowing his status.

"Wild Turkey," the bar regulars' favorite song, was on the jukebox and, unfortunately, a few of those most inebriated were attempting to sing along with the chorus:

> I hear your wife just up and left
> He said it with a grin;
> I made a fist and in a flash
> His blood ran down his chin.
>
> Then when he rose and drew a knife
> I knew I'd crossed the line;
> But when more blood spilled on the floor
> I knew it wasn't mine.
>
> The barkeep said the man's hurt bad
> I said, "He isn't dead";
> And when he warned the Law might show
> I turned to him and said:
>
> "Just pour Wild Turkey in my glass
> It keeps my devils still;
> Just pour Wild Turkey in my glass
> 'Cause if you won't I will."

Winny sat in the booth across from me downing a cheeseburger and fries while checking the previous night's bar statement and whatever was there made him scowl. He grumbled without looking up: "Read the paper today?"

I began nibbling on some of his french fries. "Not yet."

"Bangkok got over a hundred crematorium temples and most don't have after-burners."

"That a fact?"

"Yeah. The first burner burns the body, the after-burner gets rid of the dust and gas and smoke and crud like dioxin. The stuff that comes out of the first burner causes cancer. Unless they got an after burner."

"So you're saying – "

"What I'm saying is in Bangkok the dead are killing the living."

I put down my french fry, suddenly having lost my appetite. "I can always count on you for interesting dinner table conversation."

"Well, I didn't want you to blame automobile and factory pollution for everything."

"You ever think of working for the Thai Tourist Board?"

"Sheet, I know more about how many tourists are around than they do. Tourism is down, everybody in this bar gets calls from bargirls wanting to come over to their place; tourism is up, the bars get busy and the phones never ring." He looked at my hand.

"Hell happened to your finger?"

"Crown-of-thorns starfish."

He shook his head. "I never can understand why the fuck anybody would want to hang around underwater in the first place. All that slimy shit is just waiting to do damage to whoever's dumb enough to go down there."

Five-Minute Jack swiveled on his bar stool to join in the conversation. "They don't want you there, man. Why not go where you're wanted?"

"Because, Jack, there are things going on down there you couldn't even imagine."

"Like what?"

"Well, the female seahorse deposits her eggs into her male's brood pouch, and he fertilizes them for her."

"You sayin' the *male* seahorse gets pregnant!"

"That's exactly what I'm saying."

He took a drag of his cigarette and his watery grey eyes stared back at me. "That's unnatural!"

Death Wish Don, still done up like a steam locomotive engineer, moved to a stool to be closer to the conversation. He poked

Five-minute Jack's shoulder to emphasize his point. "That's unamerican, is what it is!"

"Or, take the parrotfish. She lays her eggs then transforms into a male. And if a male square-blotched anthias dies, a female in the harem changes into a male and takes over."

Five-Minute Jack banged his fist on the counter, accidentally breaking his cigarette. "I knew it! The fucking feminazis have taken over the ocean too! I fuckin' knew it! They're everywhere!"

"And there's the transvestite cuttlefish," I said.

Now it was Death Wish Don's turn to be outraged. "You mean the ladyboys are down *there* too?"

Winny stopped eating a french fry long enough to speak. "Didn't you read your Paul Fucking Revere: 'Straight if by land; gay if by sea'."

I decided to pile it on. "The harlequin shrimp eats crown of thorn starfish starting with the legs and working inward to keep the starfish alive and delicious as long as possible."

Death Wish Don waved off the bargirl who was about to massage his shoulders. "Fucking Jeffrey Dahmer, man. That's cannibal shit! I'm staying out of the goddamn water!"

Five-minute Jack gave forth with a nasty laugh and gestured toward Don's beer. "You're *drinkin'* it, is what you're doin."

"And in the case of some critters, the mouth and anus are the same."

Five-minute Jack stood up. "That's fucking disgusting!"

Winny laughed. "Romantic as hell!"

Death Wish Don puckered up to Jack. "Gimme a little kiss, will you, huh?"

Jack grabbed his wad of bills. "Gimme my fucking bill! I'm not gonna sit here and listen to stories about fucked-up faggot fish and cannibal fucking shrimp what can't tell there esophagus from their asshole."

When I merely shrugged, Winny went back to grumbling

about irregularities in the bar statement. For a few minutes, I listened to the desultory comments of Death Wish Don and West Texas Andy now sitting in a booth behind us. There was something about the conversations that relaxed me; made me feel I was underwater, drifting by exotic coral reefs full of clownish fish.

"Thirty-five million women in Thailand, and I've bought ladies drinks for about thirty million of them."

"Yeah? Well, I've bought *somtam* for about the same number. All they do is eat."

"Thais don't eat; they graze."

"Tell you what I've decided: I'm going to leave all my personal possessions and all my money to the bar girl I happen to be in bed with at the time I croak."

"You haven't got any fucking money. And you don't own shit."

"So? It's the thought that counts."

"Not with Thai bargirls, it ain't."

"Yeah, I know, but I can't help lovin' 'em. I'm a damn sucker for a pretty face and sexy body. That's my trouble. But I been tryin' to do what the Buddhist masters say."

"What's that?"

"They say when you feel yourself becoming turned on by a woman you should concentrate on what kind of being is really standing before you: bones, blood, pus, urine, shit, that kind of thing. That way you can stop yourself from indulging."

"So does that work for you?"

"Not yet."

"How long you been tryin'?"

"Goin' on twenty-three years."

When their conversation petered out, I asked Winny for his cellphone. He handed it over without looking up. That's when I remembered I had my own again. I handed his back.

Not unexpectedly, the two phone numbers for Da had both been cancelled; which meant the best way of questioning her would be to make an appointment with her where she worked. The woman on the phone at Jezebels spoke English with only a trace of a Thai accent. She carefully articulated her words and took a few seconds to weigh my replies before responding. She sounded neither unfriendly nor overly friendly.

I explained that I was calling because I would like to have a session with one of their mistresses. When she asked how I had heard about their services, I mentioned a conversation with someone at the Emerald Club who wished to remain anonymous but who had highly recommended Mistress Angst.

I could hear women talking in the background. The woman on the phone said something to them and it grew quiet.

"You understand we accept only bottoms, no tops." When I said nothing she expanded on her meaning. "Submissives only. No switching. You may not assume a dominant role."

I assured her that I understood my role would be that of a submissive, which caused Winny to give me a curious glance.

"Would you like to serve only Mistress Angst or Mistress Angst and a friend?"

"Just Mistress Angst, thank you."

"And how long a session would you like?"

She seemed so nonchalant about the subject of our conversation that it almost felt as if I were ordering pizza. "How long are they usually?"

"Anywhere from two hours to two days."

"I'll take the two hours."

"You understand that will be ten thousand baht payable before the session begins."

"Ten thousand baht." Winny winced. "Yes, no problem. But I'll need your address."

"With first time customers we prefer to pick you up. When would you like to come to Jezebels?"

"Tomorrow night?"

"Just a moment."
I waited, trying to shelter the mobile phone from the noise of the bar:

> I said to him (or all of them
> My vision wasn't clear);
> "Just pour Wild Turkey in my glass
> And leave the bottle here.
>
> "Just pour Wild Turkey in my glass
> It keeps my devils still;
> Just pour Wild Turkey in my glass
> 'Cause if you won't I will.

"All right, Mistress Angst is free at eight. Kindly give me your address and we will send someone to pick you up."

I gave her the address of the Boots and Saddle, she repeated it. We confirmed the time and hung up.

I replaced my cellphone snugly into its case and moved it back on my belt. "Great news."

Winny raised one eyebrow as a polite way of feigning interest.

"Mistress Angst is free at eight tomorrow night."

Winny dropped his eyebrow and raised his beer bottle. "May it prove to be a sublime experience for both of you." Then he buried his nose once again in the previous night's bar statement. And the whole bar, girls included, joined in on the last chorus:

> "Just pour Wild Turkey in my glass
> It keeps my devils still;
> Just pour Wild Turkey in my glass
> 'Cause if you won't I will!

19

A few hours and several beers later I was back in my apartment. I looked at the clock. Time to call New York. The phone in my apartment had been more-or-less repaired and I had now lived above the bar long enough so that I was one of the privileged few allowed to make long distance phonecalls from the room. The Phonenet cards from places such as 7-11 would have been cheaper but I had always been too lazy to learn how to use one. I opened a Singha, took a long swig, and pushed some buttons. It had been a while since I had called area code 212.

It rang several times before Chinaman picked up. His muffled attempt at voicing a "Hello" told me I had pulled him out of a sound, probably not too sober, sleep.

"Hey, Chinaman, how you doing?"

"Scotty? That you?"

I had grown up with that nickname. Chinaman was the only one from my New York neighborhood who still used it. "Yeah. I wake you?"

"That's all right, I was up late finishing a couple of cases."

"Detective or beer?"

"One of each, actually."

"Hard to believe I haven't seen you since dad's funeral. Three years, is it?"

"Almost."

"So you're still in the East Village."

"Yeah, for now, but people around here are getting younger every year. NYU students look about twelve. I may be the oldest guy in the East Village."

"People getting younger everywhere, what can you do?" After a few seconds of silence, I decided to get right into it. "Listen, do you remember a young woman named Lisa Avery?"

"Lisa Avery. Nope, can't say that I do."

"Immigration here in Bangkok gives her real name as Janet Burgess."

"Ah, now, her I remember. Blue eyes like those are hard to forget. She contact you?"

"Yeah, she did. But she shied away from confiding anything. Seemed to think she was about to get whatever information she was after and wouldn't be needing me after all. Then somebody…she was found dead in her Bangkok apartment."

"Christ."

"Yeah. She give you any background?"

"Not much. When she hired me I warned her I was wrapping up another case but would get to hers as soon as I could. We were supposed to meet again. She said a man had borrowed a lot of money from her and she was afraid he had skipped town."

"She say how much money?"

"No. But the guy's name was Robert Sanford. An architect in a firm on Park Avenue. I got the impression she had been calling his home and his company and pestering him about it. Anyway, she said one day she called and he was gone. His company wouldn't give out any information nor would the doorman at the building where he had lived. That's when she came to me."

"But you had to put it on hold?"

"I would have but I decided to take a long shot first. I picked up the phone and called his office and asked if they knew where I could contact him."

"And because they liked your Chinese accent so much they told you?"

"Not at first. But once they understood I was a loan officer at the First Manhattan Bank of Commerce calling to give him the happy news that his loan was approved and we just needed him to come in to sign a few papers they let it slip he had been transferred to their Bangkok office."

"I assume there is no 'First Manhattan Bank of Commerce'?"

"Probably not a second one, either."

"You devil, you. Employing cunning and craft not to mention deception to ferret out confidential information. How do you sleep at night?"

"What can I say, I grew up with American brothers who led me astray."

"So it sounds like once she knew he was in Bangkok, she flew out here to find him."

"It sounds like it. Look, Scotty, I'll check my notes and e-mail you if I find anything else."

"Much obliged. But what would be great is if you could dig into it a bit at your end. If you've got the time."

"I'll do what I can."

"Got a pen?"

"Shoot."

"Janet Alice Burgess. Place of birth Scarsdale, New York. Passport was issued in New York City. DOB twenty-seven April nineteen-eighty."

"Jesus, life can be brief."

"Yeah."

"Scotty?"

"Yeah."

"This personal?"

"Tell you the truth, Chinaman, I don't know what it is. Didn't go to bed with her; not even sure I liked her. But something told me her party girl persona was an act."

"That old Sterling sixth sense?"

"Must be."

"You think there's more to this than just a loan that needed repaying?"

"You know what the Chinese say."

"I'm Chinese. How the hell would I know what the Chinese say?"

I switched to mandarin: *"Wu feng, tsao bu dung."*

"'Where there is no wind, the grass does not move.' Didn't I teach you that one?"

"Could have been."

"You figure the grass is moving in this one?"

"Blowing all to shit."

"OK. I'll call in some favors on this one but some of the database searches will cost you."

I thought again of my late father's admonition that "databases don't solve cases" and, of course, he was right. It takes a human with a brain to know what to look for and where to look. And to interpret the results intelligently. But the power of the computer has revolutionized the detective business and with skill and luck background investigations which would have taken weeks in the pre-internet age, now could take days, hours or even minutes. "It's all right, I'll pick up whatever tab you run up."

"I'll get on it. Just watch yourself, Scotty."

"Will do. Take care, Chinaman."

As I hung up, I remembered the day dad brought an eight-year-old boy home and announced to us that Liu Chiang-hsin would be staying with us. He wore a black knit cap, a silk neck scarf, a heavy fur coat and boots still wet with snow. A well-scrubbed, well mannered, red-cheeked, sensitive-looking boy from a scholar family, a boy about my age who spoke English with a heavy Beijing accent full of diminutive "r"-suffixes, with grammar too perfect to have been learned in America. My father, the legendary detective, Jimmy "The Tiger" Sterling, whom I worshipped, announcing that the strange boy had been orphaned and brought to America from a place called China, and that we would be adopting him. My brother Larry and I were told to treat him as one of us: a brother.

I did harbor some resentment at first, but not for long. As time passed, Chinaman and I became close, protected each other's back in street fights, once or twice came close to fighting each other, then learned to respect and to love one another as brothers. But I always thought of him as I first saw him that white winter morning in the hallway of our New York apartment: as the boy who had been through unspeakable hell during a so-called Cultural Revolution. Over the years, he hadn't lost quite all of his mandarin accent; or any of his boyhood nightmares.

And I thought of Lisa. I had been right about the temporary nature of her furnishings. She hadn't planned on staying in Bangkok. And she may have been a good-time girl but she wasn't only that. She was here on a mission. Whatever that mission was had got her killed.

DAY SEVEN

20

I made another check of the situation inside the refrigerator and threw out most of what had faded, gone sour, turned green or partly evaporated, which was just about everything, then did some serious shopping to replace it. As I needed information, I also withdrew some money from an ATM machine; money which I could ill afford to withdraw.

Once I'd finished putting things away, I climbed on the back of a motorcycle taxi and headed for Lisa Avery's apartment. I had thought of impersonating someone interested in renting an apartment but this being Thailand crossing someone's palm with a bit of silver seemed the right way to approach things.

In Bangkok, motorcycle taxi drivers are great sources of information. They hang around small lanes and back streets waiting to take people to their destinations and I always made sure I knew a few of them pretty well. I had more than once shared a bit of Johnnie Walker Black with the ones inside the entrance to Washington Square and knew a bit about some of them. I wasn't quite sure what else he did for money, but the one I took was the only one I knew of who could afford both a major wife and a minor wife.

We were about halfway there when he received a call on his cellphone but, unlike several I had taken, he ignored it until we reached our destination. I had him continue on a ways past the door to the building, then got off and paid him his twenty baht. As I walked off, I could hear him explaining something to someone who wasn't pleased with him. I wondered if his major wife had found out about his minor wife. Or if his minor wife had found out about his new girlfriend.

I entered the hallway as quietly as possible but also with an air that I belonged there. I could hear a saccharin Thai love song playing in the restaurant but I saw no one.

I made an abrupt left and walked up the stairs to the first floor. I heard a door shut but except for sounds of motorcycles passing by in the street, all was quiet. I walked up to the second floor, then the third. The angry whir of an electric drill and intermittent hammering came from somewhere down the hall. The door of Lisa's apartment I had entered a few nights before had yellow police crime tape across it in the form of an X. The living room door had nothing.

I continued on up to the fourth floor. I heard the maids before I saw them. They were laughing about something and didn't hear me approach. This is why I made certain my visit was in the late morning; about the time maids should be cleaning apartments.

A plump barefoot maid somewhere in her early twenties exited an apartment and breezed by me holding a load of neatly folded ironed shirts. She smiled and wished me good morning. I approached the open door of the apartment where one maid still busily swept the bedroom floor. She was a tiny, almost shriveled, birdlike creature with the beady black eyes of a sparrow. Her jerky movements were those of an animated clock figurine, and her skin was a wrinkled, nutmeg brown, almost the same shade as her dress. At first I thought she was whispering to someone then I realized she was muttering to herself. I knocked on the open door.

She looked over at me, hesitated for just a moment, then continued sweeping. I slipped out of my loafers, left them beside her sandals, and walked across the room. The bed had been made so I sat on it. I used my best Thai. "Excuse me, I was a friend of the American lady in room three-oh-two. I am also a private detective. I wonder if you are the lady who found her."

She stopped sweeping but continued to grip the broom with gnarled fingers. She stared at me, firm-jawed and unsmiling. Her thinning black hair stopped just below the line of loose flesh below her chin and her gaunt, swarthy cheeks were pockmarked. She was crinkly-eyed, broad-nosed, with thin lips in an almost abnormally thin face.

She nodded.

"I would very much like to have a look around her apartment. Do you think you could let me in?"

Her head began shaking in abrupt movements. Surprisingly, there was nothing twittery about her voice. It was throaty and distinct. I got the impression that her voice was all that was left of the real personality before illness or misfortune took their toll on her; the personality which had once been confident and unafraid. "The police said no one goes in."

"Well, I just want to look. I don't want to move anything or touch anything. It would – "

She mumbled something I couldn't catch then continued her sweeping. I had hoped to find a maid a bit more approachable than this one but, in fact, I wasn't particularly disappointed. A young maid would be overawed by the police and afraid to let me in. An older woman like this, one whom I suspected had medical bills to pay, might be far more susceptible to suggestions backed up by cash.

I reached into my pocket and pulled out a one-thousand baht note, about the equivalent of twenty-three American dollars. Quite a bit for someone on her maid's salary. "I only need ten minutes. That's one hundred baht a minute." She stopped sweeping and stared at the bill. "And if you saw anyone or heard anything that is useful, I will pay you more."

She lifted her head up and squinted her eyes as if trying to get a better view of me. "You were really her friend?"

"I knew her. She wanted my help but she waited too long. I

157

want to find out who killed her."

She propped the broom against the wall and shuffled her way over to me. She gave me a brief wai, snatched the bill, and told me to follow her. The bill disappeared somewhere inside a pocket of her brown dress. Following her shuffling gait down the hallway and down to the third floor was close to the opposite of following Bright Eyes through the various rooms of the Emerald Club. I hadn't seen her strange kind of movements since I had observed mantis shrimp scuttling along an ocean's floor.

She walked over to the living room door of Lisa's apartment, inserted the key, and walked in. I followed. The living room was a mess. The computer was still there and knickknacks were still in place on nearby tables but drawers had been searched and left open, the cover had been slipped off the harddrive, and paper littered the floor.

"Was it like this when you found her?"

She pursed her thin lips together into a kind of a jagged "U," squinted and nodded.

I pressed the message machine and got what I expected: silence. The computer had been disconnected and I found no sign of floppy disks or any other backup system. I did a quick search of what few desk drawers there were. There was nothing of value or of interest. I quickly shuffled through receipts, bills, statements and instruction books for the computer, printer, scanner and message machine. The dates on the receipts, bills and statements were all dated well before the present month. I assumed the police had taken any diary, address book, recent bills and statements. I checked the blades of the fan, behind the curtains, and the area behind the computer. I checked the flower pots along the balcony. I looked over the balcony chairs. Again nothing.

The kitchen was too tiny to hide much of anything but I did a cursory search. A sink, a grill, a microwave, one set of cupboards. I walked into the bedroom. The bed was unmade and clothes and VCD's littered the floor. The dresses, blouses, slacks and jeans were quite stylish as far as I could tell, which wasn't very far. The photographs I had seen previously remained where they were. The VCD's were current features she had bought for cheap Thai prices at Panthip Plaza and the tapes seemed to be only of music groups I had barely heard of. I began asking questions while I opened and checked out the air conditioner. "Was the room like this when you found it or did the police mess it up?"

"It was a big mess when I found her. Of course, she was never very neat, but it was never like this."

I wondered if the police dusted for fingerprints or ran checks on phonecalls or talked to neighbors. Some Thai police were competent, some were incompetent, some allowed the institutionalized corruption to alter their investigation and some didn't. After accidents, it was often an independent group which collected bodies and took fingerprints as many policemen were actually too superstitious to take any fingerprints of a dead person. I decided that the most prudent course would be to go on the assumption that I was the only one investigating the death of Lisa Avery.

I finished with the air conditioner and gestured toward the bed. It was covered with what appeared to be a colorful northern hill tribe quilt. "Where exactly did you find her?"

She shuffled over to the bed and made a motion with both hands which made her look as if she was practicing some kind of bizarre dance step. Or an autopsy without the instruments. "She was on her back. Her head was here." She gestured again. "Blood." Then she surprised me by speaking in English: "Have many blood get out!"

Something about her grammar as well as the way she gestured made the death of Lisa Avery very real to me. I thought of the young woman with beautiful blond tresses, big blue eyes and the lovely face turned into a corpse at the pull of a trigger. And then

I thought of "have many blood get out." I continued on in Thai. "What was she wearing?"

She described a far more modest outfit than the one I had last seen Lisa wearing. It sounded as if she had changed clothes to meet someone.

"Did you hear or see anyone that night?"

She shook her head.

"Did she ever have people over? A boyfriend?"

Her lips pursed again. Her eyes squinted until they were just about shut. I wasn't sure if that expression was a typical one for when she was lost in thought. Or when she was filled with disgust. Or if it was simply that she had gotten old before she should have. "About a month ago. I saw her leave with a man."

"A foreign man or Thai?"

"Foreign."

I knew ten minutes was up but she seemed to have forgotten about any time limit. Money does that sometimes. "How old? What did he look like?"

"Maybe forty-five. Maybe fifty. Not tall like you." She held out a hand. It shook slightly and she withdrew it. "Not fat but getting there."

"He have all his hair?"

"No."

Drawing information out of her was like pulling teeth from the mouth of someone who hates dentists. "Hair on the face?"

She shook her head.

I went for her jugular. "Were they in love or was she paying him?"

She stared at me a few seconds before her face assumed the usual pinched prune appearance.

I pressed on. "I mean people do confide in their maids sometimes, right? Maids know things. She was a woman alone in a foreign country."

She avoided my eyes. "Not my business."

"Did she have woman friends over?"

"One Thai woman. She came many times."

I figured that would be Da. "And the woman stayed with her overnight sometimes?"

She nodded.

"Do you know her name?"

"She called her 'Da.'"

I looked over the bedroom. It was always possible anything valuable belonging to Lisa had been stolen. By her murderer, by the maids, by the police, by anyone with a key to the apartment. But her TV and VCR player were there. A cable was coiled on a shelf under the VCR player like a two-headed snake. I picked it up, ran it through my fingers and replaced it.

Her books had been stacked into two untidy piles near the bed table. Most were guidebooks to Thailand, a few novels on Thailand, and more classic fiction. I noticed the book on detectives I had spotted previously. I picked it up and saw that the title was *Detective Techniques in the Computer Age*. I couldn't help remembering dad's admonition: "Data bases don't solve cases." They solved them even less in Southeast Asia than they did in New York. But Lisa Avery had been a good detective; good enough to get herself killed.

I riffled through the book, found nothing, and put it back on the pile. Then I noticed Henry Miller. I picked up *Crazy Cock* and riffled through it. I wasn't sure if the bookmark was any closer to the end of the book then when I had seen the book on her table, but it was the bookmark itself that interested me.

What Lisa had been using as a bookmark was some kind of marker from the Emerald Club. On one side was the club's emerald logo, the address and the words, "member's bottle ticket." On the obverse were six lines: "Name," "Purchase date," "Expiry date," "Bottle brand," "Mixer count" and "Bottle number."

In the place for name, something had been written in Thai.

The ink was smeared as if from a spilled drink. The purchase date was just over a month before, the expiry date was a few days ago, the bottle brand was "Chivas," the mixer count had nine out of ten boxes checked and the bottle was number "118." Someone had written in the number "38664" and I had no idea why. I palmed the card and then slipped it into my pocket. It might have nothing to do with anything but I thought I would like to get the anglicized name of the Thai gentleman Lisa had been having drinks with at the Emerald Club.

I turned to the maid. "OK. Give me one minute to check the bathroom then I'm finished."

I checked inside the toilet tank, behind it, around the sink, inside the laundry basket, under the laundry basket, inside each neatly stacked towel and facecloth, behind a mirror, and behind a water heater. And found nothing.

I reentered the bedroom. I briefly looked at the photographs of Lisa and her friend; both bundled up and standing in snow. At least one of the photographs had been taken in Manhattan and it had been taken before September 11, 2001, because I could see a glimpse of the World Trade Centers in the background. I checked behind the photographs and found nothing. I dug a card out of my wallet. "If you remember anything else, call me."

She took the card and held it in front of her. I had no doubt she couldn't read English but she pursed her lips, anyway.

She followed me out the door and locked it. I started down the stairs.

"Wait."

I stood where I was. She walked slowly up a flight of stairs. I heard her unlock a door, presumably to her room. I heard the door shut. I waited. I could hear intermittent hammering and the dull roar of motorcycles. I heard a vendor of fruit in a pickup truck cruise by advertising his rambutan over a microphone. His voice grew louder then softer, then died out altogether.

I heard the maid's door open. She made her way slowly down the steps and walked toward me carrying a brown envelope about half the size of *Time* magazine. She stopped on the stairs and held it out to me. I walked to her and held it. After a moment of hesitation she let go.

The envelope had been well sealed. After a few tries, I slowly peeled back some Scotch tape and opened it. It contained something like a dozen Polaroid photographs of people having fun. Nearly naked people or people in bizarre clothing having fun. Handcuffed wrists, ball-gagged mouths, legs held open by spreader bars. A woman's shapely ass being paddled. A man dressed as a woman kissing someone's breasts. A woman wearing a strap-on dildo kissing a woman dressed as a man. Vampire masks and a few other masks even Anne Rice couldn't have imagined. No one was playing up for the camera or posing in any way. And the camera angle never changed. Which might have meant the people having so much fun hadn't known there was a camera.

But the pictures were of poor quality and each had part of the frame of a TV screen at the edge. Lisa had taken Polaroid photographs of a video tape. Why? A guess: To prove to someone that she had the video tape. Why? I didn't know. Where was the tape now? I didn't know that either.

I put the pictures back in the envelope then dug another thousand-baht bill out of my pocket and handed it to the maid. No change of expression. Same disappearing act with the bill. She had shown no curiosity as to what was in the envelope. But she had guessed correctly that it might put more money in her pocket.

"She asked you to keep this envelope for her?"

She nodded and responded with a "Yes, sir." Since she'd first seen me, I had gone up in her estimation. Two thousand baht worth.

"When?"

"Maybe two weeks ago. Maybe less."

"What did she say?"

"She just asked me to keep something for her for a few weeks."

I thanked her for her help.

While I waited on the corner for a motorcycle taxi to take me back to Washington Square, I thought about the photographs. Of the faces in the pictures, six were clear enough to be recognized. I recognized only two. Lisa was one and the man I had thrown into the deep end of a swimming pool was another.

21

The rain had stopped, so I waited for my ride outside the Boots and Saddle passing the time by observing the "Tradition Thai" massage parlor girls exercising across the way and watching girls from the Wild Country bar replace the tea and rice they had left for whatever spirits they believed lived in a nearby tree. No one seemed particularly interested in or alarmed by the fat brown rat that bulldozed its way into a nearby black garbage bag, still glistening from the rain.

A few vendors had set up their pushcarts in the midst of banana trees and untended wild foliage. An elderly female vendor removed steaming ears of corn from her wire grate and scooped charcoal briquettes from a green plastic bucket. She lifted the grate, dropped the briquettes in, replaced the grate, then replaced the ears of corn. I thought for a few seconds of what painters could do with the steaming yellow corn, the emerald green bucket, the ink-black grill, the drenched and dripping vegetation, the woman's robin's egg blue straw hat, russet tunic and wrinkled, dark brown skin.

I had checked with Len's Dive Shop in the morning. George hadn't been in but his assistant knew he had no clients for me here or in Pattaya. So once I had stashed Lisa's photographs in my apartment, I'd taken a bus to Pattaya, anyway, and done a bit of diving. Sometimes I wondered if observing the silent wonders beneath the sea wasn't my substitute for religion. Solo diving is totally peaceful and relaxing and, if I have ever had ideas that could be described as intelligent or insightful, they most likely came to me underwater while I was diving alone.

When I dive with students as an instructor I'm constantly looking out for them. With solo diving I can concentrate purely on the pleasure of diving. That's when I can truly appreciate the meditative aspect of underwater marine life – the feeling of being underwater, the solitude, the quiet, the beauty.

Other than the usual curious, incurious or startled sea creatures, I hadn't seen anything spectacular. So with plenty of time to spare, I had spent my afternoon using my knife to pry open the wire gate on wood-and-wire fish traps and releasing the fish inside. I didn't know if it would help my karma or not but it certainly seemed good for the fish.

The traps had caught mostly angelfish, butterfly fish and squirrel fish but I did release a blue spotted ray and a porcupine puffer. The puffer fish swam out of the trap right into my hands. I held it gently and watched as it gulped water and, in seconds, puffed itself up like a balloon. That and its tiny but effective spin projections were its defense mechanism.

I was careful to let it calm down and deflate before letting it go or else it might have shot up to the surface and died. Many of the traps were old and forgotten by those who had set them and I did my best to ensure whatever traps I came across would never again ensnare anymore fish.

Other than ripping up fish traps, my main excitement for the day had been fending off importuning bargirls and crossing Pattaya streets without being run over. I can't say my underwater activity edged me any closer to solving Lisa Avery's murder, but sometimes the subconscious shoots something out later – not unlike the puffer fish.

After about ten minutes, the car arrived – a Honda Civic – and I got in front beside the driver. She introduced herself in English as Gee Gee, the owner of Jezebels. She looked about 35 and, as many Thai women seem to appear perpetually young, I guessed her age to be about 45. She hadn't *waiied* me or offered to shake my hand but she was not unfriendly either. As on the phone, her attitude seemed to be perfectly balanced between restrained pleasantness and attention to business. Perhaps she thought it would appear unseemly for the head of a house of domination to engage in small talk with a client.

She was wearing a cleavage-revealing, low-necked white blouse, purple slacks and thong sandals. She had an oval face, an almost Negroid nose and very dark brown skin, and I would have bet my bottom baht she was originally from the northeast of Thailand, say, Buriram or thereabouts, and had spent more than a few years in Bangkok bars before scraping enough money together to start Jezebels. Her English was good but she only replied to my queries and asked nothing about myself. So after a few minutes I settled back as much as one settles back into a Honda Civic and we headed along Sukhumvith Road in the direction of Pattaya.

The traffic was light but it was a good twenty minutes before we left the highway and entered narrow lanes lined with concrete shophouses. Every now and then we would pass fences of wood or bamboo beyond which I could glimpse attractive wooden houses which somehow had escaped Bangkok's building boom. I wondered how many times Gee Gee had chauffeured men to Jezebels to be humiliated and spanked and otherwise happily abused by young Thai women. The thought occurred to me that dominatrixes no doubt wear skin-tight black outfits and so do scuba divers (theirs leather; mine neoprene), but I had no doubt whatever that their occupation paid far better than mine.

If I had expected a palatial estate with immaculately kept grounds similar to the Emerald Club, or some mansion built to the specifications of an erotic imagination, or a bit of elegant decadence from *The Story of O*, I quickly realized my error when we reached our destination. The car pulled off a relatively quiet street into a long dirt driveway which paralleled a canal partly visible behind shrubbery and fruit trees. We pulled up beside a rambling wooden house and spacious but shabby lawn. Torn fronds of banana trees languidly reached out over a bamboo fence as if begging for change. Across the quiet canal, a few lights set far back from the bank did nothing to disperse the darkness.

As I exited the car, dogs which had been occupied in barking at one another now found the foreigner a far more inviting target. Gee Gee made half hearted attempts to shush them as we headed for the front door. She seemed to know them all by name and they quickly settled into tail-waving whines of familiarity. As far as I could tell they were merely *soi* dogs, useful to property owners for their warning barks rather than any ferocity. Once they were more or less quiet, I could hear the clamorous croaks of frogs from somewhere in the direction of the canal.

Light pouring out of the ground floor and upper story windows allowed me only a limited and somewhat distorted view of the house, but that was enough for me to conclude that this was no ordinary Thai house. It was as if a Thai architect with unlimited funds but limited sense had decided to try his hand at combining Victorian Gothic with early Ayuthya period. Or perhaps when he was young, the *House of the Seven Gables* had been his favorite bedtime reading material. Bangkok's architects had created some of the world's most bizarre architecture combining – some might say desecrating – various styles from Classical Greek to traditional Chinese to Art Nouveau but this house was certainly in a class of its own.

From the way the roof peaked here and drooped there it was difficult to tell if it had been constructed as a two-story or three-story house. It seemed as if the builders had made half-hearted attempts to fashion projecting wall dormers into a kind of clipped gable roof and then gave up in despair. It was difficult to tell if the eaves were flared or if the roof had simply sunk in over the years making it appear as if the roof had flared eaves. The front porch was a mixture of wood and brick and seemed to have been tacked on as an afterthought in case any stray water buffalo needed shelter in a storm. At the moment, two motorcycles – one glistening from the rain – had been parked under the porch's roof.

As I looked up, I had a brief glimpse of a woman in black staring down at me from a casement window on the second floor. The light spilled out around her unsmiling face and long black hair. For a moment I wondered if I was entering a movie set for Poe's "Fall of the House of Usher." When light again poured from the window I knew the woman had moved away.

Beneath a banyan tree, two boys about six or seven were energetically trying out their muay-Thai skills on one another. As the dogs quieted down, the grunts of the boys continued on, providing a contrapuntal variant for the unrelenting amphibian chorus. On the lawn itself, untrimmed bushes seemed to be growing wherever they pleased, unattended and forlorn, and burlap bags bulging with what might have been cement were piled against the remains of what once must have been a functioning automobile. The yard gave off the musty scents of decaying plant life. Someone had abandoned a torn banana leaf wrapper in the middle of the path, from which lumpy scraps of still pungent curried fish oozed out into the mud. The grass was damp and wet, and as I followed Gee Gee into the house, the scent of papaya wafted over to me.

Just inside the front door were several pairs of sandals, no doubt left inside to prevent the dogs from appropriating them as toys. None seemed large enough to fit a man but in Thailand one could never be sure. Of anything.

I slipped out of my shoes and followed Gee Gee through the hallway and into a spacious area which seemed to pass for a living room. If there were other sounds in the house – the screeching of mistresses, the cracking of whips, the pleading of clients, they would not have been heard over the saccharine Thai love songs emanating from the Bose speakers along the wall. The furniture was not exactly stylish and the room was untidy, but far more effort had gone into the interior of the house than into the yard outside.

Gee Gee stood near a door leading to a kitchen. "Please sit down. Would you like something to drink?"

"Singha Gold, if you have it." I had been getting too drunk too fast on regular Singha and had only the month before reluctantly switched to the lighter brand. Gee Gee pushed open a door and disappeared into the kitchen. As the door closed, the aromas of garlic and curry and fish sauce permeated the living room.

An attractive young woman in a low-cut honey yellow blouse and colorful *phasin*, a Thai-style sarong, brought me the beer. I thanked her and she smiled and reentered the kitchen. An attractive maid, perhaps. A mistress without a client, perhaps. I wondered what she would be like when she transformed into her dominatrix role. A bit of training and thorough knowledge of what make-up, dress and attitude can do for a woman. And, voila! The rice farmer's daughter from Nakorn Nowhere becomes Mistress Mangosteen or the Guava Goddess or the Durian Dom. The butterfly emerges from the larva – whip in hand. Gee Gee reentered the living room with what looked like a glass of Mekhong coke. She took a sip and placed it on a table. "I believe your Mistress is ready to receive you."

"Fine."

She hesitated. "If you could pay now?"

"Oh. Sure." I reached into my back pocket and handed her ten one-thousand baht bills. "Fresh from the ATM machine so they must be real."

My attempt at levity was lost on her as she was totally absorbed in slowly counting out the bills before folding them and sticking them in her pocket.

I followed her upstairs and into a room. "Please wait here. Your *chao-meh* will be right in."

So folks in the domination business in Thailand used the term "goddess" for dominatrix. I doubted if Bangkok's many language schools bothered to teach useful information like that.

The room I was in now had obviously been professionally decorated. Behind black leather couches and chairs, large oil paintings by an obviously talented artist lined the wall, each emphasized by the crisp white halogen beam of a spotlight. In each scene, a woman in red latex and black leather was disciplining a man dressed in women's underwear and stockings. The man – his face obviously made up – cowered at the boots or under the lash of the woman. The woman was clearly Asian and the man Caucasian, and each painting had Thai-style tables or chairs or cabinets somewhere in the background. Other touches that could only have come from the vivid imagination of a Thai were the way the woman's free hand elegantly curved backward in the style of a Thai dancer; the diminutive mythical beast from the *Ramakien* holding a tray of whips and leather restraints for the woman; the bold colors, decorative motifs, and stylized gold borders; the lack of shadow or perspective. I had no doubt some gifted but poverty-stricken Thai artist had been commissioned for the job. I wondered what he'd thought of the assignment.

A rack of whips and paddles and leashes had been installed on one wall between paintings. Metal handcuffs, leather restraints, ropes, leather face masks and what appeared to be a dog collar dangled from hooks. A narrow cot had been pushed against the far wall. It too had handcuffs and leather restraints. I pulled up a kind of director's chair without restraints and sat down. It was as uncomfortable as it looked.

In less than a minute, Mistress Angst appeared in the doorway, barely glanced at me, and shut the door again. She was dressed in shiny, studded black leather, stiletto-heeled leather boots and held a coiled cat-o-nine-tailed whip in her right hand. She had let her hair down and it reached just below her shoulders. Her makeup was not excessive but she had done an excellent job of emphasizing her eyes. Eyeliner and whatever else had highlighted and accentuated them. They reminded me of the eyes I had seen on Nepalese stupas.

She sat back into a plush leather chair and stared at me with the same seductive challenge as in her head shot. "So you've been a bad boy?"

I took a swig of my beer. "That's quite possible."

"And you need punishment?"

"What I need, Mistress Angst, are answers."

She frowned slightly and ran the leather tails of the whip through her left hand. Her narrowed eyes suggested that I would pay for my insolence. "Answers?"

"Answers to what you know about the murder of Lisa Avery."

It was at that point that the penny dropped for her. "You. At the bar!"

"Me. At the bar. And at George's party."

She stood up and pointed to the door. "Get out of here before—"

"Before what? Before the police get a tip-off that you were her lover? That you spent many nights at her apartment? And therefore a suspect?"

She thought that over. "What do you want?"

"I want the person or persons who murdered your lover behind bars."

She thought that over as well, then sat down in the chair, sighed and placed the whip in her lap. "I have no idea who killed her. Despite what you may think, we weren't all that close."

I tried a long shot. "A number of sources tell me you were very possessive of her."

"It didn't matter. She had a lot of girlfriends whether I liked it or not!"

"Lisa have a boyfriend?"

"Lisa had clients. Period."

"And where were you on the night she was murdered?"

"I had clients here. An old Englishman stayed all night until after breakfast. You can check with Gee Gee."

"I would if I thought I'd get an honest answer. But as far as I know now nothing was stolen from Lisa's apartment. I doubt she had much to steal. She wasn't raped. So why was she murdered?"

"I told you, I don't know."

"What would you know about a video tape?"

She seemed genuinely puzzled. "Video tape? I don't know a damn thing about a video tape."

"Did she have any persistent men clients at the Emerald Club? Anyone she complained about to you?"

"Not a client." Mistress Angst fidgeted with the whip. "Somebody who worked there kept trying to get her into bed."

"Who?"

"A guy named Somnuck. One of the boss's men."

"Describe him for me."

"Thin. Dark. Carries a gun."

"He make any threats?"

"Not exactly. But Lisa made it clear she wanted nothing to do with him. Went to the boss, complained."

"Did it do any good?"

"Sure. But Somnuck lost face. You don't want to make a man like Somnuck lose face. He's a killer." She thought for a few moments, her hand still fondling the leather tassels of the whip.

"There was one customer. An Australian. Hotel GM or something. Rod somebody. He took her out a few times."

"He threatened her?"

"No. Lisa just said he and his Chinese wife had some weird scenes with her in their apartment. Some of it scary."

"Such as?"

"You know. They wanted a threesome for bondage games with masks and whips. Music, weird lighting, acting out roles. They liked scenes that had the illusion of danger. Lisa said they started inviting their friends over and the games kept getting more and more bizarre."

"And how did Lisa like it?"

"She said she didn't. She thought they were really nuts. But they tipped enough to keep her going for more."

"But you weren't convinced."

"With her looks she could make money without doing that kind of thing. Something kept her going. I don't know what. Maybe she was into it."

I had made a smaller size picture of the man from the swimming pool on my computer. Just the face. The man who had slurred his name when we were introduced at Len's Dive Shop. But now I was quite sure I knew why. And I was quite certain I knew his name. I took the picture from my shirt pocket and handed it to her. "Do you recognize him?"

She handed it back. "Never saw him before."

"All right. I'll need Rod's name and address."

"I don't have it and they sure as hell won't give out a customer's name and address at the Emerald Club."

I decided to change the subject. "Gee Gee the owner here?"

"Gee Gee fronts for a Chinese-Thai businessman who owns this place and lots of bars and brothels."

"How well do you know Frank Webber?"

"He was my date once when I worked at the Emerald Club."

"He didn't know Lisa?"

"Not as far as I know."

"But he invited you to the Halloween party?"

"Frank? No. George invited Lisa. I just tagged along."

"George? He knew Lisa?"

"Yeah. He hangs out at the Club a lot. One of his sister-in-laws works there. She makes a fortune."

"Why'd you quit there to come here?"

For the first time, Da seemed evasive. "I make good money here. And lots less competition."

I managed to extricate myself from the director's chair, dug a namecard from my wallet and handed it to her. "You think of anything else you give me a call."

She glanced at the card. "You're a diver?

I nodded.

"I thought you must be some kind of cop."

"I never said I was a cop."

"So you are what I said."

"What's that?"

"A bad boy." The sensual challenge returned to Da's eyes. As she gripped the handle of the whip her voice dropped to that of a husky contralto on downers. "And we've still got a lot of time left."

I used my usual excuse to extricate myself from a sticky situation. "It's the rainy season so I guess I'll take a rain check." I would have to give some thought to what excuse I would use with beautiful women after the rainy season ended.

"You don't mean to say you're one of those immature people who prefer only vanilla sex?"

"'Vanilla sex?'"

"Most of my clients are intelligent and creative. Many are businessmen. They're looking for a bit more in a relationship with a woman than just animal coupling. Something involving a forbidden fantasy or two."

"Looks like they've come to the right place. You help them forget their failures, is that it?"

"In fact, most of my customers are too successful. Men at the top of their professions get tired of giving orders all day and shouldering responsibility and making every decision. They need the refreshing change that abject submission and absolute obedience to a beautiful woman provides."

"You're saying you shackle your customers physically so they can unshackle their fantasies."

"Exactly!"

Da seemed pleased that I understood. She pursed her lips and let her whip's leather thongs trail back and forth along the floor beside her chair. "We are ruled by emotions, not logic. Isn't that right?"

"Not sure about women but men certainly are, you got that right."

I stood facing her with my legs apart and my hands on my hips. I started to speak again when she suddenly and expertly cracked the whip, its leather thongs passing within a whisper of my crotch. With a practiced flick of her wrist, she snapped the whip back to her lap and began coiling it. "It's possible you simply aren't successful enough to feel the need to submit to me."

"I must say I admire your insights into human sexology" – I glanced down at my crotch – "not to mention your perfect aim. But I'll still take a rain check."

"As you like." I almost made the door before she spoke again. "But it's customary to tip the mistress."

I reached into my pocket and pulled out a thousand baht bill. As I handed it to her she continued to stare invitingly into my eyes. I leaned forward and kissed her on her lips. Softly. Gently. Much to my surprise I enjoyed it.

I left her sitting there. A beautiful Thai woman dressed in leather who made her living with whips and fantasy fulfillment and who knew more about what made men tick than I did. A New Age psychologist ready to assist highly successful men by humiliating and punishing them. It made me more than ready to get back to the relatively uncomplicated life of Washington Square where humiliation and punishment came in the more traditional form of excessive drinking and the occasional barroom brawl.

As I reached the bottom of the stairs the woman who had given me a beer – the one I had thought was a maid – passed by.

Only now she too was dressed in a leather outfit and black leather boots. As she passed me, she gave me a far more knowing smile than the last time around.

I couldn't help marvel at the way young Thai women handled new situations without trauma. Girls who had been brought up on countryside farms came to Bangkok and were trained to dominate men who wanted to be dominated. Women who worked the lamyai fields or who fermented tea leaves or who bound rice seedlings into bunches quickly and effortlessly learned the intricacies of the different types of whips, paddles and brushes. From Thai-style sarong and water scoop to leather outfit and riding crop, from the agitated squeals of frightened pigs to the frantic squeals of submissive clients, from tying up rice seedlings to tying up foreign men. There was something in the Thai character that was fluid enough to handle abrupt changes and new experiences without trauma. Perhaps it was the Buddhist world view that all in this world was illusion, anyway, and the reluctance to pass judgement on others.

A door opened and I heard the sounds of an angry woman berating someone on a Thai television station. Gee Gee appeared, opened the front door for me, and gave me a brief wai. "You are leaving so quickly?"

I shrugged. "My first time; I figured to take it slow."

"I hope you enjoyed your session."

"It was very instructive," I said.

She pointed toward a window. "There are taxis out on the main road. Only about a three-block walk. But I can drive you to the road if you like."

"No, thank you. Three blocks I can handle."

"Some of our clients...." She thought for a moment, as if choosing her words carefully. "When they finish their session, some of our clients find walking three blocks is a long and somewhat painful journey."

"And yet they come back for more?"

"Of course."

I moved quickly through the door. "You have a pleasant evening, ma'am."

As I started down the walk, a rather large woman with an exaggerated walk headed in my direction. As "she" got closer, I realized it was a ladyboy, a *katoey*. Thai ladyboys were either transvestites or transsexuals and it was obvious some client would soon be arriving who, for whatever reasons, wanted one. The ladyboy smiled, I nodded. It was at that moment that I noticed still more papaya trees along the fence. Which was appropriate: papaya plants have the ability to bear male flowers, female flowers or bisexual flowers. And some male and bisexual papaya plants transform into female plants. Like plants, like people.

DAY EIGHT

22

The day was overcast and its gloomy darkness cast sinister shadows in every corner of the lobby of the Falconview Hotel. Perhaps the architect had been hired from abroad and he hadn't taken Thailand's rainy season into account in his design. Or perhaps he was the same local architect who had designed a school for the blind with no railings along the verandahs. During Thailand's wet season, up-market tourists were few and far between and the hotel lobby was as deserted as a Chinatown brothel that had been tipped off to an impending police raid.

Hotel offices were on the 14th floor. I shared the elevator ride up with a petite reservations clerk whose bright Thai smile and lustrous black eyes helped to dispel the gloom. Although never mentioned in tourist brochures, a Thai smile can mean many things. I have encountered Thai smiles which clearly conveyed how much people liked me; and smiles that suggested I had inadvertently embarrassed someone; and smiles that implied someone would prefer to see me dead. The clerk's smile had been of the simple, polite, down-to-earth, pleasant variety and if it didn't exactly make my spirits soar, it did make my day a little brighter.

My hotel friend in Pattaya had given me the full name of the only Australian "Rod" he knew of in hotel management in Bangkok: the general manager of the Falconview. I had gone to the hotel's website and found Rod's picture in the hotel's "activities section." He was seen several times shaking hands with important guests. There was no question that Rod was the same man appearing in one of Lisa's Polaroids. Although in the Polaroid, he wasn't wearing the chalk-stripe suit – only his birthday suit; and his activity was decidedly different.

The cave of the sorcerer always has a dragon as guard. In this case the dragon was a middle-aged Thai secretary whose smile in my direction was several shades more calculated than that of the reservations clerk. I gave her one of my most masculine yet enigmatic grins; as if suggesting we shared a secret. In a way we did: I wanted to see her boss – she was there to make certain such ne'er-do-well, time-wasters as me never even got close.

Her face had more than a few lines and her forehead was a bit high but she was an attractive woman somewhere in her late forties. Or at least she would have been had it not been for her eyebrows. She had plucked and redrawn them in dramatic new configurations. I suspected she had spent most of her life in the far north, and it may have been the slash-and-burn methods of cultivation which she had seen as a child that inspired her method of eyebrow art, as not only were the redrawn brows unnatural, uneven, not to say unwise, but her slash-and-burn, search-and-destroy methods of plucking had irritated her skin and where those brows had once been were two bright salmon pink streaks. Also, her choice of highly arched eyebrows on her already round face was, to put it kindly, unfortunate.

Her office was actually little more than a desk, some maiden-hair ferns, and some shelves outside the door of her boss's office, but it was not the size or glamour of her office which gave her power; rather her position as decision-maker.

I greeted her pleasantly and handed her my card. I decided if I could head her off at the pass it might throw her off balance. "Let me say right off the bat that I have no appointment but I'm not selling anything and I do need to see Mr. Larkin on a rather urgent matter."

She looked at my card and back up at me. Her English was

flawless. This dragon had been to London. "I am sorry, Mr. Sterling, but Mr. Larkin's schedule is already overloaded and unless you already have an appointment I can't possibly – "

I gave her my most boyish smile. "Ma'am, believe me, Mr. Larkin will be very pleased to hear what I have to say. Would you just be good enough to give him my card? If he says he's too busy to see me then I'll leave. No problem." Actually, I wouldn't have but the average non-bargirl Thai usually finds it hard to believe a *farang* would have so little shame as to tell a bald-faced lie. The bargirls, of course, know better.

She stared at the card and looked up at me. "You are sure you are not selling something?"

I held my hand up in scout's honor position. "I swear on my ex-mother-in-law's honor."

She gave that attempt at humor more of a laugh than it deserved, got up, knocked lightly on the door, then entered the inner office. She closed the door and I stood waiting for about one minute.

When she returned she didn't have my card which I took for a good sign. Sure enough. "Five minutes."

I thanked her profusely and entered the office. Rod Larkin sat behind a wooden desk, its smooth surface not quite large enough to serve as an aircraft carrier. I guessed his age at about forty and he appeared in excellent shape no doubt from frequent squash sessions with his business associates. He sported a blue-and-red regimental tie and the kind of powder blue suit Raymond Chandler's characters sometimes wore. He had an unruly but very full crop of red hair, a rough reddish complexion and oversized eyes beneath thick brows. All of which reminded me of a Spotfin Squirrelfish with its huge eyes, scabby scales and reddish-orange coloring.

The room's *décor* was in warm earth tones, brown and green. Lining the shelves behind him were the usual sandstone Khmer

Buddhas and wooden Burmese nats and Thai celadon plates all of which were *de rigueur* in the displays of cultural awareness for foreigners living in Bangkok. At the center of the center shelf was a framed photograph of Rod and an Asian woman in bathing suits happily prancing in the waves at some beach resort. The woman wore a skimpy bikini and looked to be a still sexy forty; Rod had unruly red chest hair and a belly almost as flat as hers.

Large pots with dragon motifs lined the floor in front of the shelves and from these pots sprang mammoth, leathery, dark green leaves of the Split leaf something-or-other plant. Apparently, Rod had learned enough about the hotel business to know that it might not be wise to display the paraphernalia of his unorthodox nocturnal hobby: Southeast Asian cultural artifacts, yes; whips and handcuffs, no.

He stood and gripped my hand to the point of giving pain, the kind of grip men in business practice after reading about the importance of firm handshakes. We asked each other how he was. I had no sooner got my hand back when his desk phone rang. He gave me a pained sorry-for-the-interruption expression and motioned for me to sit down.

He leaned back in his chair and picked up the phone. For an Aussie, he had very little accent: I could understand at least every third word.

"Rod Larkin…What room is that, sir?… I'm very sorry the hair dryer doesn't work, sir, but may I suggest you dial house-keeping? They will send someone up right away."

I wondered if the clock kept running on my five minutes or if phone calls indicated a time out had been called. Rod looked at me for confirmation of the guest's ridiculous behavior and shrugged his shoulders in exaggeration. "Not at all, sir, I thank you for telling me. Have a great day."

He hung up the phone and shook his head. "The hotel business. But it does have its benefits." He picked up my card. "Now,

Mr. Sterling, what can I do for you? No, let me guess. You'd like to place some sort of ad for your diving skills in every room of the Falconview and in exchange…?"

"Actually, I'm not here about diving, Mr. Larkin. I'm investigating the death of an American woman named Lisa Avery. A week ago, she was murdered in her apartment on Sukhumvith *soi* 31."

Rod made almost the same kind of clicking sound Spotfin Squirrelfish are known for. I was beginning to alter my views on evolution at least as it occurred Down Under.

It took him a few seconds to recover, and when he did his accent had moved a considerable distance from the fair-dinkum, Aussie outback, Crocodile Dundee stereotype he had affected. "I see. So, you are also a detective?"

"I used to be attached to the American Embassy. Now I help out friends in a non-official way."

Rod straightened his tie the way a man might loosen a noose. He chose his words as cautiously as a Philadelphia lawyer. "I'm not quite certain how I could be of help to you in your investigation, Mr. Sterling."

I decided to start with a touch of discretion and, if that didn't work, proceed from there. "My information is that you and your wife were acquainted with the deceased."

I could almost see Rod's mind working. Should he simply stonewall, deny everything and order me out of his office or should he admit what he must suspect I already knew: that he and his wife had enjoyed some bizarre fun and games with Lisa Avery. He glanced out the window as if the 14th-story, bird's-eye view of Bangkok in the rain might aid in his decision. The transformation of his manner of speech from Outback Aussie to Suburban Sydney was now complete. "My wife had the person in question over to the house on a few occasions. But I certainly wouldn't say we knew the woman well."

'The person in question.' The distancing had already begun. My, how soon we forget. I decided to be kind but a little snotty. "Well, Mr. Larkin, let me be clear. I'm aware that you met 'the person in question' at the 'house in question,' but at this time I know of very little that suggests you were in any way involved in her death."

That said, I was fairly certain Rod was smart enough to know that I was visiting him because he was still somewhere on my list of suspects. I let that sink in and continued on. "I am interested in anything Lisa might have mentioned to you and your wife, anything at all, about other people in her life. Perhaps other customers she was afraid of or having trouble with."

He shook his head. "No, nothing like that."

"Did Lisa make any threats?"

"Threats?"

"Did she in any way suggest that unless you paid her money she might expose her activities with you and your wife? In plain English, was she blackmailing you for money?"

He seemed about to give an automatic denial, then stopped. "You said you knew of 'very little' to suspect my involvement in her death. May I know what that 'very little' might be?"

I reached into my bag, took out the brown envelope and pulled out the Polaroids. I leaned forward and dropped them in front of him.

He looked them over slowly, one at a time. He seemed to visibly age with each picture. When he finished he cleared his throat and lowered his voice. "Not blackmail, exactly. Not for money. During…I mean, when we were playing some hide-and-seek games, Lisa must have found the camera."

"Camera?"

He looked into the middle distance, sighed heavily, and began fiddling with a silver pen on his desk. "I had the bright idea of videotaping a few of the sessions. I thought my wife and I could see them when we wanted to. Enjoy them at our leisure." He suddenly stared at me as if reading my mind. "I was not going to use the video as blackmail or anything else. I'm in it, for God's sake!"

"So you and your wife set up a spy camera in…."

"A clock. A Sony wireless."

"You and your wife set up a spy camera in a clock and took a video. Somehow the video disappeared."

"My wife and Lisa were very close. She apparently hinted to Lisa that they could enjoy the moments more than once. Of course, I found that out after the tape was missing." A venomous anger crept into his voice. "The stupid, trusting bitch."

"Did you contact Lisa?"

"My wife did. She begged her to return it. Lisa refused. But she said something about how my wife and I had nothing to worry about. It wasn't us she was after. My wife was hysterical. I wasn't much better."

I reached over and took the photographs. He made no effort to stop me. He probably figured I had copies. Or maybe ever since the day he first realized how much he enjoyed kinky sex games, he had dreaded but never doubted a moment like this would come. His voice was a bit scratchy now. "So I called her and offered money, whatever she wanted, for the tape. She just repeated that my wife and I had nothing to worry about." He whacked the edge of the desk with the pen. "Oh, yeah, I got an indignant lecture about the type of people who use hidden cameras to spy on their friends. You understand, I was getting the lecture from a thief and a lesbian whore and God knows what else."

"How long ago was this?"

"Two, two-and-a-half weeks."

"Do you know a woman named 'Da'; Wattana?"

"I heard of her from my wife. She wasn't part of our group but my wife said she was crazy over Lisa. My wife said Lisa was afraid of her."

"Afraid?"

"Of her jealous rages, I mean. Da wanted Lisa all to herself or else."

"Or else what?"

"How would I know? I heard she's a dominatrix now. That's the right profession for that ball-breaking bitch." He gestured toward the Polaroids. "You realize these pictures could ruin me."

"They won't. Not unless you killed her."

"Killed her? I never touched her! I never even saw her again!"

The phone rang again. He picked it up. "Yeah?...Jesus Christ, would you call housekeeping, sir? Or use a bloody towel!" He slammed the phone down.

Rod was beginning to crack. "Rod, it's like this. Lisa had a fire wire cable in her apartment. I believe she also had a camcorder but that was taken, most likely by the murderer. I think the murderer also took the video. It isn't difficult to transfer a video tape onto a computer and the fire wire cable is high bandwidth and provides a very fast connection. I think this is one lady who knew what she was doing. But she was cautious enough to take a few Polaroids as an ace in the hole in case anybody tried to get their hands on the video. And to hide them well. But before she could get the video transferred to the computer, she was killed. You and your wife seem to be the only ones who knew what she had."

Another heavy sigh. I was worried if he kept that up he might hyperventilate. "I discussed it with my wife. We decided we were obligated to tell anyone who could be recognized on the tape."

"And you did?"

He nodded. "We aren't the most popular people in town at the moment."

"How many people did you contact?"

"Four." He gestured to the photographs. "They're all there."

I pushed the photographs half way between us. "And they are?"

He pointed to a man wearing a woman's panties and a bra

being ridden by a blonde woman naked except for brown leather cowgirl boots. "The guy is a therapist. English. The sheila is his girlfriend from Holland." He looked at the next one. It was a picture of the same woman wearing nothing but boots and a turquoise dildo. Another man, completely naked, was kneeling by her as if ready to perform fellatio on the dildo. My swimming pool friend: the man who had told me he was a computer specialist. "This guy is an architect." He pointed to a picture of a woman passionately kissing another woman. I recognized the women. One was Lisa and the other was the woman with Larkin in the photograph on the shelf behind him. Larkin was naked and on his knees between them performing cunnilingus on Lisa. "My wife and Lisa." His voice dropped to a whisper. "And me." He passed over pictures with the same people in different clothes or poses then stopped at a picture of a beautiful bare-breasted Asian woman dressed in a man's Paisley tie and striped trousers. She also wore a large white cowboy hat with the cord tucked beneath her chin. Someone just out of camera range was handing her a paddle. "That's a woman Lisa met at the Emerald Club. Noy. Maybe Oy. I forget which."

"She works there, you mean?"

"Yeah."

"And where is Sanford's wife?"

He started at the fact that I knew the name. "She never played in the games. I don't think she knows about them."

"What do you know about Sanford?"

"I know he lost a lot of money in the stock market. He was a partner in an architectural design firm in New York that went bust. Not many new buildings going up in Manhattan so now instead of designing buildings he specializes in doing corporate interiors."

"Not that many buildings going up here, are there?"

"Nah. But the bottom may be in sight. Anyway, the firm has a branch in Shanghai so they make their bundle there. Sanford spends a lot of time up there."

"What about his wife?"

"Sally's from a wealthy family. What she sees in him, I don't know. He puts on airs but he wouldn't have a stick of furniture if it wasn't for her."

"I'll need his home address."

"Cherbourg Villa. But it's exclusive. You won't – "

"I've been there before." A thought occurred to me. "And Da never played in these games?"

"Hell, no. My wife says she enjoys her work as work. Watch out for that bloody bitch; from what I hear, she is fucking nuts!"

I stood up. Larkin looked up at me with a mixture of shame and hope on his face – like a little boy who wanted desperately to believe that he would get his ball back even if it did smash the neighbor's window. "Thank you, Mr. Larkin. What Lisa said was correct. If you weren't involved in anything, and if these aren't needed as evidence, I'll destroy them."

"What about the video?"

"I'll see what I can do. If I find it. But you should understand I won't destroy anything police consider evidence in a murder case."

I nodded and closed the door. I couldn't help but feel sorry for the man. His predilection for kinky games hadn't hurt any-one but if it became public it was very possible his career in hotel management had a short future. Rod was learning the hard way what a psyops specialist at the Farm used to say in his lectures: "Society punishes those who deviate from its norms."

The friendly dragon looked up at me with her redrawn eye-brows knitted. "That was quite a bit over five minutes."

"What can I say? Your boss and I hit it off."

23

The day had started off bright and sunny and filled with as much promise as the first few weeks of a love affair. Now it was just after two in the afternoon and storm clouds were rushing in as if late for an appointment, abruptly jostling aside any remaining patches of blue sky which had dared to linger over Bangkok.

I had been to the Cherbourg Villa before. As a dinner guest of the French attache. Fortunately, he was still the attache and he agreed to have his wife let me in.

Cherbourg Villa was located on a quiet sub-*soi* off Petchburi Road. The 18-story condominium was surrounded by beautiful Thai houses, both old and new, each with a spacious lawn and landscaped garden, and, when it was being built during the boom years of the mid-90's, Cherbourg Villa had no doubt demolished beautiful Thai houses, lawns and gardens just like them. The logo of Cherbourg Villa was a fancy gold *CV* set against a stylized orchid *fleur-de-lis*, or, flower of the lily, the royal flower of France. The logo-lily flower combination was carved several times into the long ivy-draped wall cum fortification which fronted the road and appeared again in the gold wrought iron gates which prevented unauthorized vehicles from entering.

I pushed open a small wrought iron door and walked a very short distance along a tree-lined stone path which took me directly to the guard shack. Except the word "shack" would be totally inappropriate for the small but elegant carriage house-style brick building where two young guards in spotless white monogrammed uniforms sat facing the gate. Both stood up and came from behind a counter but only one smiled. The other eyed me suspiciously.

I flashed my best happy-harmless-*farang* grin and explained in Thai that I had an appointment. The suspicious one wrote down what I said on a clipboard, held out his hand for some ID, then went inside the guardhouse to verify the appointment. The other stood motionlessly and smiled. I decided this was probably the Thai guard way of playing "good cop, bad cop."

For anyone accustomed to Bangkok's daily tumult, the quiet was eerie. I could hear the distant laughter of children playing, what sounded like a body diving into a swimming pool, the repetitious "wop" of a tennis ball being hit back and forth over a net and the lilting calls of whatever birds had been deemed refined enough to remain in the area. A plane droned overhead but high enough so that the sound was somnolent and pleasant. Another minute of this and I was sure I'd need to take a nap.

The guard returned revealing just enough of his front teeth to indicate that I was welcome after all. My ID would be returned on the way out. He made an elaborate gesture and I began walking up the stone path toward the building with a huge *fleur-de-lis* on the façade of the lower two floors. An elderly gardener was trimming shrubs in a topiary garden into one ornamental shape or another. He had already finished transforming a hedge into a swan and was now putting the finishing touches on a shrub which in his skilled hands had assumed the shape of an elephant.

I passed through a professionally landscaped flower garden with flowers every color of the rainbow but I had no doubt there were TV cameras watching my every move, and I knew that any attempt at pocketing an orchid or picking a lily would bring some kind of immediate response from a ready and waiting SWAT team. The far end of the garden was bordered with traveler's palms and poplars, and so I couldn't spot the tennis court but I got a glimpse of the heated outdoor swimming pool and had no doubt there would be an indoor one as well, complete with saunas and jacuzzi and a fitness room to the rear.

I did get a glimpse of one Caucasian male near the building. He walked out from the lobby and stood as if trying to decide something. Probably wondering if it was his day for the putting green or the squash court. He must have remembered it was a squash court day because he walked back inside.

The path to the building skirted a large lily pond with huge circular trays of amazon waterlilies floating on the surface. Just before I entered the lobby, I glanced up but the windows had tinted glass and the balconies seemed deserted. I wondered if anyone residing at Cherbourg Villa had ever dared hang wash out on their balcony and, if so, if they were still a resident.

The lobby doors slid open by themselves and led into a spacious high-ceilinged room about three times the size of the Boots and Saddle. The carpet was of course gold with orchid curves in the center in the shape of a stylized *fleur-de-lis*. The furniture and fixtures were done in an elegant golden yellow and nutmeg brown and if I'd had to guess I would have said it was in the style of Louis between-one-and-sixteen. At the far side of the room, above a marble guard's counter, was a huge mural of the Normandy coast and wind-tossed waves rocking fishing boats off Cherbourg.

A uniformed guard stood erect behind the marble counter. He called upstairs, made certain someone at my stated destination recognized me in her central closed circuit TV monitor, then led me to the elevator.

I took the elevator up to the appropriate floor, then, taking the stairs, made my way down to the 6th floor. I walked quietly through the deserted hallway. A wall lizard scampered down the hall as if his presence were urgently needed elsewhere.

During the dinner, I had seen enough of the French attache's apartment to know each apartment had a large balcony, a separate maid's quarter, high ceilings, marble fixtures and parquet floors. The Sanfords were doing very well indeed. Or at least one of them was. I stopped before their door and pushed a button.

Plangent door chimes: The first eight notes of Beethoven's Fifth sounded from within. I had known a contract officer for the Company in Beijing who, in another life, had been a mathematician and composer; and he had told me that if Beethoven returned to earth and composed his tenth symphony it would simply be an embarrassment; because music had moved on. I told him I would have to think about that. I still am. But I wish people wouldn't tell me things like that.

The door opened a few feet and the woman from the swimming pool peered out. There was still the same elegant simplicity to her that I had found attractive the first time I'd seen her. Her red hair had been swept back into a rather severe bun and she seemed to have applied very little makeup. She also seemed on the verge of offering an apology for whatever she thought had forced me to stop by; a type of woman they don't make much anymore.

Everything about her from her looks to her expression to her beige kitchen apron over the lower part of her sensible blue-and-white dirndl dress suggested her personality: diminutive, docile, and conservative. The puffed white sleeves of her bodice were large enough to serve as water wings. She looked like a librarian before librarians stopped looking like librarians.

She stared out at me through eyes as green as recently transplanted rice, but as soon as she recognized me, she drew her shapely lips tightly together as if in anticipation of some unpleasant event. The aroma of some delicious dish about ready for eating drifted out to me. Whatever it was, I had no doubt she was a great cook. I gave her my best hi-it's-only-me grin. "Mrs. Sanford?"

"Yes. You are the diver."

"Right. I'm sorry to bother you. I was wondering if I could speak to your husband for just a minute?"

The television set was on inside the apartment and I could hear a CNN reporter giving gory details on the latest Hindu/Muslim clash.

She hesitated. Then stammered. "I'm sorry. My husband isn't home now."

"Would it be possible for me to wait for him? I just need five minutes of his time."

As she stared at me, her eyes ever so slowly increased in size and fear seemed to seize hold of her. She stumbled over a few words. "Mr. Sterling, is that right?"

"Yes."

"I don't think my husband – I mean, I don't think he would wish to see you. I'm so sorry but I don't want any trouble."

"Well, ma'am, I don't intend to make trouble. I just need to ask him a few questions. And then I'll – "

I heard the television set snap off, heavy footsteps, and a terrified look on the woman's face. She disappeared. The door slammed shut. I heard a man raising his voice. I took a step back and waited. The man who opened the door completely filled the doorway. Something about his body language suggested to a stranger that Robert Sanford could take care of himself – so watch it. He was casually dressed in polo shirt and slacks with the open shirt revealing a few inches of gold chain.

He stood in the doorway for several seconds looking me up and down without expression. His voice was as cold as I wish my air-conditioner would be during the hot season. "And you want what?"

"I'm investigating the murder of Lisa Avery, Mr. Sanford. I'd very much like to talk to you about – "

"Listen, I don't know who Lisa Avery is and I don't want you bothering us again. Is that clear?"

"Your showing up for diving lessons was a coincidence, was it, Mr. Sanford?"

As he narrowed his blue-green eyes a few wrinkles appeared on his otherwise smooth forehead. He looked as if he were going to take a swing at me but then started to close the door.

"You can talk to me now or you can talk to the police later."

That line has worked beautifully for detectives in every book I've ever read or movie I've ever seen. The anger and resentment remain on the face of the suspect but, realizing he is caught between a rock and a hard place, he chooses the lesser of two evils and opens the door. The detective enters and digs out information useful in solving the case.

Unfortunately, in real life, that line never works. Sanford replied with a two-word curse suggesting I should be intimately involved on the receiving end of sexual intercourse and slammed the door in my face.

I walked down the elegant hallway toward the stairs under the observant, unblinking gaze of a wall lizard. Maybe the same one. Maybe the one the other one was running from. Maybe like me he was wondering why a louse like Robert Sanford gets to marry an attractive mousy type for money; why some guys have all the luck. Or maybe like me he was wondering what the hell I was doing chasing down leads in a case with no pay for a deceased client I had hardly known.

DAY NINE

24

It was another lovely morning. I knew it wouldn't stay that way but as I walked up the gravel driveway of the Emerald Club, the sun's rays bathed the fluted pillars and marble statues and bamboo thickets in a brilliant yellowish-white light. The glow of the rich. It was the kind of club Jay Gatsby would have belonged to if he had lived in Bangkok; and if he hadn't been so hung up on what's-her-name.

There were only a few cars parked about and one spanking new robin's egg-blue SUV. I pressed the diamond-shaped bell, trying not to wonder why a club called the Emerald would have a brass bell shaped like a diamond.

As I feared, at this time of day, there was no Bright-eyed Susan to greet me. A young Thai man I had never seen before shielded his eyes; whether from the glare of the sun or from the unwelcome sighting of a *farang* so early in the day, I wasn't sure. He wore a short-sleeved shirt with the club's logo, well-pressed khaki slacks, brown socks and flipflops.

I mustered up my best grin. If this case continued on much longer I knew I would need someone to massage my aching smile muscles. I asked to speak with the man in charge. He hesitated only a second before shaking his head. A man of few words, but if I read his head movement correctly, it seems the club was closed to outsiders cum intruders during the day. As I dug into my shirt pocket for the bottle ticket I heard a vehicle scrunching up the gravel driveway in my direction.

And a strange vehicle it was. A very fat Thai man had somehow managed to cram his corpulent body inside the safety cell of a BMW C 1 CityScooter. He rode it almost up to the steps before he stopped. As he untangled his girth from not one but two seatbelts and stepped out he appeared a bit too conventional for such a futuristic machine. He too wore a club logo and slacks. He walked toward me and smiled. His eyes were partly hidden beneath his heavy lids, his cheeks were as plump and round as a toy Santa, and just above his double chin was a pair of almost girlish, bow-shaped lips. His massive chin either hid his neck or else he didn't have one. He waddled his way over to me and spoke in English with a pleasant but surprisingly whispery voice, "May I help you?"

I held up the bottle ticket. "Yes, if you would. I just wanted to ask the bartender a few questions about this ticket."

He reached out his hand. "May I?"

I handed it to him. His pudgy fingers surrounded the card like the tentacles of a giant octopus gripping a swimmer. He nodded approvingly. "Chivas Regal."

He handed it back. "I am in charge of the club during the day. What was it you wanted to know?"

His English was just about flawless so I continued on in English. "I was hoping you might tell me what this five-digit number is. Also, the ink is smeared and I can't make out the name."

He took the card back and pointed to the first line. "You mean here?"

"Yes."

"That is not a name. That is a number." He held it close to his face and squinted to make it out. "Let me see, three-four-four-nine."

"And the five-digit number?"

"That is just a stock control number."

"So there is no way of telling whose ticket this is?"

He raised his eyebrows, which in turn revealed a bit more of his beady eyes. "Of course there is. But, for the sake of discretion, we use numbers here, rather than names. But we keep the book of numbers which correspond to the members' names."

"Could you tell me whose ticket this is?"

"I could check inside easily enough." He smiled and ran his pudgy hand across his missing neck as if it were a knife. "But then I would have to look for another job." He held one stubby finger to his lips and gave me a conspiratorial smile. "Members names are top secret." At that he chuckled.

"I can understand that. The thing is I was here the other night and had a chat with your boss. The man behind a desk on the second floor. Corner office. Would you be willing to call him? Just tell him the *farang* with the black eye is back again and needs to know whose ticket this is."

He hesitated for just a second, then gestured toward the door. "Why don't you wait inside while I give him a call?"

The younger man had kept quiet through all of this and I had the distinct impression he didn't much like the fact that I had been invited in. But he wasn't in charge.

Once again I sat in a straight-backed emerald green chair near the front door facing an upholstered emerald green couch. Everything was in its place: the intricately carved woodwork, the profusion of plants, the statuary on gold-trimmed, marble-topped tables, the chandeliers, and the paintings. The only things missing were the sounds of happy voices and soft laughter. And Bright Eyes.

Truth to tell, I had been thinking of Bright Eyes every now and then and was determined to stop. Over the years, I had seen the way a Thai woman could enslave a *farang* male's soul and occupy his every thought with just a coy glance and an enchanting smile and the promise of more to come. And I had met several men who thought they had lived in Thailand long enough to become impervious to the charm of Thai women. Several million baht down the drain later, they learned they hadn't. And each now passed his time drinking alone in the Boots and Saddle or in a bar like it wearing an inane smile and a rueful expression of stunned disbelief.

The jolly fat man returned wearing a huge grin and beckoned me to follow him. We walked in silence over the ruby red carpet and entered the room with the bar I had seen before. He motioned for me to sit on a barstool then disappeared behind a paneled door. He returned in about twenty seconds holding a bottle of Chivas Regal. He smiled broadly and held it up, like a proud fisherman who had just caught the fish nobody else could catch. "Here it is. Bottle number one-oh-eight."

He managed to fit his body behind the bar and handed it to me. I looked at the large label stuck to the back of the bottle. Three items were printed on it. The words "Date," "stock control number" and the stylized "E" logo for the Emerald Club. The date had been stamped in the proper space and the number "38502" had been stamped in the space beside "stock control number." At least the number mystery had been solved.

He pulled out a large ledger and riffled through a few pages. Then ran his finger down a page. I had the feeling that whoever had bought Lisa Avery these drinks had been very much involved in her life. And just possibly in her death. And I was willing to bet some money that the name we would find would be that of Robert Sanford.

He smiled and turned the book toward me holding his finger in place. "Number three four four nine." He ran his finger across the page to the name. "Mr. George Russell."

25

When I called George and told him I needed to talk with him, he agreed to meet me later that afternoon at Bumrungrat Hospital where Winnie was recovering from surgery. I knew Dao wanted to visit Winny as well, so I arranged to meet her at the hospital. In her white blouse and blue skirt she looked like a student on her way to her university. Several male heads turned as she walked through the downstairs lobby.

Bumrungrat had once been written up in the *New York Times* under the headline, "Sea, Sun and Surgery." The *Times* failed to mention that it was located off Sukhumvith Road just a ten minute walk from one of the world's most notorious nightlife areas, Nana Plaza.

Nonetheless, it was a very well respected hospital with western-trained doctors and the cost of an operation was a fraction of what American hospitals charged. It had also become popular with Middle Easterners, so I wasn't surprised to find Muslim women covered from head to toe as well as Caucasian women in casual tops and shorts.

The lobby and mezzanine floor had restaurants and fast food outlets including Starbucks and McDonalds and Au Bon Pain. The joke was that someone recovering from a heart operation could call down for a Big Mac. Which they probably did.

Dao and I took the elevator to the 11th floor and knocked on Winny's door. His live-in girlfriend of two years opened the door. Malee was a tiny but irrepressible 30-year-old from Chiang Mai with the kind of natural light skin that thousands of Thai women spend fortunes on whitening cream to achieve. She gave us a bright smile, planted small kisses on our cheeks, then ushered us in. Chattering in Thai, she led Dao off to join with three of her girlfriends sitting on a couch near the window.

The room was a private one with wall to wall carpet, refrigerator, TV, VCR and private bath. A blood pressure gage was coiled on the wall above the bed like a snake ready to strike. One wall was a window which looked out upon the buildings along *soi* three.

Winny lay in bed under a sheet with a saline drip in his arm. The bottle contained a clear solution of dextrose and saline. A blood line leading out from under the large bandage on his neck was attached to a container which was about ready to be emptied of blood. His face was pale but he was alert.

A smaller bed was just a few feet from Winny's. For very little money Thai hospitals would bring in an extra bed so that a loved one could stay overnight.

George Russell sat in a chair near the bed. I exchanged greetings with him and stood beside the bed. I wheeled the bed table out of the way. "How we doing, Winny?"

"Piece of cake."

"I hear it's not malignant, that right?"

"That's it. It was just a bump on the neck."

Malee had called Dao and filled her in on every detail of the operation and on Winny's progress. I knew how relieved she and Winny had been when the doctor gave them the happy news that the tumor was benign.

Winny gestured for me to be quiet and listen to Malee gossip in Thai. He explained that Malee had overheard the nurses enough to have learned some medical terms in English. The ones that most fascinated her were "bowel movement" and "urination." She in turn had been repeating them to her visiting Thai friends as if they were magic words, almost as if she were a sorceress casting a spell, an incantation that might help lead to her boyfriend's recovery. She spoke them as someone who was proud to be able to speak of intimate body functions in English.

And so she might attempt to speak them mysteriously or cavalierly, but at some point before a visitor left, she would be certain to lower her voice, glance toward Winny and, leaning forward toward the visitor in confidence, speak just above a whisper: "But don' worry because today he awready have urinachun and bowen momen'."

Winny listened for the words as Malee filled Dao in on his condition. When he heard them he threw his head back and roared with laughter.

I joked about with Winny for a few minutes then a nurse came in to take his temperature and empty the container of blood. She closed the curtain around the bed. I moved away and sat down beside George. "George, have you ever seen the garden they've got on the sixth floor?"

"Garden? No. Can't say that I have."

"It's outside on a wide terrace. Runs the length of the building. I'd like to show it to you."

He looked at me as if he were about to protest then must have realized I wanted to talk with him in priv ate. "All right, let's see it."

I turned to Winny. "We'll be right back."

His voice came from behind the bed curtain. "Take your time. I'm not going anywhere."

We walked in silence to the elevator, stood in silence inside the elevator, and walked in silence along a balcony path winding its way through trees, fountains, plants and flowers. I led George over to a gazebo and we sat facing one another on wooden seats. George looked around at the trees and plants, then at the view of Bangkok. "Nice up here," I said.

"Yeah, it is." He stared at me through his gunmetal gray eyes. His gravel-voice sounded almost mournful. "That why you brought me up here?"

"No. I brought you up here to find out what your relationship was with Lisa Avery."

He nodded as if it was a question he had one day expected to be asked. "She came to the dive shop, maybe three months ago. Said a mutual friend in New York gave her your name and work address. But when I offered to call you she asked me not to. Not right away."

"And you agreed?"

"Hey, I figured the lady had her reasons."

"And she was drop dead gorgeous."

He ran a hand through his thinning hair as if there was enough to need smoothing down. No doubt there was a time when there had been. "That she was."

"And like a lot of men you're a sucker for a pretty face."

"Yeah." His smile widened. "That I am." He lost his smile. "That's not a crime yet, is it?"

I shook my head and waited.

He took a pack of cigarettes from the pocket of his long-sleeved shirt. "OK, so she said she needed a job. She'd worked in some upmarket nightclubs in New York, never said exactly where or doing what. Just high class entertainment kinds of places."

He stopped to light a cigarette. The wind had picked up and the flame of his lighter seemed unwilling to cooperate but he kept at it. His square hands had liver spots. He took a deep drag and exhaled. "I got two sisters-in-law get their spending money making nice with big spenders at the Emerald Club. So I told Lisa about the club."

"She like the idea?"

"She jumped at it. I told her we had a couple of Eurasians but no American. Thought she'd be a big hit, especially with the Chinese-Thai customers. Something different, you know?"

"And she was."

He nodded. "You got that right. Got popular enough with

some of the big spenders to piss off some of the other girls."

We halted our conversation for several seconds as an elderly Thai patient in bright blue pajamas hobbled by on crutches followed by a concerned looking and very shriveled woman with leathery skin.

"Why did you leave a message on my phone, reminding me to go to your Halloween party, George?"

He hesitated before answering. He watched the cigarette burn down between his stubby fingers. Sunlight glinted off a ring and turned his watch into a mirror. "She asked me to try to get you there. She wanted to meet you."

"You invite Da, too?"

"Her girlfriend? Naw. They met at the club. They hit it off. Inseparable."

I saw flashes of white pass behind a mass of pale red bougainvillea. Nurses on their break were walking slowly in our direction. "They were bedmates?"

"Da was crazy about Lisa. That much I know."

"You take Lisa to bed?"

He stared at me. His smile was of the wistful variety. "I wanted to. My wife would have heard about it from one of her sisters. That kind of trouble I don't need." He patted his crotch. "She's the type that might feed it to the ducks."

I thought of the maid's description of the man in Lisa's apartment. "You were seen in her apartment."

He took my statement in stride. "Yeah. She took me up there. *Once*. For a drink, she said. And that's all it turned out to be. The bitch was a dicktease with a capital 'D'. Never put out." He eyed me curiously. "At least not for me."

I ignored his implication. "When did you last see her?"

He thought for a few seconds. He was a man telling the truth. Or else a man who had learned to lie very well; and has learned to assume a questioner knows some part of the answers so some part of the truth is best.

"Must have been at the club. About three nights before she got bumped off."

"You were a member there?"

"Yeah, of course. She said she was tired and about to call it a night. So I bought her a drink first. Must have been about one o'clock."

"Who do you think killed her, George?"

"Me? How the hell should I know? Maybe some sex-crazed guy at the club she wouldn't put out for. She was something of a dicktease, you know? And, frankly, from what I heard and saw, I think she went both ways."

"Were you involved in the kinky parties she went to?"

"Hell, no. I'm not into that shit. But I heard about them."

"Why did Da quit the club?"

"For one thing, she was getting drunk and disorderly. Every time somebody went near Lisa, there was trouble. Lisa couldn't do her job and the customers were complaining. So Da got fired." His smile contained more than a hint of contempt. "I hear she's a whip-snapper now."

I nodded. "That she is."

"Then she found her true calling."

I didn't see that George had more to offer or at least that he would volunteer anything else he knew so I stood up to leave. George looked up and then away. "Sit down for a minute, will you? I need to talk to you about something."

I sat down. A gust of wind blew hanging boxes of orchids together, imitating the soft clicking sounds of wind-chimes.

George reached into his shirt pocket and handed me what looked like receipts. His eyes still avoided mine. I looked the receipts over. All three were dated within two weeks of one another. The latest was dated ten days before. All were receipts from the Ritter Hotel off Sukhumvith Road. The hotel wasn't a short-time hotel, but it wasn't a giant step up from one either. I looked at George.

"You're a detective, right? You keep things close to the vest? I mean if you do something for me it would be on a confidential basis, right?"

I nodded. More nurses floated by behind a row of potted palms. "I never talk with others about my cases, George. What is it you want?"

He took a long drag on his cigarette. "I found those in my wife's drawer. I think she's seeing another guy. I want you to check it out, see if you can find out who the guy is."

I looked at the receipts. No credit card number; probably paid for in cash. "I can do that. If that's what you want."

He looked at me.

"I mean a better way to solve this might be for you to have a talk with your wife."

He shook his head. "Nah. I want to know what I'm up against before I go into battle." He reached into the same shirt pocket and pulled out a folded photograph of his wife. I had seen her a few times at the Boots and Saddle. She was middle-aged now but whatever her age there was no denying her beauty. In the photograph, she was smiling into the camera, even while her wind-whipped hair blew across her chin. Behind her was an expanse of deep blue water. "Phuket."

George spat out the word as if Phuket was responsible for his troubles. "All right." I put the receipts and the photograph in my pocket. "I'll find out what I can."

"I don't want her to know I know."

I nodded.

"I'll pay whatever your fee is."

"Understood." I stood up. "Coming?"

"Nah. I'll finish this first." He shook his head. "Jesus Christ, she's always been the jealous type. I can't believe she'd...."

He looked away.

I went back to Winny's room. Dao and I said our goodbyes and took the elevator to the ground floor and walked outside.

Outside the hospital, I was about to hail a taxi when Dao led me over to the nearby shrine. We circled around it and walked up the steps. The shrine was to Phra Mae Laksmi – goddess of wealth and good fortune, and the many plants which encircled her no doubt had been chosen for their auspicious names. The goddess herself was surrounded by dozens of small elephants, fruit, garlands, roses, censers of incense and a tiny clay orchestra. The squat pillars of the shrine had been wrapped in colorful strips of cloth. Riding on top of several of the elephants were miniature tin turtles with the Chinese character for "wealth" on their backs.

Dao withdrew a packet of incense sticks from her purse, lit them, and knelt down before the goddess to pray for Winny's recovery. I watched her kneel in the legs-tucked-under position and observed the reverent way she leaned forward and prayed for his recovery and – as much as I hated myself for doing so – wondered if she were really capable of murder.

27

There are some nights – when I've had enough to drink – that my living in Bangkok almost makes sense. And on those nights when I've had more than enough to drink, Bangkok itself almost makes sense. Not by Western logic, of course. Attempting to grasp the nuances of the Thai way of thinking through Western logic would be like trying to spoon water with a sieve.

Thailand is without question a Land of Smiles. That's what the Thai Tourist Authority assures everyone. They forget to mention that it also has the highest homicide rate in the world. Shortly after I'd first met her, Dao had introduced me to a muay-Thai trainer. We'd chatted quite a bit and then he excused himself for an appointment. When I mentioned he smiled a lot and seemed very pleasant, she remarked casually, "Yes, and he hates foreigners." As she explained it to me later, I still had a lot to learn about *wai na, lang lok* – Those who *wai* to your face, but deceive you behind your back.

Sometimes I wondered how people withstood the pressures of a complex modern city – especially one in which every relationship was hierarchical rather than equal – without spending several hours a week immersed in the serene tranquillity and mystical beauty of an underwater wonderland.

Whenever I traveled to so-called exotic countries or met people from those countries, I found that the more I scratched the surface, the more similar they were to me. With the Thais, on the other hand, the more I dug down, the more inscrutable they became.

Bar wisdom had it that Thai reactions were inappropriate; that the Thais were indignant when they should be forgiving, and forgiving when they should be indignant; tolerant when they should be stubborn, and stubborn when they should be tolerant; shocked when they should be amused, and amused when they should be shocked, and so forth. But that didn't stop anyone spouting such bar wisdom from living in Thailand – including me. Lisa had it right: The Land of Smiles was a Tar Baby that ensnared foreign men.

I finished my glass of Mekhong and coke, rinsed out the glass and sat back down. That was my technique of trying not to drink too much. A rinsed-out glass means the drinking session is over. At least until next time. But there was no question I had a buzz.

I unlocked the lower drawer of my desk, unlocked a small steel box, and brought out the Smith & Wesson five-shot revolver Buen had given me. In Thailand, it's illegal for a foreigner to own a gun but, of course, guns are available to those who feel the need. Buen had filed the serial number off and the weapon would be untraceable. I had never used it but cleaning it once a month had become a kind of ritual. I placed my hand around the grips, drew back the hammer spur with my thumb and cocked it, sighted on a nearby snake plant, carefully lined up the front and rear sights and, without issuing a Miranda warning, pulled the trigger. The hammer fell. The snake plant shrugged it off. I had shot him before. One day I would load a few .357 Magnum cartridges before firing and the smug bastard wouldn't be so smug then. Neither would the wall behind it. Neither would the massage parlor girls across the square. Such cerebral thoughts come with the third glass of Mekhong Coke.

I retrieved my gun cleaning kit from the back of the closet and went to work. I spread out some pages of *The Bangkok Post* on a chipped maple desk and opened the kit. I lined up the cotton swabs, the barrel bore brush, the can of gun oil, the powder-removing solvent, a filthy Oral-B toothbrush (medium) and went to work. Until now, I had always doubted that the day would come when I would ever use it, but keeping a weapon well cleaned in the heat, dampness and humidity of Thailand seemed a good idea. And with this slum business looming, it seemed a better idea than ever. Ten minutes later I lined up the front and rear sights, steadied my right hand with my left, and squeezed off one last imaginary round at the snake plant. I left the gun on the desk, washed my hands of oil and grime, and took off my shirt.

I reached into a drawer and withdrew an Uncle Mike's belly band which according to their brochure would protect my skin from "chafing, perspiration and discomfort." Although I doubted the Oregon-based company had tested it out in Bangkok's heat and humidity. But it was made of a light-weight synthetic mesh material, smooth and porous, and whenever I had worn it just as a test, it had worked well.

I sat down in one of two rickety bamboo chairs beside a rickety wooden table. I hadn't checked the Santa Fe payroll bag for my mail lately, so the maid had slipped some letters under the door. I'd forgotten about them but I looked them over now: An American Express bill, an advertisement for a new Thai restaurant specializing in northeastern cooking, and a letter from a New York lawyer. The lawyer was just keeping me up to date on a suit filed against me when I had once made the mistake of trying to save someone's life.

Before leaving the Company's Directorate of Operations in Langley and heading to Beijing, I had taken a week's vacation and flown to North Carolina to stay with a diver friend. On the third day he'd sprained his leg and had asked me to substitute as instructor in a private class of one; an airline pilot who supposedly had lots of diving experience. In those days I didn't need the money but I did it as a favor. Besides, I loved to dive.

The student suited up and we headed off shore. We were

doing a deep dive; when we hit bottom, we were at one hundred feet down and there was maximum water pressure and poor visibility. Nitrogen Narcosis can happen at that depth, the narcotic affects of the nitrogen that we breathe. It affects everybody – it's just how you deal with it. It produces an impaired, intoxicated feeling – people do stupid things.

In the case of my student he took the regulator out of his mouth and tried to feed it to the fish, then flailed his arms when I tried to get him to accept mine. It only lasted about thirty seconds before the air ran out of his lungs, after which his lungs filled with water and he became immediately unconscious. He went limp, and dropped down five feet to the bottom, and lay there. So I went down to lift him up. At that depth, he was very negative (heavy), so I couldn't just bring him up to the surface; I had to take off his weight belt, grab him and inflate my buoyancy control device.

We shot up to the surface, a bit dangerous for me, because I had to make sure I wasn't holding my breath, and going up that fast I might have gotten a lung expansion injury. But I chose to get to the surface as quickly as I could to get this guy breathing again. I wanted to keep him alive.

I started giving him artificial respiration in the water and while doing that I was slowly bringing him toward shore. I yelled to my friend on the beach to call 911. I gave him AR by mouth and after about forty-five seconds we got to the shore and he started breathing on his own. The first thing he did was to puke all over me. I was elated because that meant he was breathing.

I went with him to the hospital for overnight observation. He had water in the lungs, and had nearly drowned but he seemed fine. I talked to his wife and kids. They thanked me for bringing him up safely. The wife had tears of gratitude in her eyes as she hugged me and kissed my cheek. After he was released, I called him at home several times and he was adamant that he wanted to finish his course.

The last time I called him there was a silence and then he said, "Sorry, I've been advised not to talk to you." He had filed a lawsuit; claiming short term memory loss, continuing lung problems, sleep deprivation, nightmares, and whatever else his lawyer's imagination had come up with.

Of course he had signed a waiver of liability acknowledging that there are dangers associated with diving. So he would need to prove negligence. My lawyer had told me on the phone that if I had had a better grasp of "legal repercussions," I would have left him down there. The last line of his letter reassured me that there is no way in hell anyone could accuse me of being negligent and the guy would never win. But I didn't like that threat dragging on and hanging over my head. I also didn't like the lawyer's enclosed bill with "Second Reminder" stamped across the top; no doubt the real reason for the update.

But I was damned if I would allow myself to let this lawyer's reminder ruin my evening. I opened a bottle of Singha Gold and put a Billie Holiday tape in the recorder. As I reached for *The Real Cool Killers*, the phone rang.

"Sterling."

"*Dzemma yang*, Sterling?"

"Chinaman! Hey, not much. What's up with you?"

"It's getting cold here is what's up with me. Gets too cold and I might just pay you a visit."

"You'd be very welcome. Just bring an umbrella."

"OK, I managed to dig up a bit on Janet Burgess AKA Lisa Avery."

I grabbed a pen and notebook out of the desk drawer. "Shoot."

"Janet Burgess had a sister June Burgess. Janet worked in publishing and June worked as a kind of high class call girl. June was known at some of the kinky scene clubs here in Manhattan, especially in the Tenderloin. One of the players in at least one of the clubs was Robert Sanford. According to some of those I interviewed, Sanford was very keen on June. According to one club member, he was nuts about her. On the night of thirteen February June Burgess fell or was pushed or jumped to her death from her balcony. After her death, Sanford was questioned by the boys at the 24th Precinct. He denied seeing her on the night of her death and his wife confirmed he was home all ev   ening with her."

"The case still open?"

"Yeah, sort of. Kind of like Jimmy Hoffa's case is still open."

"Oh, *that* kind of open."

"Yeah, it was labeled a 'suspicious death' and will remain that way, I was told, until other investigatable leads develop."

"You were a creative writing teacher and you use a word like 'investigatable'?"

"It's the company I keep: Homicide detectives love words like that."

"Sounds like Lisa wasn't telling you the full truth."

"Any client ever tell you the full truth?"

"I see your point."

"It sounds like said Janet Burgess had no doubts about how her sister died and who killed her and she went after the guy."

"And got herself killed in the process."

"Yeah. That she did, Scotty. That she did."

"No suicide note?"

"Negative. But half the number of suicides leave no note. Although not too many people wrapping things up do it by jumping."

"So this is a tough one to call."

"It is. But I got lots of cooperation from your brother."

"Larry's still in License Division?"

"Yeah. But he's got a buddy at the 110th precinct who helped in checking out Sanford's background. Plus some database searches I ran. Your Mr. Sanford was married before. Charged twice with beating his wife. Lots of domestic disturbance calls to their house in Queens. She filed for divorce. Also filed for a restraining order against him. I saw some pictures of her after he beat her up; it wasn't pretty."

"Macho man, huh?"

"Yeah. Database searches turned up his SS number, driver's license, hunting license, and lots of stuff you don't need for this one. He was a partner in an architectural firm which filed for bankruptcy several years ago, not long before he married his present wife. And he had a bank loan outstanding for over one hundred thousand dollars which was paid off in full just before he left for the Land of Smiles. I could be wrong but I'm getting the picture of a man with money problems. So I checked out his wife, Sally, a bit. Her background presented an opposite picture. Yale background for generations, property in her name in Scarsdale and a lot more in her family's name in Westport, Connecticut."

"So we may have a man of straw married to a woman of substance."

"Hey, Scotty, where'd you learn to talk like a lawyer?"

"During my divorce."

"Oh. Right."

"OK. Maybe I'll take another crack at talking to this clown. He wasn't too cooperative the last time I tried."

"Watch yourself. He sounds like a real loser."

"I will. Thanks, Chinaman."

"Anytime."

I checked the time. In an hour or so a young girl would be waiting to be snatched out of the slums. The snatchee. I was the snatcher. I strapped on Uncle Mike's belly band, placed the .38 inside it and adjusted my shirt over it. It wasn't perfect but it would do. Uncle Mike had considerately provided space for handcuffs as well but I wouldn't be needing those. It wasn't going to be a handcuff-type event.

I confess having the gun did not make me feel more secure. Most likely because I had learned from Thai police friends that they knew of over seven million pistols and rifles owned legally, and estimated that another one million were owned illegally. I remembered being told there were nearly two million guns registered just in the capital. I was simply joining the party.

I placed a bottle of Johnnie Walker Black in a shoulder bag, put George's wife's picture in the bag as well, then turned out the lights, turned off the air-conditioner, pushed in the door lock and left the apartment. It was going to be a busy night.

27

The Ritter Hotel was off Sukhumvith Road on *soi* 4 not far from the city's notorious go go bar area known as Nana Plaza. Despite its name it could more accurately be described as a two-story U-shaped motel. It was set back far enough from the road to assure its guests a good night's sleep – assuming guests staying in the midst of every kind of sensual pleasure known to man had flown to Bangkok for the purpose of getting a good night's sleep.

The guard shack was at the end of a narrow path just to the right of the office. A middle-aged Thai man in a short beige shirt and brown trousers sat beneath the slanting roof framed by the leathery, dark green leaves of a eucalyptus tree, still shiny with rain.

The features of his face were distorted by tubes of white fluorescent light lining the interior of the guard shack roof but, as I approached, he sat motionlessly, watching me as a wall lizard waits for a careless fly. On the small table before him were packs of Falling Rain cigarettes, a badly chipped ashtray, a thermos bottle, a battered flashlight, a clipboard, and a transparent plastic bag containing spice-laced noodles.

I decided a formal *wai* would only make him suspicious of my motives so I gave him a big smile, bid him a "Good evening" and whipped out a loose salute. He returned my greeting without the salute or smile and without any discernable display of enthusiasm as to who I was or what I wanted.

He didn't ask me to pull up a nearby stool and sit down facing him so I stood where I was, left hand on my hip, right hand grasping the strap of my shoulder bag. "I wonder if you could help me." He remained about as friendly as a furniture mover during an eviction. I plunged onward. "A friend of mine is looking for a lady who spent some time here."

A sparkling conversationalist he wasn't. But he did reach for the open pack of cigarettes. As he flicked his lighter to light up, the yellow flame revealed a face quite a bit older than I had realized. His dark eyes were set deeply into a wizened face and the wrinkled hand holding the lighter was none too steady. But now that he had a cigarette in his bony hand, he appeared ready to hear whatever bullshit the *farang* was about to throw. The only sounds were those of persistent crickets and the muffled din of motorcycles roaring down *soi* 4.

I removed my shoulder bag and unzipped it. I withdrew the photograph of George's wife and placed it on the table beside his cigarettes. I decided I'd been standing long enough so I pulled up the plastic stool and sat facing him. "Have you ever seen this woman before?"

He glanced at the photograph, took a deep drag on his cigarette, then shook his head.

"Are you sure?"

He stared at me as if to say the question had been asked and answered.

I placed the shoulder bag on the table, reached into it and pulled out the bottle of Johnnie Walker Black Label. A complex scotch whisky had no problem in gaining the attention of a simple Thai watchman. I kept one hand on the bottle. "Maybe you could take one last look at the picture."

His gaze remained on the bottle for a few seconds more and then focused on the photograph. He nodded. "She's been here."

"Many times?"

He shrugged. "More than once."

"Why do you remember her?"

"There was a complaint."

"Complaint?"

"Lots of loud noise and laughing and some broken glasses. And singing. About four in the morning. I had to ask them to quiet down."

"They were very drunk?"

He nodded. "And not wearing much." He stared into the middle distance as if remembering the happy sight of a nearly naked and uninhibited woman just a foot or so away.

"OK." I pushed the bottle toward him. "This is yours. I just need you to describe the man she was with."

His eyes widened in surprise and his slash of a mouth favored me with a lopsided grin.

I was about to repeat my request when the meaning of his grin suddenly hit me. "Oh, no. You mean she wasn't with a man?"

He shook his head and held up three fingers. "I saw her. Three times. Always with the same *farang* woman. That's also why I remember her. Mostly *farang* men and Thai girls come here. Not *farang* women."

I reached into the bag and took out my pen and notebook. I thought I would get a description of the woman just in case George would recognize her from it. As he began describing the curls of blond hair and big blue eyes I stopped writing in the notebook. I thanked the watchman, politely refused his offer to have a drink with him, and put the picture back in my shoulder bag.

I walked off wondering exactly how best to share the unexpected discovery of his wife's lesbian activities with an already distraught client. George had suspected Lisa was a bi-sexual but he had also been so sure his wife had been the jealous type. He'd shown some genuine insight into what Lisa was up to but was completely ignorant of what was happening under his nose. George seemed to know as little about what makes a woman tick as the next man. I would have to break the news to him about his wife's lesbian affair; and I would have to add his wife to the growing list of suspects.

Just as I exited the path onto *soi* 4, a foreign male somewhere in his 40's and a heavily made up Thai ladyboy of indeterminable age turned onto the path. The ladyboy gave me a limp-wristed wave and a falsetto "hello" while the foreigner turned his head to avoid being seen. Which might mean he was a local. Bangkok seemed to be the kind of place that brought out latent tendencies and deep-seated desires in people who hadn't even suspected they'd been harboring any deep-seated desires. I had known a covert action officer at the embassy, a real playboy, who had bedded what he described as "acres" of Thai women. He told me he most likely had never been to bed with a Thai woman who hadn't herself at one time or another been to bed with a Thai woman. I had laughed at the time. Not now.

28

Along Thailand's urban streets or rural lanes, especially when night falls, the banal and the bewitched are often one and the same. At the kingdom's dimly lit open-air street stalls, those fiendish figures almost invisible in the darkness surrounding a charcoal stove may simply be waiting for their pork and chicken satay; or they may be sorcerers practicing witchcraft and invoking evil spells. Inside drab shop houses, dark figures and their shadows flit about in rooms lit only by a fluorescent light or bare bulb. The people inside may simply be an average lower income family sitting on their wooden or concrete floor discussing the most mundane subjects, and the space they occupy may be empty of all but sacks of long-grained rice and piles of bamboo baskets tinged a blood red by the bare crimson bulb set before a shrine to a Chinese or Thai deity, but in the play of dim or flickering light and pools of Cimmerian darkness each room and its occupants appear almost as part of a stage setting for an episode of the *Ramakien*. Beneath an insect-shrouded pink, green or white glow of fluorescence there is, at least to the foreign eye, something mysterious, something mystical, something almost sinister. It is impossible to believe that these indistinct figures are not part of a cabal uttering strange mantras and practicing arcane rituals that will remain forever unfathomable to a passing foreigner; or that in this atmosphere of mystery, they are not engrossed in secret intrigues, dark schemes and endless conspiracies. The silent stares, the furtive whispers, the undercurrents of stealth – surely all this is directed at the stranger.

Multiply the intensity of that atmosphere by one hundred and you have some idea of what a Bangkok slum is like at night. Except in the slums there is no mystery, only misery, nothing mystical, only malodorous, and what dark schemes there are are born of poverty and despair.

In the taxi ahead of us were Amnart, Narong and one of the professional boxers from the camp. In our taxi, Dao, Buen, and I rode in the back; an ex-fighter friend of Buen's, now a promoter, rode in the front. I wasn't surprised to find that others who had trained under Amnart had volunteered their services for tonight's showdown: The friendships developed among boxers from the same camp were so intense that such friends were known as *phuen dai* (friend to the death).

We rode in silence, down rain-soaked streets and partly flooded narrow lanes. Our headlight beams illuminated drenched pedestrians inching their way around expanding pools of dark water as carefully as trekkers along the edge of a steep cliff. The only sounds were the hissing of rubber tires on water and the desperate thumping of our own windshield wipers.

Eddies of wind-swept rain swirled across the roofs of buildings. They shot out from the darkness, passed briefly through areas of light and then hurried on into darkness like panic-stricken actors rushing offstage. A Skytrain sped through the night, its lighted windows dimmed by rain but magnified by reflections in glass exteriors on nearby buildings into some kind of malevolent ghost-train.

Much of Bangkok is a mere one meter above sea level. During the rainy season, the high tides of the Chao Phraya River can raise water levels two meters, causing flooding, stopping traffic and paralyzing the city; especially a city built on swampy, soft clay beside a major river.

I was already feeling guilt at having got people I cared about into a dangerous situation. And beside me, dressed in shirt and jeans, Dao hardly moved. I resisted glancing over at her and tried to concentrate on the task ahead.

We crossed a highway. More narrow lanes, narrower still, and then we stopped. As if by signal, so did the rain. All around us were enough tropical trees and vegetation to make one think we were far out in the countryside, but lights from distant steel-and-glass office towers and high-rise, luxury condominiums revealed clearly that we were still well inside Bangkok.

We exited the taxis and the drivers seemed pleased to speed away from the area without looking for other customers. Buen motioned that he would see us inside and then disappeared into a muddy stretch of overgrown weeds, wild shrubbery, and straggly trees. Banana plants crowded along the length of a crumbling brick wall, stretching their long, bedraggled, green fronds over the wall and down, like bold spectators hoping to glad-hand passing politicians. But when I squeezed through the narrow garbage-strewn lane, they brushed against me like skilled pickpockets or irate cops patting me down for weapons.

The lane widened slightly and I emerged with a shirt soaked with rainwater from banana fronds as well as from perspiration. Just as the first cluster of wooden shacks appeared the soft, soggy ground gave way to a rickety wooden walkway. The walkway briefly disappeared under a riotous growth of dark green heart-shaped taro leaves and then continued on through a maze of tin-roofed ramshackle dwellings with wood-and-cardboard sidings.

People sat in open doorways or on crates in front of their shacks drinking from brown bottles with red labels (*Lao Yi sip Baat* (Rotgut No 28) chatting with their neighbors. As soon as they spotted us they stopped talking and stared; not exactly with hostility but it was close enough. Unwashed urchins lining up to wash clothes in plastic red buckets beside a single water tap also grew silent. Diseased slum dogs continued pawing at piles of discarded plastic to reach some fetid garbage beneath but their wary eyes stayed on us. Open doorways revealed glimpses of rice cookers, cheap battery-powered fans, scurrying rats and sleeping bodies. Several doorways were littered with thin bits of tinfoil used to smoke speed tablets and against the wet earth their aluminum sheeting reflected light like a fallen galaxy of tiny stars.

We walked for about five minutes single file along still more meandering walkways, a fe w times having to leap across putrefied rubbish, oil-soaked slime and pools of stagnant water from which the planks had been taken. If I understood the plan correctly, we would go to the small restaurant owned by the girl's grandmother, she would take us to the girl, and we would then be on our way. Of course, that assumed no one was going to try to stop us.

After passing through a stretch of land with very few lights, we came out into an area which seemed a notch above what we had seen of the slum so far. For one thing many of the dwellings had been built of brick and cinder blocks and the tin roofs had been properly cut and fit. They were also wired for electricity and boasted running water. A radio blared out a popular Thai love song. Across a lane were a few shops, and beside a small hairdresser's shop was the restaurant we were looking for.

We followed Amnart, crossed the lane and headed for the one-room, open-air restaurant. A Butane gas cylinder had been positioned at the entrance, connected to the cooking area. Facing the lane were glass shelves offering trays of food to those who could afford them.

At the front of a small glassed-in cart, drops of water dripped from four skinned ducks hanging side-by-side on hooks. Three of them had their wings tied behind them like bound hostages and their nearly closed eyes lent them expressions of great sadness, suggesting that these hostages had given up any hope of rescue. The fourth had one of its wings tied with string at an upward angle, which brought the tip of the wing near the head, suggesting the duck was throwing me a military salute. If so, it seemed to be the only one in the entire slum who thought my presence an asset.

The six of us sat on rickety plastic stools around a chipped wooden table on a warped tile floor. Customers stopped talking and continued eating in silence. Behind us, among pots of constantly simmering food, and enveloped in steam from woks, pans, steamers and saucepans, three sweat-drenched women and their children bustled about preparing food.

The tiny woman who appeared to be the owner was dressed simply and practically in bodice, sarong and sandals. Her sarong was a methamphetamine-pill pink and the huge dish of beef she was working with had turned her hands blood-red. She gave a steady stream of orders to the other workers and even gently scolded customers who ate too little or drank too much. It was obviously a nightly regimen of good humor but the presence of out-of-slum strangers in the restaurant precluded any atmosphere of levity.

In addition to mistrust and foreboding, the air was heavy with the pungent odors of Thai curries, barbecued meat, sauces and garlic and the crepitant sizzling of noodle and rice dishes being stir-fried in woks.

Along the wall were advertisements, posters of Spiderman saving his girlfriend and Rambo firing his RPG, and a calendar with a slightly pudgy Thai woman in a two-piece bathing suit holding a bottle of beer. Above a wall clock were pictures of the king and queen of Thailand in military uniforms. The Spiderman poster was spotless; the Rambo poster was torn, yellowed and the speckled black soot spots made it appear that somebody had been firing back at him.

The only item in the room of any interest was a mass of blackened fuse boxes which, with their many switches, innumerable shades of brown and black and various square and rectangular shapes had inadvertently given the restaurant its only genuine decoration; as if a Thai artist used to painting temple scenes for tourists had attempted to copy a Mondrian painting and that painting had then been fired at by Rambo's rocket-propelled grenade launcher, melted in a fire and sprinkled with the remains of a leftover Thai curry.

The woman spoke to one of her staff, a cross-eyed, teenaged girl whose nearly bald head indicated she might have recently returned from spending time in a temple. With the girl in charge, the grandmother glanced at us and exited the restaurant. We stood up and followed. Rambo glared but stayed where he was. We had walked about five minutes and entered a dimly lit dirt track lined with a few squalid shacks when the boyz-n-the-hood finally made their appearance. There were nine of them. Except for the leader, they moved in pairs and then stood in the lane, effectively blocking our progress. They were all well built and obviously in shape. It was pretty clear that these boys didn't smoke the pretty pink pills they most likely sold to others, they didn't sniff glue out of paper bags, and they sure as hell didn't inject the drug-of-the-month to forget their troubles. Somebody somewhere – a much respected, wealthy gentleman in a beautifully decorated home with one or two well kept spirit houses, one or two minor wives and a bevy of Laotian maids – was taking care of these boys. And they in turn made sure his business – whatever it might involve – had no interference. My finely honed CIA instincts kicked in to warn me that in their eyes it just might be that we represented interference.

They stood about, most with muscular arms crossed over wide chests and narrow waists, and made themselves appear as large and as menacing as they could. It was too dark to make out any tattoos but I had no doubt their glistening bodies had them: dragons, tigers, various charms and emblems and sacred writing in old Khmer script to ward off danger. It was a close call, especially in the dim light, but it looked as if ominous stares prevailed over outright scowls by about six to three. They reminded me of male puffer fish puffing themselves up as much as possible to frighten male intruders away from their territory.

The path they were blocking was overrun with rain-soaked weeds and hundreds of bachelor's buttons, their tiny magenta heads spreading in all directions like a contagious disease. A stretch of screwpine grew almost to where they were standing and it was there that I noticed Buen. His head was framed by the feathery leaves of nipa palms and he stood motionless staring at the confrontation.

The grandmother had been walking slightly ahead of us and now seemed rooted to the spot. Dao walked forward, took her by the hand, and led her back to where we were standing. The leader of the boyz-n-the-hood stepped forward and stopped just a few yards from us. He was very large for a Thai, large by any standards; and he had a face that made the hitman at the Emerald Club look like a choir boy. His voice was loud and menacing; he would have made a fine actor. He probably made a fine murderer. His manner of speech was insolent and his clipped Thai was as crude as his looks. "We know who you are, Amnart, and we respect you. And your family. But the kid doesn't leave with you."

Several seconds of silence passed. No one moved. I didn't move but mentally I drew my right hand up slowly under my shirt to touch the reassuring metal ensconced inside Uncle Mike's belly band.

"That's right. She doesn't leave with them. She leaves with me."

The boyz-in-the-hood hadn't noticed Buen and at the sound of his voice some of them visibly started. When they realized who it was several took a step back. Buen moved forward into the penumbra of dirty yellow light thrown by bare bulbs of several shacks to his right. In the darkness, pinpricks of light reflected from cans and bottles like watchful eyes of an unseen audience. People who had been sitting in the doorways of the shacks seemed to have evaporated into thin air.

With his hair cascading down to his shoulders, and swinging his well muscled arms as he walked, Buen appeared less like a mortal and more like a nightmarish apparition emerging from the darkness. He strode slowly but confidently up to the gang leader and stopped less than two feet from him. "I am taking the girl. I am leaving her grandmother. If any harm comes to the woman, I will kill whoever did it. I will kill whoever gave the order to do it. Is that clear?"

I glanced at Dao but her face was devoid of expression. She stared at the leader and hugged her chest with her arms as if she were cold. Which most likely brought her hands close to whatever weapon Buen had given her.

For several tense moments, Buen and the leader faced one another. I knew Buen was armed. I wasn't sure how many of them had weapons. Or what kinds of weapons. The wet and soggy evening had a chill to it now. And the night had grown very still. I heard a dog bark far away. I could only wait. It was their move. But if gunfire broke out, it was my intention to throw Dao down to the ground, place myself in front of her, and fire from that position. I knew she would never forgive me but I also knew that might keep her alive.

Finally, without a word, the gang leader turned abruptly and stalked off in the direction he had come. His gang hurried after him. For now, at least, the danger was over. And I had a feeling they would let this one go.

On the way back, inside the taxi, the girl sat in between Dao and myself with Buen riding in the front. Dao reassured her all would be fine, but the girl was the matter-of-fact type raised in slums who seemed little affected by such events. She had seen the violence of poverty and despair all her life. She even described herself as a *khao nok nah*, "rice grown outside the paddy," that is, an illegitimate child. She harbored no illusions that in her life "all would be fine."

As I stepped out of the cab in front of the Boots and Saddle, I had an overwhelming urge to kiss Dao just for being safe and alive, but I merely touched her shoulder and said, "See you soon." I said goodbye to the girl and gave Buen a half salute. I stood watching the taxi speed off through the dimly lit shadows of Washington Square.

29

The tension of the evening's events had left me emotionally drained so I passed up a beer at the Boots and Saddle and headed up the dark stairs to my apartment. If I'd been thinking properly I might have paid more attention to the open window on the second floor landing. It looked out over the tin roof of a shed five or six feet below. I'd never seen it open before, even during the hot season. For one thing the roof was littered with debris and the foul odors were even too much for the local alley cats to deal with. I would have to break bad news to George but the problem with the girl had worked out well enough and I was both tired and relieved. And careless.

I put the key in the door, entered the apartment and reached for the light switch. Something crashed into my shoulder bouncing me violently off the wall. My hand whipped out wildly and a face mask and snorkel fell from a shelf above onto my head. A dark figure made a lightning-fast movement and I felt a shoe land near my solar plexus. I ignored the pain and threw a straight right to where I thought his face was. My fist connected with the side of his head.

He recovered his balance then moved in close. He had easily shaken off the pain of my best shot but his ability to do so had made him overconfident. He fainted a right kick then threw a straight right to my face. I ducked under it. He lashed out with a jumping roundhouse kick which, had I not anticipated it, would have done some serious damage.

As I twisted away the sole of his shoe narrowly missed my

face. I spun about to trap his foot with my hands but he was as agile as he was skilled and I ended up grabbing two handfuls of air.

The side of his foot delivered a painful blow to my left shin. He followed up with an elbow thrust which just missed my chin. I was getting tired of acting as a punching bag for a muay-Thai expert, and dropping any pretense to technique or tactics, threw myself against him and jammed a knee into his crotch. He let out a cry of pain but, in a surprise move, spun me away from the door and opened it. I tackled him and we fell hard with me gripping his legs and him kicking to free himself. He managed to evade my grasp but something slipped from under his shirt and bounced down the stairs. By the time I was on my feet, he was already on the stairs. I took the steps two at a time but I heard him hit the landing with a loud crash on the tin roof. Cats mewled. I watched from the window as he scrambled across the roof, leaped a fence, and landed in some bushes in the next yard. It was dark but not so dark I couldn't get a glimpse of him running off.

I turned back to the envelope that he had dropped. I opened it and counted the pictures. They were all there. I counted my scrapes and bruises and aches and pains. They were all there as well.

A door opened. A sleepy-eyed, barefoot bargirl in a stolen hotel bathrobe yawned, stretched and rubbed her eyes. She had far more success in keeping her eyes open than she had in keeping her robe closed. "So-cott! What you do? Have fight with girlfriend again?"

30

A rooster woke me. It was confined in a yard several houses behind the Boots and Saddle but his frequent and insistent clamor for attention easily penetrated the walls of my room. I was exhausted from both tension and violence of the night before and managed to doze off quickly. But shortly after I had managed that feat I was woken by the sound of a door slamming on the landing below. Another argument between a bargirl and her customer. It seemed he wasn't paying her what he had promised because she hadn't performed as advertised. It sounded like other female voices were taking her side. I heard the Thai word for "cheapskate." I heard his expletives in English as his loud footsteps rang through the hall and down the stairs. Excited and angry bargirls briefly exchanged opinions of the man. Of all men. Then the door slammed again.

So I got up, threw on my jogging clothes and went for an early morning jog at Benjasiri Park. The battle of the night before had left me with bruised ribs, aching shins and a sore elbow. I ran as if I thought I could outrun my aches and pains. Sometimes it works. Back at my apartment, I shaved and showered and made some coffee. While the coffee was brewing, I rubbed some Tiger Balm on various areas of my body crying for attention. Once I'd had enough coffee and a stale blueberry twist, I picked up the phone and called the GM of the Falconview. The secretary wasn't much fun on the phone but then neither was I.

"Larkin here."

"The fellow you sent to get the pictures back didn't get them."

Silence. Then: "I didn't send anybody to get anything."

"No one else knew I had them, Larkin. Only you." Not exactly true. But I was quite sure from Da's reaction she had no idea who Larkin was let alone what he was involved in. Unless, of course, she was a consummate actress which I imagine successful dominatrixes have to be.

He sighed. "That's not true."

"Who did you tell?"

"I told the others."

"*All* of them?"

"I wasn't going to but my wife said people had a right to know what was happening. Especially since all this is our fault."

I was torn between anger and sympathy but, whatever I should be feeling toward the man, what was done was done.

"Well, Larkin, one of the people you or your wife told about the pictures is a murderer. You think about that before you worry quite so much about their feelings."

I hung up and poured the last cup of coffee. Bitter and black. Just like my mood. A few of Winny's mynah birds had entered the playroom adjacent to my kitchen window and I heard one of them tell someone or something to "get out!" I pulled out the kinky scenes from the envelope and looked them over, one by one. If I had thought I might find some kind of clue by studying them closely I thought wrong.

I thought of Da and her unorthodox view that I wasn't successful enough to feel the need to be humiliated by a beautiful woman. I wondered if I would feel successful enough if I solved this case. I glanced at the clock. In eight hours I would be watching Dao in the fight of her life.

I rolled the envelope and jammed it down inside an arm of my wetsuit, picked up my coffee and sat near the living room window. And tried to think things through.

There is almost as much deception and artifice in the detective business as in the world of espionage. And I was beginning to think I had been very careless in accepting things at face value. Lisa had lied to Chinaman about her name and why she wanted to find Sanford. Chinaman had lied to Sanford's company to get information. Lisa had used her sexual charms to enlist George on her side. She had lied about her name and had documents made up to pass herself off as Lisa Avery. Frank Webber had either let me think he had invited Lisa and Da to George's party or I had mistakenly assumed that fact from his part of the phone conversation. Lisa had lied to me when she said Chinaman had given her the address of the Boots and Saddle but I had naively accepted her version without checking with Chinaman. If I had I would have learned he had put her onto George. When a detective starts accepting people and their versions of events at face value, it's time to get out of the business; and I had been unobserving, credulous and sloppy.

I picked up a pad and a pen and drew a few lines. I marked the heading "Suspects": And then I simply doodled as I thought. Da was jealous of Lisa's affairs with other women and had threatened her. In a fit of rage Da had killed Lisa. That was always a possibility. George's wife had fallen hard for Lisa and in a fit of rage George's wife had killed her. Another possibility.

Lisa had insulted a Thai hitman by not returning interest. She had gone over his head to his boss to complain; not a smart move in Thailand. He had lost face and killed her. That too was a possibility but I wouldn't have put money on it. A man like that would kill someone when told to do so; he wouldn't expose his employer to the bright lights of an investigation the murder of a foreigner would bring; an investigation which might possibly put the club out of business. Or, this being Thailand, he would at least be putting the club in a position where it would have to pay an enormous bribe to remain open. He hadn't struck me as a candidate for a good citizenship award, but he hadn't struck me as stupid either.

And then there was Sanford. And about half a dozen other people who desperately wanted to get their hands on that video tape. But Sanford was the one who had played games with Lisa's sister in New York. Her sister was dead. Sanford had played games with Lisa in Bangkok. Lisa was dead. Sanford was a womanizer and a wife-beater. And he loved kinky sex. A video tape of his activities on the internet would have ruined him. "Where there is no wind, the grass does not move."

And, of course, there was always George. A man who seemed to be living several lives simultaneously. And his lesbian wife. The wife who had an affair with Lisa. Had George killed Lisa in a fit of rage when she chose his wife over him? Had he known all along about Lisa and his wife and simply hired me to investigate as a way to establish the fact that he hadn't known?

And, finally, the unthinkable possibility that a beautiful muay-Thai boxer had killed Lisa out of jealousy. One part of me dismissed the thought of Dao being a murderess as absurd; the other part remembered having seen the look in her eyes as she went out to demolish a muay-Thai opponent. I had seen that look before only in Buen's eyes. He and his sister were alike in many ways.

Whatever, it was time to head over to Len's Dive and let George know what I had found out. Then I was going to splurge on a fast taxi to Pattaya and do some solo diving; the kind that would clear my head and just maybe give me a new perspective on the case. If nothing else, I would see some pretty fish.

31

The hall was on the outskirts of Bangkok and was about the size of a college gym, maybe a bit larger. Bleachers lined three walls and there were few empty places on them. The crowd seemed a mix of diehard boxing fans and entire families who came to enjoy the free entertainment.

An official stood on a small platform in front of the flags of the eleven nations participating in the event. There was a slight echo from the microphone. He spoke in passable English mixed with a bit of Thai and briefly described the development of professional women's muay-Thai and how it was finally coming into its own; how the ring at the center of the room was regulation size, and how, unlike amateur boxing, the women would not be wearing head or body guards. He spoke of how most male boxers no longer considered a woman touching the ring ropes to be bad luck. And how, except for the use of elbows being proscribed, women's muay-Thai was little different from the men's muay-Thai.

He admitted that seeing women being bloodied with elbow thrusts and elbow strikes would have been too much for the public and that it had made sense to ban the use of elbows in women's fighting. But, muay-Thai, he stressed, was no longer an all-male sanctuary.

In one sense, female muay-Thai was very different. The men often used the first round to feel one another out and generally fought at a leisurely pace, the round ending in a draw. In most bouts between women I had seen, the women were there to fight from the first second.

The fighters were lined up, already in their boxing shorts and jackets. Twenty-six women in red trunks and twenty-six in blue trunks. Three slim female referees stood nearby, all dressed alike in black bow tie, white blouse and black slacks.

In a corner of the gym an orchestra consisting of four middle-aged male musicians waited patiently. The small bronze cymbals, a hardwood-and-ivory clarinet-style Javanese oboe, and two cylindrical goatskin drums would soon be put to use during pre-fight rituals as well as during the fight itself. The time keeper was busy speaking with judges and issuing last minute clarifications for the fighters' cornermen.

When the speech was finished, the boxers disappeared into a waiting room to scattered applause. The first bout was between a Thai and a Canadian and as they appeared, their names, nationalities and the names of their boxing camps were announced. The four-man band began playing at a stately tempo as the fighters performed their *wai khru ram muay*, ritualized dances in homage to their teachers.

Dao was pleased whenever I showed up at her fights but asked that I not sit near her corner. She needed full concentration on defeating opponents and was afraid seeing me might distract her. And so I sat on the bleachers with the excited crowd of Thai and foreign fans.

The Canadian boxer TKO'd the Thai boxer in the fourth round, a Thai boxer defeated a French boxer by a decision, and a Japanese boxer beat a hopelessly outclassed Australian with a knock out in the second round. And then it was Dao's fight.

She was to fight Janice Olsen. Janice was in red and she stepped over the ropes as male boxers do. Dao was in blue and, in deference to male boxing tradition, she stepped through the ropes as most Thai women still did. Both women wore the *mongkon* headband, a kind of sacred circlet, which would come off before the fight began, and *prajied* armbands around their biceps containing sacred words and symbols which would remain on. I knew that inside Dao's armband was a strand of her late mother's hair.

The women paid homage to their teachers and began their balletic rituals to the music. Dao walked around the ring with her arm over the rope scowling toward the crowd. Fans knew she was simply sealing the ring off from evil influences and not scowling at them. Janice stamped her foot in Dao's corner and posed as if she were Rama shooting an arrow. But this too was part of the accepted ritual. For the most part, the women ignored one another. Unlike Western boxing, there was never any nasty scenes between opponents. All fighters were to be respected and no Mike Tyson displays of arrogance or ill temper would have been tolerated.

Dao was by far the most graceful with a smooth and flowing slow-dance as if taught by an expert choreographer. Janice's stockiness prevented her from appearing graceful or light-footed and she kept her warm-up and ritual dance short.

Dao finished her dance-ritual and stood in her corner of the ring reverently facing her father with her gloves in a *wai* position. He spoke words of encouragement to her and removed the circlet from her head.

The referee abruptly gestured for the stools, pans and buckets to be taken from the ring. The bell sounded five seconds later. When it did, both women charged out of their corners as if each had something to prove: Janice that her previous victory wasn't a fluke and Dao that it was. They circled one another warily, Janice pawing the air with her front leg as if reminding Dao of her ability to end the fight with a sudden kick. Mostly in time with the music, they traded cautious jabs, and a few less cautious kicks. Dao was first to take the aggressive and lashed out with a beautiful leg kick which just missed her opponent's head. Janice made a half-hearted attempt to capture the leg then simply bounded out of range.

They circled again. Janice suddenly unleashed her own series of lightning-fast kicks. Dao blocked them with her arms and the two women clinched and spun and fell into the ropes. The tempo of the music was already accelerating. The women traded knee-jabs to the sides and ribs while gripping one another's neck with their gloves. Dao managed to get a knee in between them and pushed Janice away. She swung several punches to Janice's face as Janice was backing up, one landing solidly on her chin. The crowd's excitement was quickly building and beside me a shriveled Thai man, obviously a muay-Thai fanatic, was shouting encouragement to Dao.

Again, they circled one another. Dao feinted a few times as if she were about to unleash a series of rights and lefts then unleashed another kick which again just missed Janice's head. Janice stepped in and forcefully thrust a knee straight upwards into Dao's chest. Dao backed out of it in time, avoiding most of the force, but Janice continued on with her own kick which landed squarely on Dao's stomach. Dao gave no sign of whatever pain she must have felt.

Again, they circled one another. Janice stepped in as if she were about to try another knee thrust, then threw a lead leg round-house kick which landed against Dao's ribs. But Dao was already countering as she stepped inside the kick and threw her own roundhouse kick, keeping it low so it landed on the back of the knee of Janice's supporting leg. It was a perfectly executed counter and Janice fell backward and landed hard on the canvas.

Dao danced into a neutral corner. The crowd roared. Janice stood up immediately but had to take a mandatory eight count. The referee gestured for the fight to continue and as the eerie music increased in tempo, the women immediately dashed toward one another. Each unleashed a barrage of feet and fists, more intent on punishing than on defense. I could hear both Amnart and Narong yelling to Dao not to get careless. Janice threw a fast, low hook to Dao's body; Dao quickly raised her knee and blocked it. Janice threw a roundhouse kick which Dao blocked with her shin.

The women backed off from one another, Janice still pawing the air with her lead leg, as if again reminding Dao of her ability to end the fight with one powerful kick. It suddenly dawned on me that her strategy might be to keep Dao's attention constantly focused on watching her feet, while planning the perfect punch. If that was her strategy it proved successful. She feigned throwing a kick, then unleashed a lightning-fast straight right which landed solidly on Dao's turned cheek, sending her reeling into the ropes. Janice pounced and in the clinch she worked her knees into Dao's kidney areas, gripping her about the neck, trying hard to bring her face downward to receive the punishment. Dao punished Janice's ribs with her own forceful knee-jabs. Both women continued gripping the other's neck with their gloves while delivering what punishment they could. I could hear Amnart shouting to Dao to stay calm, to focus. The referee moved in to break them.

The bell rang ending round one.

The men working Janice's corner were both well-built young Americans who looked as if they had just come from a Marine boot camp. They exuberantly rubbed Janice down while giving her advice.

Amnart and Narong worked with Dao. At this stage the cornermen mainly gave advice; after a few rounds they would be fanning their exhausted boxers with towels, pouring water onto them, giving them water to drink, and just possibly applying ointment to cuts.

The bell sounded. Janice was the first to reach the center of the ring and the first to attack. She punished Dao's thigh with a solid, lightning-fast blow from her shin. Dao retaliated by turning her hip and putting all her force into a straight right which glanced off Janice's ear. Janice delivered another well-aimed kick but failed to penetrate Dao's guard. Janice pressed her kicking attack but Dao bobbed and weaved, evading or blocking each kick and countering with her own. Loud whaps echoed throughout the hall as Janice's roundhouse kicks landed against Dao's arm and leg blocks.

As they circled one another like panthers on the prowl, their bodies gleamed with perspiration. Again, Janice kicked out lightning fast, just missing her target, but dropping her guard just enough for Dao to land a hard right on her neck. Janice countered and both women exchanged a flurry of punches, none landing solidly.

Janice leapt to the attack with a jumping knee technique which again forced Dao to back up. Janice stepped closer and, holding Dao's neck, began delivering a series of knee jabs. As Dao countered, the two women grappled for position. The referee separated them.

Just as they started to circle, Dao threw a sharp left jab. Janice quickly brushed it aside with her right hand and managed to thrust a knee into Dao's solar plexus. Again, whatever pain she must have felt, Dao refused to reveal it. Janice followed up with a sudden kick which just missed Dao's neck, but Dao managed to grab the leg and hit Janice with a right to the head. Janice expertly folded her trapped leg and moved in, forcing Dao into the ropes, and flailed away at her head with an almost insane flurry of lefts and rights. The musicians increased the tempo of their playing to a feverish pitch. Members of the crowd screamed. Dao fought back but was trapped in a corner and before she managed to knee her way out, got the worst of the exchange.

The women circled again, feigning punches and kicks and missing real ones. Both women expertly ducked and dodged and shot out fierce punches and kicks while rivulets of sweat spun off them.

The bell rang ending round two.

Narong vigorously rubbed Dao down while her father doubled

his fists and moved his body to explain some technique to her. It was clear he thought she wasn't putting into practice what she had learned in her training. The rhythm of the fight was not going her way.

She sat wearily on the stool, gloves on her legs, and listened to her father's advice while her brother fanned her with a towel. I felt a surge of pride in being loved by a woman with so much spirit and so much spunk. And I knew how much she needed this victory.

The bell sounded.

Janice rushed to the attack with a roundhouse kick. Dao raised her leg to block it. She stepped forward and push-kicked with her right leg, then delivered a real kick with her right. Both women kicked and punched in combinations but both missed or else had their punches blocked. Dao connected with a right to the stomach but missed with a left to the head.

Dao delivered a fast kick but Janice caught her leg with her right hand and managed to land a punch on her chin with her left. They held each other, knees slapping sides and the crowd shouting with each slap. As they grappled, both tumbled to the mat, still embracing one another. The referee rushed in, separated them and waved them up.

The women circled. Their exhaustion was clearly visible but so was their determination. The polyphonic music slowed and the oboe produced an especially haunting sound, the drummers' fingers tapped on the differently pitched drums, and the cup-shaped cymbals set the slower pace with their alternating brief and elongated ringing sounds. The music seemed to freeze the women in time, weaving a spell around both of them. For several seconds, they appeared mesmerized by the eerie music's resonance and trapped in some kind of meditative trance.

The cymbals crisp sounds suddenly intensified and the music picked up its tempo. Dao swung a wild hook and missed then barely managed to dodge Janice's straight punch. Janice landed a fast and low roundhouse kick against Dao's thigh and followed it up with a left hook which glanced off Dao's ear. Dao appeared tired and seemed to be slowing down. Janice began backing her about the ring as each stared daggers at one another. Janice was now clearly on the offence. I began to wonder just how badly Dao was hurt.

Janice threw a long left hook which glanced off Dao's ear and immediately followed it up with a vicious uppercut that landed smack on Dao's chin. Dao turned and took a step away as if trying to avoid her opponent, but glanced back at her over her shoulder. As Janice rushed at her to do more damage, Dao unleashed a spinning back kick which caught Janice flush in the midsection, knocking the air out of her. I heard the man beside me excitedly call out the name of the technique in Thai: *jerakhae faad hang*, or "the crocodile thrashes its tale."

Janice's face was a mask of pain and she covered her midsection with her gloves. She gamely raised her arms again to fight off Dao's charge. It was too little, too late. Dao had obviously decided at some point to accept pain and punishment to make her opponent overconfident and to gamble everything on one well practiced technique. Dao swung her right leg up and out from her knee, and landed a kick to her weakened opponent's jaw. Janice crumbled to the mat.

The fight was over.

32

I had no sooner switched on the light of my apartment when Dao started to laugh. She kicked her shoes off and threw herself on the bed, almost giddy with joy. She bounced a few times as if testing out a defective trampoline. She was euphoric after her win. And I couldn't blame her. I joined her on the bed and for awhile we hugged and kissed, interrupted only by her tension-release laughter.

She reached inside her blouse and massaged her stomach with her hand. "My body aches."

"Take your clothes off. I'll give you a massage."

"I will take a hot bath first."

I walked into the closet and checked the arm of my wetsuit. The envelope was still there. When I turned around, Dao had disappeared into the bathroom and her clothes were neatly folded on a shelf by the bed. As I pulled my shirt off, I felt the aches from my own battle the night before. I finished undressing, grabbed the rubbing liniment bottle and lay on the bed.

I must have dozed off for about fifteen minutes when some noise outside in the Square woke me. I got up and walked into the living room. The message light on the phone was blinking. When I pressed it I got the name of an insurance adjuster asking me to call him back. It was a Bangkok number so I dialed it wondering if it was about the man suing me. It wasn't. A diver had drowned in the waters off Phuket and his family was suing the instructor as well as the dive shop. The insurers needed an expert diver to go down there and see if there had been any negligence on the part of the instructor or the shop itself. I would be getting paid by the adjuster so I knew they would prefer I find no evidence of negligence. I also knew regardless of what I found I could be called to testify by either side. The money was good. Very good. But it would mean leaving in the morning for a few days at least. The problem was, after her fight, Dao would have some time free and she was already making plans.

While I was trying to decide what to do, the bedroom door opened. Dao leaned in the doorway wearing only my BCD, a pair of violet lace panties, and my diving knife strapped to her leg. Her breasts were barely covered by the black nylon jacket which opened down the center and closed with velcro tabs at the bottom. The contrast between the black nylon and its pockets and straps and buckles and the texture of her smooth skin was erotic in itself.

She gripped the attached inflator/deflator tube, pressed the blue button and blew into the tube. She gave me a seductive smile and spoke in Thai: "Is this how I make it bigger?"

I stared at her for several seconds, then made my apologies to the claims adjuster.

I walked to her and ran my hands up under the BCD jacket to hold her breasts. I kissed her but she pulled away and smiled.

"Massage first."

I hung up the BCD while she lay naked on the bed. I spread the oil and began massaging her.

"Tomorrow I will go to the temple and give thanks for my victory."

"Tomorrow is supposed to be a storm."

"I must go. I promised the temple spirit."

"Wait and see what the weather is. You can always –"

"Don't worry. I can take the Skytrain to Phakanom. The temple is not far from the station."

I knew I couldn't talk her out of it so I decided just to remain grateful that I wasn't asked to go.

After about ten minutes, I slapped her buttocks. "That's it, sweetheart. Massage over."

She mumbled something incoherent.

I went into the bathroom and washed the boxing liniment off my hands. When I returned to the bedroom, she was sound asleep.

I ran my fingers slowly through her swirls of glossy black hair as they cascaded down the white pillow case onto the bed then covered her up. I checked the door, put out the lights and quickly fell asleep beside her.

DAY ELEVEN

33

I was on my second cup of coffee when the phone rang.

"Mr. Sterling?"

"Speaking."

"Um, this is Mrs. Sanford. Bob Sanford's wife. You came to our apartment."

"Yes, hello."

"I'm very sorry about…the way you were treated."

"That's quite all right, Mrs. Sanford. Not everyone likes to talk about their past." When she said nothing, I continued. "Was there something you wanted?"

"Yes. I…I need to talk to someone about my husband." She said the "my husband" in such a small voice it was hard to hear.

"I'm listening."

"Oh, no, not this way. Not on the phone. Is there any chance we could meet?"

I glanced toward the window. "Of course. But today looks pretty wet."

"Mr. Sterling, what I have to say…I'm afraid my husband is about to do something very foolish. I need to see you alone. Today. Please. I will come to you wherever you are."

"Well, I live in Washington Square. I doubt that you – "

"I know it well. Bourbon Street Café is where we often have Cajun food. May I come to your apartment? Please."

I couldn't think of when I had heard a woman so scared. I told her where my apartment was and where the stairs were. She apologized again, thanked me profusely and said she'd be there as soon as possible.

I hung up the phone then stared at it for what must have been half a minute. Dao had already left for the temple. If I was going to call Buen and ask about what it was he gave his sister now was the time. I picked up the receiver and pushed for an outside line and dialed his cellphone number. When he answered I heard voices in the background but he assured me it wasn't a bad time.

"Buen, you mentioned the other day that you gave your sister some 'personal protection.'"

"Yes."

"I was just wondering what type of weapon it was."

"Weapon?"

"I mean, what caliber?"

He was silent for a moment, then I heard him burst into laughter. "I didn't give her a weapon, *khun* Scott."

"You didn't?"

"No. I gave her a silver neck chain with three amulets. Very powerful amulets my abbot gave to me when I was a monk...Scott? Are you still there?"

The realization hit me that I had been thinking like a Westerner; not a Thai. "You mean that was the 'personal protection' you gave her? Buddha amulets? No weapon?"

"Scott, the amulets are very old. Extremely powerful. And they were blessed by a devout forest monk near Burma. People say he could work miracles. I would never give my sister a gun."

I tried to say something. I couldn't.

"And Scott, you see, they worked very well. No harm came to her."

"Buen, you are a wonderful brother. And, as I know you are a wonderful friend, there would be no point in mentioning my silly question to your sister."

He laughed again. "What question? Take care, my friend."

I put down the phone and began formulating the best possible way I could make it up to Dao. Without her knowing why I felt guilty.

34

The storm was so loud I almost didn't hear her knock. I walked to the tape deck and turned down the wild Rhythm & Blues squeals of Big Jay McNeely's tenor sax. Big Jay played tenor sax the way some men fired sawed-off shot guns: with unwavering concentration and intense pleasure. I opened the door.

And despite the rain, Mrs. Sanford was as neatly and properly dressed as ever. No spaghetti straps or cleavage-revealing blouses for her. Even her movements were precise. Her red hair was protected by a sensible dark blue scarf which matched her sensible dark blue dress under a transparent rain jacket. Her face was still sprinkled with raindrops. She blinked her green eyes and gave me an apologetic smile. "I'm so sorry I'm late. The storm is getting worse."

"No problem, Mrs. Sanford. Come right in. I've got coffee brewing." She noticed my shoes against the wall and a pair of sandals in my hand and realized I was one of those foreigners who had picked up the Thai habit of leaving shoes outside the apartment door. She placed her black umbrella against the wall, unsnapped the leather straps of her black ankle boots, slipped them off, unzipped her rain jacket, folded it neatly on top of her boots, and, with just a small purse hanging from her shoulder, entered the apartment.

I dropped Dao's leather thong sandals at her feet. "These should fit. Coffee all right?"

She slipped her small feet into Dao's sandals. They seemed a perfect fit. "Yes. That would be lovely."

I pointed to the living room. "Most people find the white leather chair is the least uncomfortable. Just make yourself at home. How'd you come?"

"I took the Skytrain, Mr. Sterling."

"A sensible choice. Especially in this weather."

"Yes. I thought so."

The woman seemed more than a bit nervous but it was quite likely she had had to work up the nerve to tell me things about her husband. Things that might change both their lives forever. I went into the kitchen, poured two cups of coffee, placed the coffee, milk and sugar on a tray and walked back into the living room.

Mrs. Sanford had apparently decided not to sit in the white leather chair. In fact, she had remained standing right where I'd left her. Except now one thing was different. The lady was holding a gun.

I was looking into the muzzle but I could see it was a mini-revolver. Her slender white hand was covering the grips but as she motioned for me to continue walking, she turned the gun to the side and I glimpsed a spot of red; leaving me with little doubt that it was a North American Arms Black Widow – a stainless steel, single action, five-shot revolver with a vented, two inch barrel. There were other .22 Magnum mini-revolvers on the market, but this was the only one that came with a small red hour glass on its grips. It also came with reliable fixed sights and comfort-able rubber grips ensuring that it took very little expertise to hit a nearby target. If Mrs. Sanford so desired, I could accurately be described as a nearby target.

Had I been in her shoes, The Black Widow is exactly the one I would have chosen. For a mini-revolver it has excellent stop-ping power, especially if it's been chambered for the .22 Magnum cartridge. It certainly could stop a woman her size in her tracks. Unfortunately, for it to be able to do that, it would have to be pointed in her direction. Which it wasn't.

I had the sinking feeling that I was very close to solving the case of Lisa Avery's murder but that I might not be around for any congratulations. I managed to spread my lips into a strained smile. "R & B not to your liking? I can change the tape."

She raised her left hand and gripped her right wrist, giving her firing hand support. This lady was no amateur. She stared into my eyes and spoke softly. I could barely hear her over the swoosh of wind gusts and heavy rain striking the living room window but if she was nervous she didn't show it. After all, she had done this sort of thing at least twice before. Practice makes perfect. "You would have done well to mind your own business, Mr. Sterling." As she spoke, Mrs. Sanford kept the gun pointed right at center mass: My heart and upper spine. Someone had taught her well. "Now place the coffee tray down and raise your hands."

She hadn't said "Pretty please with sugar on it" but nonetheless I put the tray on a nearby table and raised my hands. One of the things my father used to teach me was this. When someone points a gun in your direction there are three basic rules to staying alive: First, keep him talking, second, keep him talking, third, keep him talking. Right advice; wrong pronoun. "So it wasn't your husband who killed Judy's sister in New York, was it, Mrs. Sanford?"

When she didn't answer I continued on. My tongue seemed awkwardly positioned, unbelievably heavy and abnormally large. Like somebody had placed a sand shark in an aquarium big enough for a puffer fish. "And it wasn't your husband who killed Lisa?"

"Lisa was just like her sister. She knew how to seduce weak men. My husband loves me very much but he is a very weak man, Mr. Sterling. Very easily led astray." From her expression of disdain, it was obvious that Mrs. Sanford had little time for weak people. "But I love him very much. No flashy whore is going to steal him away from me. And no flashy whore's sister out for revenge is going to destroy my marriage."

I tried not to stare into the muzzle of the Black Widow, but it seemed to be expanding in size, arresting my line of vision and dwarfing all else in the room. Some detectives might smile at the dangers of being confronted with a small frame size, small caliber gun but being shot dead by a large frame size, large caliber weapon wouldn't have made me feel any more macho. "Did you know Lisa was involved in fun and games with your husband and others?"

"Of course. I warned my husband that she was a very sick woman. She even assumed a false identity to get close to him here in Bangkok. At first, I didn't know what she thought she would gain from involving him in her filthy little games but then I heard of the video tape and I realized who she was and how she was out to ruin him."

She stood several steps away from me, perfectly placed with the gun out of reach. Her hands were steady. Any attempt on my part to rush her would have been suicidal. My mouth was feeling parched. My saliva seemed to have evaporated like water in the desert. This left my tongue sticking to my palate like a little boy too shy to come out and play.

"Lisa's sister in New York played the same kind of games with your husband, didn't she?"

"My husband – "

" – Loves you very much, I know. You told me. But he doesn't love diving. Learning that was *your* idea, wasn't it?"

"Of course. I found your namecard and notes about your involvement as a detective in her apartment and knew I would have to deal with you sooner or later."

Sheets of rain struck the living room window with increasing intensity. As if accepting the storm's challenge, Big Jay McNeely's sax wailed and honked in ever wilder squeals, bluesifying anything and everything within hearing distance. "So the alibi you provided for your husband in New York was actually to protect yourself, wasn't it? Only he didn't know that. He thought you were lying for him. He really was home the night Lisa's sister was killed; it was you who were out. That right?"

Her green eyes just stared back at me without emotion. I wasn't talking to some mad woman beside herself with anger. Nor to someone beyond feeling. She was a lady who knew just what she was on about. And there was certainly no struggle raging inside her. She was simply determined to keep her husband at all costs. And if that included the taking of human life, so be it. "Did you give Judy the same line you gave me, Mrs. Sanford? Did you call her and tell her you needed to talk to her about your husband's confession?"

"She was just as gullible as you are, Mr. Sterling. And as careless." She gave me a look of pity. "You seem to be a reasonably intelligent man. But did it never occur to you that you might not know enough of human nature to be a very good detective?"

"I'm beginning to suspect I don't know enough about *women* to be much of a detective."

"Did it never occur to you that not every woman in what on the surface appears to be an abusive relationship is interested in getting out of it? When two people stay together, there are always reasons."

I wasn't sure how long I could stall her or exactly what I was gaining by doing so; but whenever someone holds a gun on me, considering the alternative, talk always seems a sensible way to go. "So he stays with you for your money and you stay with him because he's a hunk, is that about it? He doesn't know or doesn't care to know that his wife is a cold-blooded murderer. He asks you no questions and you tell him no lies. You on the other hand give him some leeway to play but when playtime gets out of hand, you rein him in by killing off the playmate. A nice symbiotic relationship: kind of like an urchin crab and a – "

Her lovely green eyes narrowed in anger. "I told you: I love my husband very much. And in his own way he loves me. People have needs; and when relationships meet those needs, the people stay together."

I certainly had needs; the most important being the need to get out of the room alive. And no sane betting man would place ten baht on my chances. "So you tossed Lisa's apartment for the video tape?"

"Yes, that. And the bitch had a diary and newspaper clippings of her sister's death. Not to mention our former New York phone numbers. Even an unlisted one. I searched thoroughly because I wanted it to end with her death."

"But it didn't."

"It would have if it hadn't been for you."

She raised the barrel of the gun from the level of my stomach to the level of my face. "And now I must ask you for the Polaroids."

"So it was you who sent the thug to snatch them. Where'd you find him? A friend of one of your watchmen?"

She gave me the slightest of smiles. "Something like that. Where are they?"

I suddenly remembered that Dao would be returning soon. The thought of harm coming to her because of me hit me like a perfectly delivered muay-Thai kick to my stomach. I decided that if I were going to die it would be better to give this woman what she wanted and get her out of here before Dao returned. "They're stuffed in a sleeve of my wetsuit in the bedroom closet."

"Lead the way, Mr. Sterling. And I do know how to use this so please don't try anything stupid on the way to the bedroom."

Ah, yes, the bedroom; where a pillow would be employed to muffle the sounds of the shot just in case the storm wasn't loud enough for that purpose. She had the same scenario for me she had planned and carried out with Lisa Avery.

She waved the gun toward the bedroom and then back to me. I turned around and headed slowly for the bedroom, my mind racing. If there was a way out of this that would lead to something other than my sudden demise I had yet to figure out what that was. I couldn't understand how I had stupidly never even considered her as a suspect. Actually, I could. I had bought into the stereotype: The abused, timid, afraid-to-speak-out, mousy woman who finally summoned up the courage to speak to someone about her husband's out-of-control behavior; no matter how much it pained her to do so. And she portrayed the role as well as any Tony Award-winning actress in a Broadway play.

There was no question my knowledge of female psychology was woefully inadequate. That had been pointed out to me first by a woman with a whip and now by a woman with a gun. Why more and more women seemed to feel a need to perform some sort of violent, destructive act against me was something I'd have to look into at a later date; that is, assuming for me, there would be a later date.

As I turned to walk to the bedroom, an angry car horn briefly rose above the sound of the storm's fury. In the old days, say, in the late 1980's and well into the 90's, traffic in Bangkok was without question the worst in the world; especially during the rainy season when the streets were flooded and nothing moved. It was a murderer's worst nightmare. If you wanted to kill someone you first had to wade through hazardous eddies of water as it rapidly flooded snake-infested, rubbish-strewn lanes, all the while trying not to let your murder weapon of choice slip into the black, swirling pools that were soaking your shoes, socks and trousers. You would try to hail a dilapidated taxi which itself most likely had noisome, brackish water swishing about along the rusty, ruptured floor drenching your socks and shoes, and then the taxi would pull ahead a few yards only to wait for the longest red light in the world.

But whatever color the light was didn't matter because days of heavy rains and high tides had overwhelmed the handling capacity of the city's pumps, and plastic bags and other garbage clogged the city's drainage pipes, and all traffic had become stationary. It would take two or three hours to arrive at the intended victim's apartment by which time you would most likely have caught a serious cold or contracted rat urine disease or some other incurable infection from the foul, filthy, polluted water you had been immersed in. Or have suffocated to death in the taxi. Or have gone mad from listening to the same *luk thung* – northeastern Thailand songs – again and again and again on the driver's radio.

But then in December of 1999 the Skytrain was finished, designed to move people smoothly and comfortably across Bangkok all the while keeping passengers well above the watery mess below. It was a murderer's dream come true. Now if you need to do away with someone on a dark and stormy night, all you have to do is take a motorcycle taxi out to any of the modern stations, head up the stairs (some equipped with escalators), and for a maximum of 40 baht (US$.95), you can quickly and safely arrive at your destination.

Once in the area where your victim lives you can even stop briefly at an elevated café and grab a cappuccino and a slice of pizza or grab some quick cash from an ATM machine before hailing a motorcycle taxi and heading off to complete your business. In fact, with the Skytrain, it's possible for murderers to squeeze in more than one victim an evening in which case killers on a tight budget could purchase the special one-day tourist pass allowing unlimited travel. Maybe Mrs. Sanford had done just that.

I walked through the living room, and entered the area which passed as a kitchen. I stopped suddenly and turned to face her. "One last question." My left hand was about three feet from a stack of dirty dishes and empty beer bottles. My chances of grabbing a beer bottle and smashing her with it before she got off at least one well-aimed shot were miniscule but better than any odds I had once I entered the bedroom.

But my plan was to faint toward the bottle as if I was grabbing it, then dive, roll and come up right in her face and grab the gun.

A move I had worked on with Chinaman as my partner about fifteen years before in a Forest Hills, New York, martial arts academy. The problem was I hadn't practiced the move for fifteen years, either. And even then I had sprained a shoulder trying it.

Her eyes narrowed again and she gripped the gun even more tightly. She cocked the hammer. The slightest pressure on the trigger would send a .22 Magnum round crashing into my chest. "I warn you, Mr. Sterling, I know how to – "

The bolt of lightning that flashed and then struck the earth wasn't all that close, probably several blocks away, but it was close enough. Suddenly, behind the curtained window above the sink, all hell broke loose; there was the loud crash of something thwacking against glass and an angry shriek: "Pay your goddamn bill!" answered immediately by a high pitched and no-nonsense "Get out!"

Mrs. Sanford jumped back and swung the gun in the direction of the curtain. She probably pulled back on the trigger out of shock. A natural r eaction. She blasted off one round shattering the window behind the curtain and causing still more hell to break loose with the birds. I threw myself on her, grabbed her right wrist with my left hand, and we tumbled and stumbled a few steps like two drunkards entwined in a macabre embrace. We spun off the sink and hit the floor just as the thunder boomed.

I banged my head hard on the way down and she landed on top of me. Despite her diminutive size she was a strong, determined woman. Amidst the tumultuous cacophony of squawks from indignant birds and sounds of the raging storm we struggled.

I shook off the explosion of pain at the back of my head and rolled her over, trying to make certain she couldn't fire. But mini-revolvers have no trigger guard and there was nowhere to jam my finger to keep her from pulling the trigger. She stretched both of her hands above her, grunting with the effort. I knew she was attempting to transfer the revolver to her free hand. And I knew I had to stop her.

As I reached up with both hands to pin her hand holding the gun, I managed to snap an elbow hard against her nose. She emitted a strange guttural sound and all strength and sense of purpose seeped out of her like a deflating balloon. She relaxed her grip. The Black Widow was in my hand.

DAY TWELVE

35

"WELCOME BACH!" "FUCH CENSOR!" The girls had draped the two long white paper banners with lipstick lettering across the front of the bar and tied them securely to columns with their bra-straps. Photographs and paintings of the Olde West were now obscured by varicolored streamers and leftover bunches of black and orange Halloween balloons. Although familiar with the spelling of the term, "Welcome," the girls were less familiar with the words "Back," "Fuck" and "Cancer," leading casual observers to speculate as to why Bach was being welcomed to the Boots and Saddle and if he was being accused of censoring fugues. But if the spelling was inexact the spirit of goodwill was unmistakable.

The bar was as busy as I'd ever seen it. The music was loud, male and female voices were loud, and small wooden cups overflowed with customers' bar bills. Most of the booths were full and there were few barstools vacant. Winny sat in his usual booth with a large, white bandage stretched across the left side of his neck. Despite losing a few pounds, he looked healthy enough. I walked over and sat down facing him. "Welcome back!"

"Thanks."

The bandage was long and if, as I'd heard, the cut had stretched from the Vagas nerve to the carotid artery, the scar would be long as well. "Good thing about getting older is that neck wrinkles hide scars."

He almost chuckled at that one. I had no doubt he was ignoring some doctor's orders not to drink alcohol for awhile. "But weren't you supposed to be in for another day or so?"

He tilted his head back slowly and carefully and took a swig of beer. "Got bored."

I ordered a Mekong and Coke and toasted his health. I cleared my throat. "Sorry about your bird."

He shrugged and spoke while looking at his beer bottle. "An accident." Then he looked right at me. "I know it was you or the psycho. And I'm damn glad it was you." He gave me the slightest of grins. "But if you had to take out one of my birds did it have to be Liberty Valance?"

As near as we could determine, Liberty Valance had slammed into the glass just as Texas John Slaughter had screamed out his trademark, "Pay your fucking bill!" The .22 round had missed Texas John but taken out Liberty.

Son-of-Loser Paul had been following our conversation and despite his alcoholic daze somehow managed to spit out what he had to say without falling off his nearby barstool. "Liberty gave his *life* for you, man! He took a round dead smack in his chest!"

West Texas Andy chimed in with his lazy drawl: "Hey, that's right! This is the Man who shot Liberty Valance!"

The Thung Lor police station hadn't questioned me for long before releasing me and zeroing in on Mrs. Sanford but local papers had somehow managed to confuse the story and had it that a shot went off during the life-and-death struggle killing a rare and priceless mynah bird. One Thai language paper, indulging in its usual creative reporting, even suggested that I had been attacked by killer birds high on some kind of methamphetamine and had fought for my life. Their story had been illustrated with the close-up of the eyes of an enraged eagle; not unlike the logo on a Black Widow revolver.

I practically shouted my denial to West Texas Andy. "I didn't shoot Liberty Valance!"

West Texas Andy removed his hand from the shapely thigh of

a nearby bargirl to wave my denial away. "Don' matter none! Jimmy Stewart didn't shoot him neither; John Wayne did. But folks thought Jimmy did just the same!"

Someone started it and then several male voices joined in singing snatches of the Liberty Valance theme song:

The man who shot Liberty Valance!
He shot Liberty Valance!
He was the bravest of them all!

Five-Minute Jack stumbled over and leaned against the bar, holding a drink in one hand and a copy of the *Bangkok Post* open to Bernard Trink's column. His Hawaiian shirt-of-the-day was eggplant purple and sunset pink. His voice was that of an indignant reader seeking confirmation for his complaint wherever he could find it. He waved the paper from left to right and back again, like a man trying to keep the embers of a dying fire alive. "You see Trink's 'Night Owl' column? He didn't even refer to Liberty by name. Just called him 'a *bird*.'"

West Texas Andy placed his hand back on the girl's thigh. "Trink's not still alive, is he?"

Five-minute Jack's watery grey eyes widened. He glared at West Texas Andy. "Course he's alive."

"He can't be. There's been a Trink column in the *Post* forever."

"Well, he's still writing. Still pissing off the feminazis."

Son-of-Loser-Paul belched loudly and wiped his mouth with the back of his hand. "You know what I think?"

Winny said: "I think you're gonna tell us what you think."

He let that pass. "You remember the *Phantom* comic strip?"

West Texas Andy furrowed his brow. "You mean the flaky white guy in Africa wore a mask and costume?"

"Yeah. All the natives thought he couldn't die. They called him 'The Ghost who Walks.'"

Death Wish Don picked up his beer bottle and moved closer to us. "Hey, I remember him! Shit, he was a cool dude. The natives called him 'The Guardian of the Eastern Dark.'"

"No shit? That's a cool name. I wonder if Dang would call me that?"

"Tell you what, Andy. Buy her a drink and Dang'll call you any fucking thing you like," Winny said.

Son-of-Loser Paul plowed on, irritated but undeterred by detours in the conversation. "Anyway, what the African guys didn't know was that the Phantom had replaced his father and his father had replaced *his* father and so on for hundreds of years."

"So, you're saying Trink is like that?" I asked.

"Yeah. Has to be! There must be a long line of Trinks but they keep it a secret to make us think there's always been the same one. Otherwise he'd be four-hundred-years old."

"So why the fuck would Trink want to make us think he can never die?" Winny asked.

"So none of his pissed-off readers will take a shot at him."

Winny thought that over. "Well…yeah, that makes sense."

"Fucking-A it does!"

Son-of-Loser Paul gave forth with another belch. "'Guardian of the Eastern Dark'. Man, that's a perfect description of me in Bangkok."

"Sure it is, mate," Winny said. "But if it is, then it becomes a question of 'who's guarding the guards'."

I drained my glass, and counted out enough baht for the bill. There was more than enough on my tab already.

Winny watched me. "What's your hurry?"

"I promised Dao I'd meet her at Emporium. I hate to say it but it looks like it's a shopping day. To celebrate her victory." I hesitated. "Liberty was expensive. What about – "

"Forget it. Like the man said, he gave his life for yours."

I nodded. "Take care."

"Give that lovely lady of yours a hug for me."

I walked out into faint sunlight illuminating a sprinkling of fine rain, and headed off toward Sukhumvith Road. I couldn't help wonder just a bit about how things sometimes do work out for the best. If Son-of-Loser-Paul hadn't given me a black eye I wouldn't have gotten the information I needed from the Emerald Club; and I might have been tossed out bodily as well. If Winny hadn't had the tumor and gone in for the operation, he would have got around to putting double-paned glass in the kitchen window; in which case the shrieks of terrified birds wouldn't have been loud enough to distract a woman with a gun. And people in the bar I just came from would be toasting me in the past tense. If there hadn't been a storm.... If. I couldn't shake the feeling that Lady Luck had taken pity on me and decided to assist me on this case. Maybe she figured I understood so little about women she'd better lend me a hand.

And I thought of Lisa. I knew I would never understand her completely. I had known her very briefly and I would never know how much of what I had seen was simply a mask and how much was real. Was her apparent attraction for the world of bizarre sexual games simply a way of getting close to a murderer or, like her late sister, was there some allurement in it which she found impossible to resist. But I knew I had done my best for her and I made a silent wish that she rest in peace.

I hadn't got far before someone opened the door of the bar a crack for my benefit. And out into the rain spilled an off-key chorus of several male voices:

He shot Liberty Valance!
He was the bravest of them aaawwwlll!

THE END

Praise for *Kingdom of Make-Believe*

"*Kingdom of Make-Believe* is an exciting thriller that paints a picture of Thailand much different from that of *The King and I*. The story line is filled with non-stop action, graphic details of the country, and an intriguing allure that will hook readers of exotic thrillers. Very highly recommended." – *BookBrowser.com*

"A tantalizing taste of a culture, worlds apart from our own.Dean Barrett paints a sharp, clear picture of the reality of life. An excellent account of one man's struggle to find the truth in his existence. Very highly recommended." – *Under the Covers Book Review*

"An absolutely astounding novel. Its depth and layers of perception will have you fascinated from start to finish. Highly entertaining!" – *Buzz Review News*

"Barrett spins a tightly packed tale that is part murder mystery, part midlife crisis love story and part travelogue, with vibrant and seductive Thailand in a leading role. This mystery keeps the reader guessing at the next plot twist." – *Today's Librarian*

"A gripping mystery documenting Dean Barrett as a writer in full possession of his craft." – *Midwest Book Review*

"Sharp, often poetic, and pleasantly twisted, *Kingdom of Make-Believe* is a tautly written fictional tour of Thailand. Author Dean Barrett has woven a compelling and believable tale about a country he knows well. Barrett's prose is spare but his images are rich: a winning combination. His obvious intimate knowledge of Thailand combined with a very considerable writing talent make *Kingdom of Make-Believe* a tough book to put down." – *January Magazine*

Praise for *Memoirs of a Bangkok Warrior*

"*Memoirs of a Bangkok Warrior* is a marvelous novel, yes-novel, about the Vietnam era. So marvelous that upon finishing it, I promptly handed it over to my brother, the Nam vet, and told him, read this – you'll love it. So, read it. You'll love it. I promise." Stars 5+
– *Buzz Review News*

"Succeeds nicely in the creation of a time and place that transcends mere setting."
– *West Coast Review of Books*

"This is M*A*S*H, taken from behind the Korean lines, set down in the rear-echelon of steamy Bangkok–titillated with the tinkle of Thai laughter and temple bells. And it is an even funnier triumph of man over military madness."
– Derek Maitland, author, *The only War we've Got*

"An Awesome read! Way out, Far out, Groovy....I can smell the smell and see the green and feel the magic of Thailand!"
– Terry Ryan, TCLB (*Thailand, Laos, Cambodian Brotherhood*)

"*Memoirs of a Bangkok Warrior* is recommended reading for anyone who ever donned a uniform and found themselves far from home."
– Midwest Book Review

"*Memoirs of a Bangkok Warrior* remains one of my favorite books about Thailand. Excellent characters and dialogue. It would make a great movie."
– Dave Walker, author, *Hello My Big, Big Honey!*

Praise for *Hangman's Point*

"Setting is more than a backdrop in this fast-paced adventure story of mid-nineteenth-century British colonial Hong Kong.... A riveting, action-packed narrative.... Chinese scholar, linguist, and author of two previous books, Barrett draws on his vast knowledge of southern China during a time of enormous change and conflict, providing richly fascinating detail of the customs, fashions, ships, and weapons of the times." – *ALA Booklist*

"An expert on Hong Kong and the turbulent time period portrayed, Dean Barrett has fashioned a swashbuckling adventure which will have both history buffs and thriller readers enthralled from the very first page. An outstanding historical novel." – *Writers Write Reviews*

"If Patrick O'Brian's Aubrey and Maturin ever got as far as Hong Kong in 1857 on their world travels, the aged sea dogs would feel right at home in China expert Dean Barrett's totally convincing novel of high adventure." – Dick Adler, *Amazon.com Reviews*

"A great epic of a historical mystery."– *Bookbrowser Reviews*

"The adventures of this latter-day Indiana Jones will leave him fleeing for his life through the town of Victoria (Hong Kong), bring him face to face with the perils of the pirate-infested waters of the Pearl River, and finally fix him a date with death at *Hangman's Point*.... The novel is peppered with well-defined characters from all walks of life.... It would be just another potboiler a la James Clavell, but Barrett's extensive research sets this novel apart: as well as a ripping adventure story, it is an intimately drawn historical portrait." – *South China Morning Post*

"There is adventure and mystery in every corner of this well-researched and well-written historical." – *1BookStreet.com*

"Rich in historical perspective and characters, Barrett's debut is good news for those who love grand scale adventure."
– *The Poisoned Pen Booknews*

"*Hangman's Point* is vastly entertaining, informative and thought-provoking. ...Dean Barrett weaves an intricate and many-layered tale. Barrett clearly has in-depth knowledge of his field, more so than most Western novelists can command.... Barrett offers more than an exciting story. He provides an understanding view of China and the Chinese, guiding readers toward a fuller appreciation of that complex culture."
– *Stuart News*

"*Hangman's Point* is a great historical fiction that, if there is any justice, will enable Dean Barrett to become a household name. Highly Recommended." – *Under The Covers Book Review*

"Excellently written and steeped in details of the times, all obviously very well researched and accurate." – *The Midwest Book Review*

"Adams's adventures take him on a thrilling chase, almost an odyssey. ...*Hangman's Point* is a page-turner that is guaranteed to keep both male and female readers enthralled to the very end. Romance and high adventure." – *Romantic Times*

Praise for *Murder in China Red*

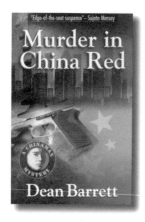

"A highly focused plot, classy prose, and a complicated protagonist merit wide readership." – *Library Journal*

"Classically toned" – *Publishers Weekly*

"A promising series debut." – *Chicago Tribune*

"*Murder in China Red* is a superior book. The writing is good, with clever, useful and apt images." – *Asian Review of Books*

"A great serial detective character." – *MostlyFiction.com*

"Fast-paced, one-liners abound, and the mix of mayhem and humor is nicely balanced. Private-eye enthusiasts will put Chinaman at the top of their list." – *Everybody Loves a Mystery* Newsletter

"A finely crafted mystery novel." – *Midwest Book Review*

"Dean Barrett has written several very good mysteries but with *Murder in China Red* he introduces one of the most original and engrossing hard-boiled detectives this side of Dashiell Hammett...*Murder in China Red* is an absolutely murderous delight!" – *Laughing Bear Newsletter*

"The next book in the Chinaman series will be *Murder in Dominatrix Black*. If Mr. Barrett can maintain the quality shown in *Murder in China Red*, this will be a good mystery series indeed!" – *Curled up with a Good Book*

"Barrett has spun a well-crafted murder mystery filled with characters that leap off the page." – *Stephen Leather*, author of *The Tunnel Rats*

Dean Barrett first arrived in Asia as a Chinese linguist with the American Army Security Agency. He has lived and traveled in Asia for over 20 years. His novels on Thailand are *Kingdom of Make-Believe and Memoirs of a Bangkok Warrior*. His novels set in China are *Hangman's Point* and *Mistress of the East*. *Murder in China Red* is set in New York, the first in a series featuring Liu Chiang-hsin, a Beijing-born private detective known as Chinaman. *Don Quixote in China: The Search for Peach Blossom Spring* recounts Mr. Barrett's adventures in China in search of a cloistered utopia described in a 4th century poem.

His plays have been staged in eight countries and his musical set in 1857 Hong Kong, *Fragrant Harbour*, was selected by the National Alliance for Musical Theater to be presented on 42nd Street, NYC. Mr. Barrett is a member of Mystery Writers of America and Private Eye Writers of America.

Sample chapters and covers of his books can be found on-line at http://www.deanbarrettmystery.com.